Elizabeth Johnston

YORK HANDBOOKS

GENERAL EDITOR:
Professor
(*University*

ST
JAMES JOYCE

Harry Blamires
MA (OXFORD)
Former Head of the English Department,
King Alfred's College, Winchester

LONGMAN
YORK PRESS

Acknowledgements

The photograph of James Joyce by Berenice Abbot on page 6 is reproduced by permission of Yale University Library. The map of Dublin on page 164 is based on the Ordnance Survey by permission of the Government of the Republic of Ireland (Permit No. 4501).

YORK PRESS
Immeuble Esseily, Place Riad Solh, Beirut.

LONGMAN GROUP UK LIMITED
Longman House,
Burnt Mill,
Harlow,
Essex

First published 1987

ISBN 0-582-96601-9

Produced by Longman Group (FE) Ltd
Printed in Hong Kong

Contents

Preface

This Handbook is designed for the student who would like to have some understanding of Joyce's total output – what exactly it consists of, from what personal and historical background it derives, how the various works relate to each other, and what their permanent literary significance is. While all Joyce's prose works are given due attention, there is appropriate emphasis on his most celebrated and most frequently studied books, *Dubliners*, *A Portrait of the Artist as a Young Man*, and *Ulysses*. *Stephen Hero* and *Exiles* are more important for the light they throw on the author of these masterpieces than for their intrinsic qualities. As for *Finnegans Wake*, although detailed analysis of it would clearly be beyond the scope of this book, it is hoped that the general account given of it here in the context of the survey of Joyce's work as a whole will at least indicate what Joyce was about in that formidable work and will thus render it more accessible.

Joyce in the 1920s photographed by Berenice Abbot.

Part 1

James Joyce and his background

Joyce's life

James Joyce was born at Rathgar, Dublin, on 2 February 1882. His father, John Joyce, had inherited property in his home town of Cork on his own father's death in 1870. John Joyce and his widowed mother moved to Dublin, where he eventually obtained a comfortable post as Collector of Rates for Dublin and, on the strength of it, married Mary Jane Murray, ten years his junior, in 1880. Between then and 1894 she bore him thirteen children of whom ten survived, four boys and six girls. Of these James, the second to be born but the first to survive, was the eldest. Next to him in age were a daughter and then another son, Stanislaus, three years younger than Joyce.

John Joyce's personality and conduct determined the character of much of James's early experience and left their mark on his books. He was a vital, larger-than-life, gifted, but reckless and irresponsible man with a fine tenor voice, a fluent tongue, and an inordinate thirst. As wit, raconteur, and ironic commentator on his kind, he revelled in admiration and entranced his eldest son. But he failed to live within his means and as successive children were born he gradually mortgaged his inherited properties one by one and finally disposed of them in 1894. Then, when he was still only forty-two, civic reorganisation rendered him redundant and he was left with a pension of little more than a quarter of his previous salary. He remained the same flamboyant wastrel and never faced the realities of life. He pictured himself as the victim of imaginary persecutors.

When James was five the family moved to a substantial house at Bray, a seaside resort thirteen miles south of Dublin, which an Irish rail magnate had tried unsuccessfully to turn into an Irish Brighton. This was to be the family home for five years until, after a year at a house in Blackrock, another resort five miles south of Dublin, mounting debts and increasing poverty drove John Joyce into the city and sent him moving from one rented house to another in a descending spiral of privation and squalor. The moonlight flit to escape rent-hungry landlords became one of the devices for survival adopted by the once well-to-do and still proud fast-talker. Fellow debtors supplied one another with references to expedite removal.

Sometimes the forsaken landlord was to discover that his banisters had been burned for firewood.

The effect of John Joyce's behaviour on his family could not but be grave. Most of his children seem to have disliked him. Stanislaus hated him. Certainly he made his wife suffer. He despised and mocked her relations. When he was drunk he abused her and once tried to strangle her. 'Die, and be damned to you,' he shouted at her in her last illness. But the man's often boisterous good-humour, his skill as a comic raconteur, his colourful colloquialisms, and his hilarious ironic shafts won and kept the affection of his eldest son. Thus, while Joyce's mother impinges on his work as little more than a stereotype of pious, long-suffering Irish womanhood, his father's persona bestrides pages of vital portraiture and dialogue in Joyce's major works.

John Joyce was still able to play the well-to-do gentleman in 1888 when James was six, and, clearly recognising his eldest son's potential, he sent him to a prestigious boarding school run by the Jesuits, Clongowes Wood College at Sallins in County Kildare. James warmed to the historical associations of the college buildings which included a restored mediaeval castle. He thought well of the college rector, Father Conmee, and he never ceased to be grateful for the intellectual disciplines which formed part of his education at the hands of the Jesuits.

Much of this stage of Joyce's life is revealed in *A Portrait of the Artist as a Young Man*,* though he fictionalises himself as a rather serious, weak, timid, and retiring boy when in fact he was a cheerful and lively one, at home nicknamed 'Sunny Jim'. Much is revealed too of the embarrassment and disgust brought on by the family's rapid social decline, which meant that James had to be withdrawn from Clongowes in 1891. He stayed at home for a time, then spent some months at a Christian Brothers' school, but was rescued from this socially inferior institution by Father Conmee who met John Joyce one day in the street and kindly arranged for his boys to attend the well-known Jesuit day-school, Belvedere College, without paying fees. James worked hard here at first, winning exhibitions in 1894 and 1895. He was admitted to the Sodality of the Blessed Virgin Mary and became prefect of it in September 1896. But at some point during that year a crucial experience came his way one night when, walking home from the theatre along the canal bank, he met a prostitute and was initiated into the sexual act. It was in November following this event that at the school retreat Father James A. Cullen's hell-fire sermons aroused in Joyce an acute sense of guilt and shame. He went to confession and in a new fervour of spiritual devotion subjected himself

*For convenience the title *A Portrait of the Artist as a Young Man* will be abbreviated in this Handbook to *Portrait*.

to rigorous disciplines of prayer and mortification. But it was not long before he began to question the sincerity of his own repentance, to lose his faith in the Church, and to transfer to the sphere of artistic achievement that strong sense of vocation which the Jesuits would have directed to the priesthood. Joyce's academic and personal successes gave him undisputed leadership in the school in his penultimate year, but rebelliousness marred his final year at Belvedere, which he left in the summer of 1898. It was characteristic of his rashness that when he played the part of Dr Grimstone, the schoolmaster, in a school performance of Anstey's *Vice Versa*, he mimicked Father Henry, the rector, unmistakably.

Among friends he made at Belvedere were Richard and Eugene Sheehy, the sons of David Sheehy, a Member of Parliament, who lived in Belvedere Place and welcomed students at his home on Sunday evenings. There was singing, games were played, and Joyce became a regular guest much appreciated for his entertaining liveliness. The Sheehys had four daughters of whom the youngest, Mary, unsuspectingly became for some years the object of Joyce's secret devotion. It is probable that she was to some extent at least the model for the unidentifiable Emma Clery in *Stephen Hero* and the *Portrait*.

From 1898 to 1902 Joyce was at University College, Dublin, where he studied English, French and Italian. During these years the Joyces' movements from home to home accelerated and the unpaid debts accumulated. Meanwhile Joyce had already begun to write poetry and had excitedly discovered the plays of Ibsen. He read a paper on 'Drama and Life' to the Literary and Historical Society, and managed to get an article, 'Ibsen's New Drama', published in the *Fortnightly Review* of 1 April 1900. Ibsen himself wrote to William Archer expressing gratitude for the article and the message was conveyed to Joyce to give him his first real encouragement as the coming literary genius he aspired to be. It stimulated him moreover to more zealous study of languages and literature, and encouraged in him the sense of inheriting a European rather than a limitedly Irish culture. The fee for the article paid for a brief trip to London by Joyce and his father, and he was invited to lunch by Archer. As a result it was not long afterwards that he sent Archer his own play, *A Brilliant Career* (with a preliminary dedication 'To My Own Soul'), and Archer replied with a careful critique of the play's merits and failings, especially the latter. Joyce also wrote an article critical of the Irish literary scene, called 'The Day of the Rabblement', and, when the college magazine refused to publish it, he published it privately and sold copies himself. In 1902 he read a paper to the Literary and Historical Society on the Irish poet James Clarence Mangan (1803–49), and next day's *Freeman's Journal* called it 'the best paper ever read before the society'.

Among student friends close to Joyce during his time at University College two in particular left their mark on his work. John Francis Byrne, a handsome, tough countryman from Wicklow, impressed Joyce by his seeming indifference to much that preoccupied his fellow-students. He adopted an air of mysterious, taciturn superiority to what was going on around him, and their rarity seemed to endow his somewhat pedestrian utterances with wisdom and solemnity. Joyce made Byrne his confidant, apparently feeling that his detachment and unresponsiveness acted like the anonymous receptivity of the priest in the confessional. It was Byrne who provided the model for the character of Cranly in the *Portrait*. In contrast to Byrne, Vincent Cosgrave was a sharp-witted but lazy and self-indulgent fellow, coarse and unprincipled. He was also a fit companion on visits to the red-light district. Cosgrave was to become Lynch in the *Portrait* and *Ulysses*; and in *Ulysses* Lynch is essentially a betrayer. The origin of this identification lay in the fact that Cosgrave once stood aside with his hands in his pockets when Joyce was caught up in a fight in St Stephen's Green.

By 1902 Joyce was assiduously cultivating literary contacts. He made himself known to George Russell (known as AE, 1867–1935), who mentioned him to George Moore (1852–1933), wrote about him to Lady Gregory (1852–1932), and pressed W. B. Yeats (1865–1939) to meet him. Gossip had it that when the meeting actually took place Joyce told Yeats, 'We have met too late. You are too old for me to have any effect on you'. After taking his BA degree in 1902 Joyce at first intended to pursue medical studies, but family poverty made it impossible for him to do so in Dublin. He decided to go to Paris, with the apparent intention of studying medicine while supporting himself by teaching English. He wrote to Lady Gregory to announce his intention with characteristic self-dramatisation: 'I am going alone and friendless . . . I shall try myself against the powers of the world'. Lady Gregory induced E. V. Longworth, editor of the *Daily Express*, to send him books for reviewing and she gave him other letters of introduction. Indeed when Joyce left Ireland at the beginning of December 1902 Yeats invited him to breakfast with him after his overnight journey to London, met him at Euston Station, and looked after him for the day before he took the night ferry to Dieppe.

Though Joyce visited Dublin for three weeks at Christmas, he remained in Paris for over three months, studying, meeting people (among them J. M. Synge (1871–1909), the dramatist), writing poems, failing to get journalistic articles accepted, and begging cash from home and from Paris acquaintances to keep alive. But on 10 April 1903 he received a telegram reading 'Mother dying come home Father' and borrowed money from his pupil to journey home at once.

Back in Dublin Joyce had time on his hands and he cultivated the friendship of Oliver St John Gogarty (1878–1957), then a medical student, and destined to distinguish himself as surgeon, poet, and highly entertaining prose raconteur. Up to this point Joyce had been abstemious in his habits, but Gogarty determined to teach him to drink heavily, and succeeded. Gogarty was a brilliant conversationalist, skilled in mockery and in the manufacture of indecent limericks. He delighted in being outrageous. When Irish regiments returned to Dublin after the Boer War in 1900 he wrote a rhetorical verse tribute to them, which was duly printed in a leading social magazine, *Irish Society*, and then he flashed the news across Dublin that the capital letters at the beginning of each line should be read downwards. They ran 'The whores will be busy'.

As for the situation at home Joyce offended his family by rejecting his dying mother's request that he should go to confession and to communion, and by refusing to kneel in prayer with the rest of them at her bedside at the last, attitudes which the sturdy-minded, plain-spoken J. F. Byrne deplored. After his mother's death in August, Joyce wrote some book reviews for the *Daily Express*, made a few tentative moves towards earning money in Dublin, and finally left the family home in disgust when John Joyce sold the piano. Thereafter he moved between rented rooms and friends' houses, toyed with the idea of a singing career, worked briefly as a teacher at Clifton School, Dalkey, and finally had to face the problem of his future career when, one June day, he met and fell in love with Nora Barnacle, an auburn-haired girl from Galway who was at that time working at Finn's Hotel. Joyce and Nora took their first evening walk together on 16 June, and that day in 1904 became the day he made famous in literature for ever when he came to write *Ulysses*.

There were some rapid changes of residence in Joyce's last weeks in Ireland. He spent some time at his maternal uncle's house and even went home to his father for a few days. The temporary refuges briefly inhabited included the Martello tower at Sandycove, a defence bastion left over from Napoleonic days which Gogarty rented. But Joyce's stay in the tower soon became onerous to Gogarty who had no wish to get saddled with a semi-dependant. On Joyce's side the new commitment to Nora was a preoccupation, and the situation in the tower became uncomfortable. For his part Gogarty had no wish to earn hostility from a writer who might get satirical revenge in print. Moreover, as Stanislaus Joyce noted in his diary, Gogarty did not wish 'to forfeit the chance of shining with reflected light'. Joyce himself, however, 'determined that if Gogarty puts him out it will be done publicly'. Here then lay the genesis of another human study in betrayal. Joyce was to turn Gogarty into Buck Mulligan in *Ulysses*, a readily recognisable exercise in mockery which the future established surgeon, not surprisingly, could never forgive. Meanwhile Joyce was gradually making his final decision to leave Ireland, to take Nora with him, and to find a teaching post in a Berlitz school in Europe. So it was that Joyce and Nora left together in October 1904, the two of them embarking separately, since John Joyce knew nothing up to this point of Nora's part in his son's plans.

After a spell of teaching in Pola, Yugoslavia, Joyce found a post at the Berlitz school in Trieste in March 1905, and Trieste became the Joyces' home for the next ten years. Stanislaus, Joyce's brother, joined him in Trieste, also teaching at the Berlitz school. Nora gave birth to Giorgio in 1905 and to Lucia in 1907. For some months Joyce made a fruitless attempt to settle in a permanent post as a clerk in Rome in 1906; he made return visits to Ireland by himself in 1909 and 1910; and with Nora in 1912; and the family spent the summer in London in 1923; but Joyce spent the rest of his life largely in exile, moving to Zürich during the First World War, returning to Trieste in 1919, and moving to Paris in 1920.

Before leaving Ireland in October 1904, however, Joyce had written many of the poems later published as *Chamber Music* (1907). He had also made the crucial literary decision of his life in determining to write an autobiographical novel in which he would fully express his own frustrations as a rebel against Irish Catholicism, and his deep aspirations as an artist. The novel would also of course turn the spotlight of satire on many of those who had crossed his path. Joyce started work on this novel, *Stephen Hero*, in February 1904 and wrote hundreds of pages in the next few months. By 1906 he had written some 900 pages, twenty-five chapters, representing, he said, about half the intended book. In fact it did not get beyond that point. It is difficult to judge the unfinished novel fairly: the larger part was lost. The surviving manuscript begins at page 519 in the middle of Chapter XV. This is the text that was published posthumously as *Stephen Hero* in 1944. It is now regarded as something of a preliminary canter over the field which Joyce was to cover so expertly in *A Portrait of the Artist as a Young Man*.

The return visit to Ireland in the summer of 1909 proved crucial in its influence on Joyce's work. Lucia was now just two years old and Nora remained with her in Trieste while Joyce took little Giorgio, now four years old, to see his paternal grandfather in Dublin and Nora's people in Galway. The visit to Dublin was effective in finally reconciling John Joyce to his son's elopement, though not to his having settled so far from home. From the literary point of view Joyce's renewed contact in Dublin with his 'betrayers' was seminal. Gogarty, now comfortably settled in a smart house, did his best to be friendly and hospitable, but Joyce was at first hostile and then not more than coolly courteous. As for Cosgrave, he produced a personal crisis for Joyce through sheer malice and vanity. He told Joyce that he had been secretly meeting Nora on alternate evenings at the very same time that she had been first going out with Joyce himself – and when on these alternate evenings she was supposedly on duty. Joyce was devastated. He wrote to Nora acutely painful and passionate letters with agonised talk of broken faith. He was rescued from desolation and despair by his friend Byrne, now living at 7 Eccles Street, the house that was to be the home of the Blooms in *Ulysses*. When Byrne heard Joyce's story he realised at once that Cosgrave was lying, and possibly conspiring with Gogarty to ruin Joyce. The truth of the whole matter had in fact long been known to Stanislaus but not communicated to Joyce until this crisis. The fact was that Cosgrave had tried to win Nora's affection back in 1904 and had been rebuffed. Joyce therefore soon had cause to feel ashamed of his mistrust, and to picture himself as even more unworthy of Nora's innocence and fidelity. He poured out his soul to her in letters to that effect.

The traumatic experience was further intensified by Joyce's subsequent visit to Galway, where he was able to talk of Nora, to visit her old haunts, and even to look into the bedroom in which she had slept as a girl. Much of the emotion focused on the experience of presumed betrayal and infidelity was to surface later in the play *Exiles*, and, more obliquely, in *Ulysses*.

The early years of exile were years of struggle, financial and literary. To some extent the financial struggle was of Joyce's own making. Improvident with money, absurdly extravagant in spending it when it came his way, an inveterate borrower, often drinking heavily, over-fond of eating out, he was frequently bailed out by Stanislaus. It was only in 1917 that he was rescued from grosser financial worries by the generosity of Harriet Shaw Weaver who began to supply him with a regular income. The literary struggle was also acutely frustrating, as the long story of Joyce's efforts to get his book of short stories, *Dubliners*, into print shows. Joyce had started work on this book too during the crucial months in Dublin in 1904. In July of that year George Russell, who had seen Joyce's manuscript of *Stephen Hero*, asked him to write a short story for his journal *The Irish Homestead*. Joyce wrote 'The Sisters' and it appeared as 'Our Weekly Story' in the issue of 13 August 1904. Two further stories, 'Eveline' and 'After the Race', appeared in *The Irish Homestead* in September and December respectively. All three were tales of let-down, of disenchantment. 'I call the stories *Dubliners* to betray the soul of that hemiplegia or paralysis which many consider a city', he wrote. He sent the collection to the publisher Grant Richards in December 1905.

Although Grant Richards was quick to accept *Dubliners*, troubles arose when the printers objected to some of the language they were asked to set up in type, and he began to press for alterations. Joyce was obdurate and Grant Richards backed out of the deal for a time. The book was not actually published until 1914. However, the sad tale of delays was not all loss, for Joyce continued to work on the collection after first submitting it to Grant Richards in 1905. Several stories were retouched and the finest of all, 'The Dead', was added as late as 1907. It must be admitted that Joyce was not an easy writer for publishers to handle. When Grant Richards asked him to emend a passage in *Dubliners* about Edward VII and Queen Victoria which was offensive to royalty and which read 'Here's this chap come to the throne after his old mother's keeping him out of it till the man was grey', Joyce obliged by altering 'his old mother' to 'his bloody old bitch of a mother'.

The year 1914, which finally saw the publication of *Dubliners*, saw also the serialisation of *A Portrait of the Artist as a Young Man* in the London journal, *Egoist*. No one can doubt Joyce's wisdom in abandoning *Stephen Hero*, which he later denigrated as 'a schoolboy's production'. In the *Portrait* there is a new economy. The focus is shifted. Instead of a masked autobiographical record we have an artistically shaped novel, a novel of growing up in Dublin at the end of the nineteenth century. Its hero, Stephen Dedalus, in moving from infancy to young manhood, has experiences which match Joyce's own. This is what makes the book an 'autobiographical' novel. It is not an autobiography, not even a 'fictional autobiography', because it is not written in the first person. Moreover Stephen Dedalus is not a direct self-portrait. Joyce has certainly given a record of the environment in which he was brought up, people he knew have been drawn upon in his portrayal of other characters, but certain facets of their personalities were exaggerated or played down so as to meet the artistic needs of the novelist. Similarly, certain aspects of Joyce's own character were intensified and others ignored in order to create in Stephen a hero who is 'the artist' of the book's title.

Joyce's alter ego is Stephen Daedalus in *Stephen Hero* and Stephen Dedalus in the *Portrait*. He bears the names of the first Christian martyr and of the arch-artificer of classical legend. Saint Stephen's ardour in preaching and healing provoked such hostility that he was hauled up before the Sanhedrin, and when he boldly stood his ground, extolling Christ's authority over that of the Temple, he was stoned to death. Thus St Stephen provided Joyce with an image of himself as the heroic martyr, inspired with a prophetic mission, who is persecuted and condemned by institutionalised powers incapable of recognising his greatness. Daedalus, on the other hand, the great Athenian craftsman, constructed the labyrinth at Crete in which the monstrous Minotaur was confined. When he found himself imprisoned in his own maze, Daedalus fabricated wings for himself and his son Icarus from wax and feathers, so that they could escape by flight. Unfortunately Icarus flew too near the sun, the wax melted, and he was drowned. As the maker of a labyrinth and as one who escaped by flight, Daedalus provided Joyce with another congenial symbol.

Once *Dubliners* and the *Portrait* were in print Joyce became known, and after the family's move to Paris in 1920 life became easier in that Joyce had established himself and found himself a literary celebrity. But two more personal worries continued to trouble him. He himself suffered from deteriorating eyesight and underwent several operations; and his daughter Lucia suffered increasingly from schizophrenia. She was to die in a Northampton mental hospital in 1982.

The generosity of Miss Weaver's patronage, however, enabled Joyce to concentrate on *Ulysses*. Its composition occupied him for seven years between 1914 and 1921. Episodes began to be published serially in the *Little Review* in March 1918, and the completed book was published in Paris by Shakespeare and Co in 1922. Joyce had long been fascinated by the figure of Ulysses, or Odysseus, and for his epic portrayal of Dublin in June 1904 he chose to represent this hero of antiquity in the person of Leopold Bloom, a modest advertising agent. Penelope is his wife Molly Bloom. The agonies of Odysseus's ten years' wanderings and separation from his wife are transmuted into the personal and commercial frustrations of Bloom, who goes about his daily business in Dublin while his beloved wife entertains her lover at home. Stephen Dedalus, Joyce's alter ego in the *Portrait*, cut off physically and psychologically from home and friends, fatherland and church, is in search of spiritual fatherhood, and thus parallels Telemachus, Odysseus's son who goes out to find his father. The realistic details of the work as a portrait of Dublin city, Dublin's personalities, and Dublin life are unmatched in literature. Yet this is but half the story of the book's significance. For structural parallels with Homer, Dante, Shakespeare and even Milton add layers of rich meaning to the documentary of twentieth-century life, and a system of symbols ties the whole fabric together. Moreover, the archetypal patterning thus achieved is further enriched by highly innovatory experiments in matching style to substance.

Serial publication ensured that *Ulysses* was highly acclaimed in literary circles long before it was generally available in book form. Influential writers such as Ezra Pound (1885–1972) and T. S. Eliot (1888–1965) recognised the magnitude of Joyce's achievement from the start. Hence the circle of admirers that gathered round Joyce in his Paris days. After the immense artistic achievement of *Ulysses* Joyce's decision to devote what turned out to be seventeen years to the composition of *Finnegans Wake* dismayed many of his admirers, Miss Weaver among them, for stylistic experimentation in this massive work is carried to a point at which only the fervent enthusiast will take the trouble to work out even a minimum of the meanings that the compressed text holds. Joyce's devotion to the task was characteristic. The man who was absurdly careless of money and over-fond of playing the wild Irishman through long nights of drinking, telling tales, singing, dancing, and joking, would at the same time be recording scraps of conversation and odd verbal usage and storing them for use in that side of his life in which he worked at his manuscripts with a patient and disciplined effort that only the toughest of moral fibres could sustain.

Such paradox is the mark of Joyce as writer and as man. He loved Nora from the moment when, as he put it, she sauntered into his life in a Dublin street. She was quite incapable of sharing his literary and intellectual interests. She was totally uninterested in the work that exacted year after year a mountainous price in its toll upon his mental and moral resources. Yet Joyce's dependence upon her and his devotion to her were central to his achievement. He was deeply attached too to his impossible father, and overcome with remorse that he had not visited him more when John Joyce died in 1931. Joyce's own last years were darkened by Lucia's deteriorating mental condition. The Second World War drove the family back from Paris to Zürich, and Joyce died there in January 1941 after surgery on a duodenal ulcer. He was buried there, and so was Nora when she died ten years later.

Joyce's Dublin

Whatever and wherever Joyce wrote it was the Dublin of his youth and young manhood that provided the central substance of his work. He was fond of claiming that if Dublin were destroyed it could be reconstructed from his books. It is evident that since the Joyce family had at least sixteen different addresses before Joyce left Ireland and since the home itself was not an attractive one to linger in there was every incentive for Joyce as a child and as a student to roam the streets and become familiar with the oddest corners of the city. As a capital city Dublin had impressive public places, dignified architecture, and a fine cultural life, yet it was small enough for there to be a sense of community at its centre, for the inhabitants to know one another, and for the city's characters to be a matter of interest to all. At its heart it was lived in as well as worked in. Its people had common contemporary subjects for their conversation and many of them a common stock of historical knowledge to draw on or fantasise about.

Dublin is an ancient city. Scandinavian invaders had made it their base in the ninth century and Danish power was not finally overthrown until the Irish king Brian Boru broke it at the battle of Clontarf in 1014. It was during the reign of Henry II in the twelfth century that English forces first invaded Ireland and took Dublin, and the chequered story of Anglo-Irish political relationships from that time has been summed up in the phrase, 'England never wholly victorious nor Ireland thoroughly subdued'. No doubt the eighteenth century was an age of some cultural splendour in Dublin. Much of the finest public and domestic architecture dates from this period prior to the Act of Union (1800) when Ireland had its own parliament. It is not surprising that in Joyce's youth the splendour of eighteenth-century Dublin was looked back upon with nostalgia. It was 'the seventh city of Christendom' Gogarty would remind its citizens. And Joyce was wont to insist upon its current dignity as 'the second city of the British Empire'.

Joyce's love–hate relationship with his native city was of intense significance to him as a writer. He may have shaken the city's dust from his feet in 1904, disgusted with its paralytic decay and angry with its cramping conventions, but he knew the city inside out and his work reveals how much he admired its dignity, its humanity, its sheer comprehensiveness and comprehensibility. These qualities made it appropriate as the locus of an epic on the scale of the *Odyssey*. Dublin could be Everyman's city, the archetypal 'womancity' like the New Jerusalem. 'If I can get to the heart of Dublin, I can get to the heart of every city in the world', he said. 'In the particular is contained the universal.'

The fact that Dublin had been the seat of government and the home of the aristocracy in the eighteenth century but had declined from this status in the nineteenth century determined the physical peculiarity of the city in which Joyce was brought up. The public face of a capital city was evident, many of the fine squares and terraces of the capital's hey-day were evident too, but encroaching upon them were slums, seedy tenements, and signs of dereliction as bad as any in western Europe. The area immediately north of the Liffey, between Marlborough Street in the west and Amiens Street in the east (which Joyce called 'Nighttown') contained a large number of brothels. Popularly known as 'Monto', the notorious area included Montgomery Street, Talbot Street and Mecklenburg Street. This once fashionable area had been taken over by British regiments in the mid-nineteenth century, girls poured in, and prostitution flourished. The brothels remained when the military departed. Thus central Dublin contained, within easy walking distance, such magnificent buildings as those of Trinity College, the old Parliament House (taken over by the Bank of

Ireland), the Custom House, the ancient castle, the Four Courts, the cathedrals, the libraries, the galleries and museums, and a plethora of Georgian mansions and terraces. It contained all these cheek-by-jowl with a red-light district that had been labelled the worst slum in Europe. There were something like 5,000 soldiers in Dublin at the turn of the century and there were whores of appropriate social status and environment to accommodate licentious soldiery of all ranks. The better-class whores sent their cards to the Officers' Mess. Cabs conveyed the traffic from garrison to brothel, and no doubt this fact encouraged Joyce to use the horse as the symbol of betrayal it was in the Fall of Troy.

The widespread poverty in Dublin spawned pawnbrokers as well as prostitutes, and indeed an enquiry made in 1904 revealed that nearly three million pawn tickets were issued in Dublin in one year. The tenements that lay in narrow lanes behind the smart squares and shopping streets housed thousands of inhabitants in conditions of great privation, sometimes ten or more to a single room.

In becoming a student at University College, Joyce was joining the less prestigious of the two Dublin colleges providing university education. Trinity College, whose charter dated back to 1601, had distinguished scholars on its faculties, but it was a stronghold of the Anglo-Irish Protestant ascendancy. The Catholic hierarchy frowned upon non-Catholic and non-sectarian educational institutions alike, and John Henry Newman had founded the 'Catholic University' in 1853 to cater for those thus excluded from Trinity College. It was taken over by the Jesuits in 1879 and became one of the constituent colleges of the Royal University, which included also the Queen's College in Cork, the college visited by Simon Dedalus and Stephen in the *Portrait*. It was at University College, Dublin, that the poet Gerard Manley Hopkins (1844–89) was Professor of Greek from 1884–9. Something of the relative social and cultural divide between Trinity and University College may be sensed in a remark attributed to J. P. Mahaffy, a renowned Trinity classicist with a European reputation: 'James Joyce is a living argument in favour of my contention that it was a mistake to establish a separate university for the aborigines of this island – for the corner-boys who spit into the Liffey.'

An aspect of a Dublin upbringing that was important to the young Joyce as it had been to the young George Bernard Shaw (1856–1950) was the musical life of the city. It is clear from Joyce's books, and from his biography, that musical gatherings in the home, musical concerts in such halls as the Antient Concert Rooms, performance of sacred music in churches, and the performances of flourishing operatic societies familiarised musical Dubliners with a considerable repertoire – if predominantly the repertoire of drawing-room balladry, fashionable oratorio, and popular operatic arias. In 1900 Dublin had over 400 music teachers to a population of about 300,000. This was the age of the itinerant organ-grinder too, as George Moore discovered to his cost when he annoyed his neighbours in Ely Place by painting his door green. They retaliated by hiring organ-grinders to play under his windows when he was penning his mellifluous prose. The bars too were places where men sang, and bars there were in plenty. At the turn of the century you could drink liquor in 900 places and buy it at another 350 or so.

In the streets of Joyce's Dublin, as he presents them, bars and churches, shops and offices, houses and hospitals flash before our eyes. There are trams in the streets and horse-drawn traffic everywhere. In *Ulysses* the trams are electric, but in the period of Joyce's childhood represented in the early chapters of the *Portrait* they are horse-drawn, for the horse-drawn trams put on the streets in 1872 were replaced by double- and single-deck electric trams in 1902 when Joyce was twenty. Tom Kettle, Joyce's friend who married his adored Mary Sheehy and was to be killed in action in France in 1916, called the tramcar 'the social confessional of Dublin'. Cabs for hire were, of course, horse-drawn. Some 656 closed cabs for hire were registered in 1904 as well as 1,030 open cars known as 'jaunting cars'. The novelty of the motor-car in Joyce's early days is made evident in his story 'After the Race' (*Dubliners*).

The river was as much a highway as the streets, for Dublin was a city of quays and docks. In *Ulysses* we see a barge laden with Guinness stout for the export market passing under O'Connell Bridge in the city centre, and we learn too of the upheavals and dangers sometimes brought into the city streets by herds of cattle being driven through them to the docks. Dublin was a city with a shore-line, offering the maximum interest to the growing, exploring child. It is on the coast that Joyce's great masterpiece *Ulysses* begins, in one of those Martello towers which were built as defensive fortresses around the Irish coast at the time when a Napoleonic invasion threatened. The walls of the tower in question at Sandycove are eight feet thick and its height is forty feet. It is a circular building, the main room entered by an iron staircase. A smaller staircase leads up to a gun-rest on the parapet. This is where Joyce's epic begins and, appropriately, it is now a Joycean museum.

Historical background

At the time when Joyce was young Ireland was still part of the United Kingdom of Great Britain and Ireland. By the time he finished writing *Ulysses* the Irish Free State was being established. By the time he died the total independence of the Irish Republic had been accepted by the British government. Joyce therefore grew up at a time of momentous political changes, the culmination of a century of unrest, and the controversies that were alive in the Dublin he portrayed were giving voice to long-standing demands for the betterment of social conditions in Ireland and for the freeing of the nation from British control. Names of key figures in the century-long moves towards emancipation were part of the conversational background of Dublin life.

Thus in *Ulysses* nationalists hark back nostalgically in their talk to the days of Henry Grattan (1746–1820), an opposition politician whose oratory was such that the hey-day of Ireland's parliament as an independent legislature was popularly called 'Grattan's parliament'. During that period, in 1791, a republican movement was founded by Wolfe Tone (1763–98) and Hamilton Rowan (1751–1834), called the Society of United Irishmen. Official attempts at suppression led to its going underground in 1795 as a secret revolutionary movement. It flourished, and official repression was intensified after a French expedition of some 6,000 troops arrived threateningly in Bantry Bay in December 1796, though in fact the force was prevented from landing by adverse weather conditions. Accompanying the fleet was the patriot Wolfe Tone himself, who was condemned to death for treason two years later, but committed suicide in prison. He worked hard to try to ensure that the French assistance necessary to successful revolution would be forthcoming, but matters came to a head prematurely in 1798 as a result of the effectiveness of the government secret service. Among leading conspirators arrested was Lord Edward Fitzgerald (1763–98) who fought desperately when cornered and received a fatal wound. In May 1798 rebels in County Wexford defeated a body of the North Cork militia but then failed to make a successful breakout from Wexford. In June they won a victory at Gorey but, having besieged New Ross and taken it, they were driven out by a relief force while still celebrating their victory. A determined rebel attack on Arklow (County Wicklow) was also beaten off, and finally General Lake stormed the rebel headquarters at Vinegar Hill, Ennisworthy, and the rebellion was over. But the bold exploits of the 'Wexford boys' passed into history and stayed there. This rebellion is the background to the ballad 'The Croppy Boy', one of Joyce's own favourite songs and one which is a moving expression of the patriotic themes that stirred the imagination of nationalists. Ben Dollard sings it in the 'Sirens' episode in *Ulysses* and its phrases re-echo through the text.

'The Croppy Boy'

'Good men and true! in this house who dwell
To a stranger bouchal* I pray you tell
Is the priest at home? or may he be seen?
I would speak a word with Father Green.'

'The priest's at home, boy, and may be seen:
Tis easy speaking with Father Green;
But you must wait till I go and see
If the holy father alone may be.'

The youth has entered an empty hall –
What a lonely sound has his light foot-fall!
And the gloomy chamber's still and bare,
With a vested priest in a lonely chair.

The youth has knelt to tell his sins;
'Nomine Dei', the youth begins:
At 'mea culpa' he beats his breast,
And in broken murmurs he speaks the rest.

'At the siege of Ross did my father fall,
And at Gorey my loving brothers all,
I alone am left of my name and race,
I will go to Wexford and take their place.

'I cursed three times since last Easter day –
At mass-time once I went to play;
I passed the churchyard one day in haste,
And forgot to pray for my mother's rest.

'I bear no grudge against living thing;
But I love my country above the king.
Now, Father, bless me and let me go
To die, if God has ordained it so.'

The Priest said naught, but a rustling noise
Made the youth look up in wild surprise;
The robes were off, and in scarlet there
Sat a yeoman captain with fiery glare.

With fiery glare and with fury hoarse,
Instead of blessing, he breathed a curse: –
'Twas a good thought, boy, to come here and shrive,
For one short hour is your time to live.

* bouchal: (*Irish*) boy

'Upon yon river three tenders float,
The Priest's in one, if he isn't shot –
We hold his house for our Lord the King,
And Amen! say I, may all traitors swing!'

At Geneva Barrack that young man died,
And at Passage they have his body laid.
Good people who live in peace and joy,
Breathe a prayer and a tear for the Croppy Boy.

The ballad attributes so much trickery and harshness to the British soldiery and so much idealism and self-sacrifice to the young Irish rebel that its emotive appeal is strong. And though in *Ulysses* Joyce's hero, Leopold Bloom, listens with ironic detachment to its performance as an indulgence of Irish sentimentality, Joyce plainly relished the song, and indeed he fastened on part of the Croppy Boy's confession – 'I forgot to pray for my mother's rest' – to add overtones to Stephen Dedalus's refusal to pray at his mother's deathbed.

Rebellious risings in Ulster in June 1798 were even more quickly defeated than the Wexford rising. It was ironic that a much-needed, though small, French expedition landed at Killala in County Mayo on 22 August. An insurgent band, thus reinforced, was defeated within a few weeks at Ballinamuck, County Longford. But the invitation to foreign invasion which Ireland presented, together with the threat posed by the rising of 1798, induced the English Prime Minister, William Pitt, to seek legislative union between the two countries. One of Pitt's promises, which won support for the Union, was that of Catholic emancipation.

Both Catholic bishops and Protestant landlords were fearful of revolution, and the bill to merge Ireland with Great Britain in 'The United Kingdom of Great Britain and Ireland' was finally passed in 1800 and became operative on 1 January 1801. A good deal of bribery was involved in achieving the necessary majority in the Dublin parliament. Grattan opposed the change. So too, odd as it may sound to modern ears, did the Protestant Orangemen of the north who, disliking the British government's dealings with Roman Catholics, were fiercely anti-unionist.

The Union was weakened from the start by the failure to grant immediate Catholic emancipation, a failure in which a crucial element was the pressure put on George III to persuade him that his coronation oath precluded royal assent to such a bill. But there was a temporary lull in Irish political activity in the early years of the new century. One name, however, was added to the list of almost legendary heroes. Robert Emmet (1778–1803), a friend of the poet Thomas Moore (1779–1852) in his student days at Trinity College, Dublin, had to forsake his studies in 1798 because of his links with the United Irishmen. He went to Paris and contacted exiled patriots, then, expecting a Napoleonic invasion of England, he returned to Ireland and built up stores of arms in Dublin. Emmet's was another story of a premature action, this time produced by an ammunition explosion at his store. All Emmet achieved was to lead a mob to a vain attack on Dublin Castle. Then, after lying low for a time in Dublin, he was captured and executed. The historic significance of Emmet's effort was in practical terms negligible, but two factors gave him legendary status in the nationalist pantheon. He made a dignified speech from the dock which was to inspire patriots for more than a century. Its concluding lines run through Leopold Bloom's mind in the 'Sirens' episode in *Ulysses*: 'When my country takes her place among the nations of the earth, then and not till then let my epitaph be written. I have done.'

Another matter gave romantic associations to the figure of the young martyr. Emmet's sweetheart was Sarah Curran (1782–1808), daughter of a distinguished lawyer who strongly disapproved of him, and it was because Emmet stayed on in Dublin to say farewell to Sarah that he was caught. She was broken-hearted by Emmet's execution and her health gave way. She married an army officer and died in England. Her sad story was the theme of Thomas Moore's touching song, 'She is far from the land':

> She is far from the land where her young hero sleeps,
> And lovers are round her sighing;
> But coldly she turns from their gaze, and weeps,
> For her heart in his grave is lying!

A major political figure who spoke against the Union from the start was Daniel O'Connell (1775–1847). In the 1820s he became a staunch advocate of the Catholic emancipation which the Union had failed to bring. When the long overdue Catholic Emancipation Act was finally passed in 1829 O'Connell himself became the first Catholic Member of Parliament in the House of Commons. O'Connell, nicknamed 'the Liberator', was an orator of astonishing power who toured the country addressing massive crowds. Recognising that repeal of the Union must be a long-term aim, he threw himself first into campaigns for reform in such matters as suffrage, tithes, welfare, and local government. Then he agitated publicly for Repeal of the Union at open-air meetings at which hundreds of thousands of people (and in one case possibly almost a million) heard him. By the time O'Connell died the failure of the Irish potato crop through blight in 1845 and

1846 had marked the beginning of the four-year famine which eroded the Irish economy. This calamity reduced the population by a million and a half. Widespread starvation, disease, and poverty that led to eviction and homelessness provoked only a totally inadequate official response. Lawlessness ensued and was answered by suppression. Indeed the 'Great Hunger' left a legacy of bitterness and distrust that transformed both the rational and the emotional impetus of nationalism and republicanism. Moreover it naturally gave stimulus to radical movements which believed in violence.

A difficulty for outsiders in trying to grasp an outline of Irish political history in relation to Great Britain in the nineteenth century is the complexity of the Irish internal divisions. The Catholic–Protestant division did not match up with the division between nationalists and unionists. Nationalist movements were split between those who believed in working through parliamentary machinery towards Home Rule and those who sought revolutionary action. Nationalists were disunited about the desirable degree of disentanglement from Great Britain. There were those who wanted a Catholic Ireland and those who wanted a wholly secular republic. The variety of cross-currents still prevalent in political controversy at the turn of the century is evident from student discussion in the *Portrait*.

A crucial cause of bitter internal dissension in Ireland which casts its shadow over *Dubliners*, the *Portrait* and *Ulysses* was the career of Charles Stewart Parnell (1846–91), a Protestant landowner who united most of the Irish nationalist movements behind him before his fall. He became a Member of Parliament in 1875. He was the first president of the Irish Land League which was founded in 1879 to oppose exploitation of land by landlords and sought equitable distribution of land among those who actually worked it. The League brought people together across religious and class boundaries. Their solidarity eventually brought about Gladstone's Land Act of 1881 which strengthened the hold of tenants on their homesteads. Parnell, called 'the uncrowned king of Ireland', now devoted himself to the struggle for Home Rule culminating in Gladstone's Home Rule Bill of 1886 which was heavily defeated in the House of Commons. Parnell's downfall resulted from his long liaison with Katharine O'Shea, the wife of Captain O'Shea, who in 1889 filed divorce proceedings, naming Parnell as co-respondent. One of the first to turn against Parnell was Michael Davitt (1846–1906) who had been closely involved with him in the founding of the Land League and who now called for his resignation. Gladstone determined that the Liberals would no longer be able to work in alliance with a party of Irish MPs under Parnell's chairmanship and Parnell turned against him in consequence. Finally the Catholic hierarchy called for an end to

Parnell's leadership. Parnell's struggle to retain it, which involved seeking support from underground radicals, left a legacy of bitterness. Joyce's father (like Simon Dedalus in the *Portrait*) was a Parnellite anti-cleric who blamed the Church for destroying the people's hero. Parnell did not survive his downfall for long. He married Kitty O'Shea in June 1891 and died the following October in England. His body was brought to Ireland for burial in Glasnevin Cemetery, Dublin. His fervent admirers were able to claim that political enemies had hounded him to his grave. The verses 'The Death of Parnell' recited by Mr Hynes at the end of 'Ivy Day in the Committee Room', one of the short stories in *Dubliners*, express popular sentiment on the tragedy:

> He is dead. Our Uncrowned King is dead.
> O, Erin, mourn with grief and woe
> For he lies dead whom the fell gang
> Of modern hypocrites laid low.

Echoes of the affair are with us on the very first page of the *Portrait*.

An event which might have terminated Parnell's career earlier occurred in May 1882 when an underground republican terrorist splinter group calling themselves 'the Invincibles' murdered the new Irish Chief Secretary, Lord Frederick Cavendish, and the Under Secretary, Thomas Henry Burke, outside the Vice-Regal Lodge in Phoenix Park. Public opinion on all sides was shocked. Parnell, indeed, believing his cause to be irreparably damaged, offered his resignation to Gladstone, who persuaded him to stay on as leader of his party. James Carey (1845–83), one of the Invincibles, turned informer and five of his fellow-conspirators were executed.

It was 1893 before Gladstone was able to introduce a second Home Rule Bill in the House of Commons and, though it was eventually forced through, it was then rejected by the House of Lords. The third Home Rule Bill was carried in the Commons in 1913 against strong opposition from Ulster Unionists. By this time the Lords had power only to delay a bill for two years, and royal assent was given in September 1914. However, the First World War had already started and it was agreed to suspend the implementation of the successful bill for the duration of the war.

Developments during the time of the abortive legislative attempts to establish Home Rule and, even more, during the war, when the successful bill was suspended, rendered the long constitutional struggle irrelevant, for nationalist demands were intensified as a result of repeated frustration. Moreover increasing interest in Irish culture added further dimensions to the political drive for independence. Douglas Hyde (1863–1947), a Gaelic scholar, was one of the founders of the Gaelic League in 1893. Its object was the revival of the Irish language. Hyde called for the 'de-Anglicising' of Ireland. He sought unity of aim in this cause across the sectarian and political boundaries, and when the League took a decisive line for political independence in 1915 Hyde and other moderate members resigned. The agitation for reviving Irish was reaching a crucial stage by the time Joyce became a university student at the turn of the century. Hyde, who was a literary man, published *Love Songs of Connacht* (talk of which is heard in *Ulysses*) in 1893.

The crucial twentieth-century moves towards Irish independence took place after the year 1904, with which *Ulysses* is concerned, but were still continuing after Joyce completed the book in 1921. The 1916 Easter Rising was plotted by members of the Irish Republican Brotherhood, an extremist body which had been formed as far back as 1858 by James Stephens (1824–1901) and which was sometimes in alliance with and sometimes at loggerheads with those who sought reform by constitutional means. The Brotherhood recognised its own president as President of the Irish Republic. A rebel force, led by Patrick H. Pearse (1879–1916) and James Connolly (1868–1916), seized the General Post Office in Dublin on Easter Monday 1916 and proclaimed the Irish Republic. After a week of fighting the rebellion was crushed and fifteen leaders were executed. These executions and the mass arrests alienated much moderate opinion and resulted in vastly increased support for the Sinn Fein ('Ourselves Alone') movement which had grown in the last decade of the century under the guidance of Arthur Griffith (1871–1922) and others. Eamon de Valera (1882–1975), one of the rebel leaders whose death sentence was commuted, became President of Sinn Fein in 1917 and together with Michael Collins (1890–1922) reorganised the movement.

The party gained a sweeping victory in the General Election of 1918, whereupon the Members of Parliament met in Dublin and proclaimed themselves the assembly of the Irish Republic. The forces who had formed the rebel army of Easter 1916 took an oath of allegiance to this body as the Irish Republican Army. Meanwhile the I.R.A. took over control in some parts of the country. They raided tax offices and made settled administration impossible. Harsh British attempts at suppression included the ferocious reprisals carried out by the 'Black and Tans', soldiers newly demobilised from service in the Great War. In 1921 Lloyd George, the British Prime Minister, negotiated with Irish emissaries. The Treaty which finally emerged (imposed on the Irish by threat of renewing the war) created the Irish Free State with dominion status in the British Empire. Six counties of Ulster, the stronghold of uncompromising unionism, were separated by partition to form Northern Ireland. Though the Irish assembly accepted this treaty, De Valera, who had remained in Dublin during the final negotiations, was among a minority who rejected it, resenting the partition and making a key issue of the oath of allegiance to the King which the constitution required. The pro-Treaty party had a substantial majority over the anti-Treaty party in the Irish General Election of June 1922, but the anti-Treaty party under De Valera refused to recognise the new government and civil war followed. The anti-Treaty forces accepted defeat in May 1923. Thereupon De Valera founded a new political party, Fianna Fail, which ultimately gained power in 1932.

Literary context

From some of the things Joyce said we might be led to believe that it was a culturally moribund Ireland on which he turned his back in 1904. The implication of the *Portrait* is that Ireland was no place for a nonconforming artist to work in. But in fact Dublin was at that time astir with literary activity. Indeed the period of Joyce's productivity coincided with an Irish literary renaissance of outstanding distinction in the history of English literature. Forsaking Ireland for a time, even for a long time, would not of itself have isolated a writer from this renaissance. Indeed many of the key figures of the Irish literary renaissance spent many years, in some cases most of their lives, in England. Shaw, George Moore, Yeats, and Sean O'Casey (1884–1964) are cases in point. Somehow Joyce's exile seems to have snapped the link with Ireland with a finality that is not evident even in O'Casey, who quarrelled with theatrical Dublin and rejected priest-ridden Ireland as decisively as Joyce did. Perhaps the fact that Joyce settled on the continent rather than in England intensifies the reader's sense of his alienation from his homeland. But the irony remains that in his work he continued to live imaginatively in his native Dublin with an intensity of love and of satire that never seemed to slacken.

There is, however, another aspect of Joyce's place in the literary context of his time. You could not write of the Irish movement without giving attention to Joyce beside Yeats and Synge, O'Casey and James Stephens (1882–1950), George Moore and Lady Gregory. Neither could you write of the revolutionary twentieth-century Modern Movement in English literature without giving attention to Joyce beside T. S. Eliot and Ezra Pound, Wyndham Lewis (1884–1957) and Ford Madox Ford (1873–1939), D. H. Lawrence (1885–1930) and Virginia Woolf (1882–1941). Nor could you write of the dominant figures of the European novel in our age without mentioning Joyce alongside Marcel Proust (1871–1922), Thomas Mann (1875–1955), and Franz Kafka (1883–1924). Yeats's international reputation may be no less secure than Joyce's, but Joyce's achievement seems to give him a status that transcends all groupings and movements.

That side of the Irish literary renaissance which was concerned to revivify the Irish language and to make early Irish writers known in translation did not excite Joyce's enthusiasm. It is the richness of the Anglo-Irish literary revival that concerns us here. It had begun in the last decades of the nineteenth century. Oscar Wilde (1854–1900) had mesmerised London audiences with his scintillatingly witty comedies in the 1890s. His masterpiece *The Importance of Being Earnest* was first produced in 1895. George Bernard Shaw had pleased and teased the London public with wit and paradox that turned fashionable assumptions upside down in *Arms and the Man* (1894), in *Candida* (1897), and in *You Never Can Tell* (1899). Shaw's ability to make the English laugh at themselves was remarkable. Indeed it might be argued that by the time Douglas Hyde published his seminal pamphlet 'The Necessity for de-Anglicising Ireland' in 1901 Bernard Shaw had already faced up to the more formidable necessity for de-Anglicising England. Meanwhile in prose fiction Edith Somerville (1858–1949) and Martin Ross (Violet Martin, 1862–1915) captivated readers with two volumes of the hilarious *Experiences of an Irish R.M.* in 1899 and 1908, and George Moore had a unique success with his novel *Esther Waters* in 1894.

The poet W. B. Yeats was the dominant figure in the Irish movement. It was he who co-operated with Lady Augusta Gregory and Edward Martyn (1859–1924), both minor playwrights, in establishing the Irish Literary Theatre. Yeats and Martyn also prevailed upon George Moore, now well established in England as both novelist and dramatist, to join them in their efforts to promote Irish drama. Moore left London for Dublin in 1901 to immerse himself in the Irish movement. One of the Irish Theatre's earliest productions was Yeats's *Countess Cathleen* in 1899 which sparked off the controversy referred to in the *Portrait*, where Joyce quotes the text. In 1902 they performed Yeats's *Cathleen ni Houlihan*, a passionately nationalistic play showing the call to heroic sacrifice coming in 1798 to a young bridegroom in a country cottage near Killala where the French fleet landed. The company took over the Abbey Theatre in 1904 and here performed the plays of their great discovery, J. M. Synge. His masterpiece *The Playboy of the Western World* was first produced in 1907. The company's early productions already included the work of Yeats, Martyn, Lady Gregory, Douglas Hyde (in Irish) and George Moore, so there was nothing absurd about the theatrical efforts on which Stephen Dedalus of *Ulysses* is made to pour such scorn – nor about the premises on which he is made to pour vomit.

A key figure in the Irish literary renaissance was George Russell who used the pseudonym 'AE'. A poet, a mystic, an enthusiast for Irish mythology, an industrious editor, and an indefatigably watchful and helpful poetic talent-spotter, he assumed the role of Dublin's literary panjandrum and was consulted by all and sundry. One of AE's discoveries was the poet and novelist, James Stephens. His novel *The Charwoman's Daughter* (1912) introduces the reader to the daughter of a Dublin tenement-dweller whose daily walks impinge unwittingly on the perambulations of AE, Yeats, Synge and George Moore. The literary scene over which these writers presided was vividly, if sometimes distortedly, depicted in George Moore's lively autobiographical trilogy, *Hail and Farewell* (*Ave*, *Salve*, *Vale*), published between 1911 and 1914. Another of Joyce's contemporaries, Sean O'Casey, scored brilliant successes at the Abbey Theatre in the 1920s with *Juno and the Paycock* (1925), which portrays the Dublin of the Civil War in 1922 and *The Plough and the Stars* (1926), set in the Dublin of the 1916 Rising.

In Joyce's *Ulysses* there are references to Yeats, Martyn, Lady Gregory, George Moore, George Russell, Synge, James Stephens, Douglas Hyde, Oscar Wilde, and Padraic Colum (1881–1972). The book can therefore scarcely be detached from the literary movement centred in Dublin. Yet Joyce's experimentation in substance and style brought him into line with writers of the wider Modern Movement such as Ezra Pound, T. S. Eliot, Ford Madox Ford, Virginia Woolf, D. H. Lawrence, and of course Yeats himself, who in verse or prose were finding new and striking ways of creating new, contemporary literature. The Movement was engaged in expanding the range of subjects to which literature made itself open – and in this respect Joyce's more accurate and detailed representation of what transpires in the human consciousness and in the physical processes of daily living inevitably challenged the conventions of Victorian reticence. It was also a matter, especially in the novel, of breaking apart the literary frameworks within which nineteenth-century novelists had conducted their readers through successive paragraphs of narration, description, and dialogue in mimicry of stage presentation. The exploration of Dublin in *Dubliners*, the *Portrait*, *Ulysses*, and even *Finnegans Wake* certainly gives Joyce's work its place in the Irish movement. The exploration of the human consciousness and the projection of its moment-by-moment life in a style and presentation fashioned specifically to that task by dozens of new devices gives Joyce's work its central place in the Modern Movement of English literature.

Part 2

Joyce's works

Dubliners

Dubliners brings together fifteen short stories written for the most part with the purpose of displaying the 'paralysis' afflicting Dublin's life. Defending the collection to his publisher, Joyce claimed:

> I believe that in composing my chapter of moral history in exactly the way I have composed it I have taken the first step towards the spiritual liberation of my country.

Indeed when the publisher took fright at the frankness of the text and demanded cuts in the stories, Joyce declared:

> It is not my fault that the odour of ashpits and old weeds and offal hangs round my stories. I seriously believe that you will retard the course of civilisation by preventing the Irish people from having one good look at themselves in my nicely-polished looking glass.

Joyce's admission elsewhere that in *Dubliners* he had adopted a style of 'scrupulous meanness' taken in conjunction with his image of the 'nicely-polished looking glass' exactly sums up the way the surface economy and naturalism of the stories is overlaid with layers of meaning and sometimes of mystification.

'The Sisters'

The first three stories are presented through the eyes of a child. Each of them recounts a momentous experience which shocks and bewilders the boy. Though the adult reader can understand things which the boy cannot understand, he nevertheless shares something of the boy's bewilderment. Like the narrator, if to a lesser extent, the reader is confronted by characters and events that are not always fully explicable.

The boy has become acquainted with an old priest, Father James Flynn, has visited him, taken snuff to him as a present from his aunt, and been informally instructed by him in the ways of the Church. He has appreciated this teaching but has found certain of the priest's habits disturbing – his stupefied dozes, his trembling hands, and the way his mouth would fall open and his tongue lie out on his lower lip. He has picked up from adults the word 'paralysis' describing the priest's condition. When the old priest dies and the boy's aunt takes him to visit his two bereaved sisters and to take a last look at the corpse, what is said by the adults gradually clears up for the reader – if not fully for the boy – the outline of the priest's story. Father Flynn had failed physically and mentally. At one point he accidentally broke a chalice; at another point he disappeared for a time and was discovered at night sitting alone in the confessional box in the church 'wide-awake and laughing-like softly to himself'. This picture and the bereaved sister's remark that the event 'made them think there was something gone wrong with him' is what the child finally remembers of the experience.

Joyce's technique was from the start to universalise the particular by means of symbols. But he did this with restraint so as not to impose on the reader anything like clear 'allegorical' interpretations. Indeed he was careful to give the reader a share in the narrator's own bewilderment in trying to interpret his experience. 'Father Flynn' is certainly an archetypal name for an Irish priest and thus the failing, half-demented priest with his background in the Irish college in Rome and his sure grounding in the niceties of ecclesiastical practice may be said to represent the Irish church or perhaps even Ireland itself. Father Flynn's increasingly paralytic condition renders him totally ineffective in practical matters. Nannie and Eliza, known by their names in the story, become 'The Sisters' in the title, which of course suggests nuns. It is significant that their 'little house' is in Great Britain Street over a drapery shop selling bootees and umbrellas that protect human beings artificially from the touch of living water. Father Flynn's priestly garments have a 'green faded look'. The red handkerchief with which he tries to wipe his snuff-stained clothes clean is itself black with snuff. (Red is always England's colour, Ireland's green.) It is worth noticing too that the little boy feels inexplicably an unexpected 'sensation of freedom as if [he] had been freed from something by his death'. Thus a few deftly dropped hints suggest a moment in the life of the youth at which a source of valued teaching, whether individual or institutional, is revealed as far advanced in debility and dementia. And it is significant for the experienced reader of Joyce that this revelation is made while the company gaze at an empty fireplace and partake in common of unconsecrated wine and biscuits.

Yet, quite aside from such readings, the story is a subtle and powerful record on the naturalistic level of how the adult world impinges on the mind of a young boy as he fastens on the comments of his elders, who so often beat about the bush in their evasive chatter.

'An Encounter'

The story brings the boy into contact with another decayed eccentric. Once more the child's eyes are opened to seedy aspects of adult life – if 'eyes are opened' is the right expression to use for an experience which the boy is too young to understand. He is old enough, however, to sense the menace of the squalid derangement from which the stranger suffers.

The boy tells the reader how an imaginary world of romantic excitement impinged on him in his schooldays to offset the drab routine of daily life. It came in the form of Wild West stories printed in boys' magazines. His playmates involved him in fierce games of cowboys and Indians. Lacking their robustness, he was a somewhat reluctant participant: on the other hand the Wild West world in books 'opened doors of escape' and fed his hunger 'for wild sensations'. This hunger leads him to plan a more practical escape from routine with two school-fellows, Mahony and Leo Dillon. They will play truant for a day and walk out to the Pigeon House, an old fort way out on a breakwater in Dublin Bay. On the morning of the adventure Dillon fails to turn up, and Mahony and the narrator go off without him, taking a circuitous route to the coast in order to avoid possible detection.

It is noon by the time they reach the quays. The busy spectacle of the shipping there is the one reward they get for their venturesomeness, for by the time they have grown tired of watching it is too late to carry out their project of visiting the Pigeon House. The adventure deteriorates, first into wandering around the dingy streets of Ringsend, then to lying in a field on the bank of the river Dodder. A curious man, fairly old and shabby, approaches, hand on hip, tapping the turf at his feet with a stick. After passing them, he turns round and comes back to sit down at their side. He embarks on a conversation which soon touches embarrassingly on the ways of boys with girls. Then he leaves them for a few minutes. Suddenly Mahony exclaims, 'I say! Look what he's doing!' but our narrator is too embarrassed even to raise his eyes. Whatever impropriety the stranger may have committed, the reader's ignorance gives him a surer share in the boys' unease. Sensing danger, the narrator tells Mahony to be 'Murphy' while he himself will be 'Smith'. When the fellow returns, Mahony goes off, chasing a cat, while our narrator is left to listen to what becomes an obsessive, neurotic monologue on why naughty boys ought to be whipped and what relish can properly be taken in whipping them. Thoroughly alarmed, our little boy gets up, excuses himself, and shouts out for 'Murphy'. Mahony comes running as if to his aid and the two escape.

The encounter with a perverted Dublin character (taken from

Joyce's own boyhood memories) makes a violent contrast with the romantic dreams which send the boy out on his day's adventure. The crumbling of dream into reality as the venture fails in its objective, then into sheer sordidness as the real adult world of Dublin impinges in the form of the obsessed pervert makes the kind of fine contrast in which Joyce delighted. Perhaps this contrast between the light and the dark in life is what was in Joyce's mind when, at the beginning of 'The Sisters' he gave his narrator a special interest in the word 'gnomon' alongside the word 'paralysis'. The gnomon is the triangular upright of a sundial which casts its shadow across the face of the clock. Joyce's sober presentation of the encounter recreates very precisely the growing fear and bewilderment of the young boy as the pervert's obsession gathers momentum. And the study contains a further nugget of morality. The boy has been initially somewhat scornful of his friend Mahony's roughness, his readiness to take on ragged urchins in the street, and to chase cats. Yet it is Mahony who is prepared to answer the stranger back boldly, and Mahony who comes rushing to the boy's rescue so that he feels mean for having ever despised him. The experience in the end is not wholly negative, for it brings our narrator an admission of penitence.

'Araby'

This is superficially the simplest of the first three stories of childhood disillusionment. The young boy is living with his uncle and aunt in a cul-de-sac in a house once tenanted by a priest and containing faded relics of his library. What brings a captivating excitement into the drab surroundings is the sister of a neighbouring playfellow. He catches sight of her framed at night in the light of the doorway as she calls her brother indoors. Deeply attracted, he contrives every morning to leave his home exactly when she leaves hers, to follow her and to overtake her, all without speaking to her. Repeatedly the boy tells us that her name stirred him and was frequently on his lips 'in strange prayers and praises'; but in fact he does not mention her Christian name. She is referred to as 'Mangan's sister'. Since the Irish romantic poet James Clarence Mangan was one of Joyce's heroes and had become for many a symbol of Irish patriotism and of passionate poethood, we may assume that if the drab cul-de-sac is representative of the Irish environment, the idealised girl is the universal beloved, inspiring to service and adoration. 'But my body was like a harp and her words and postures were like fingers running upon the wires.'

Be that as it may, a moment of revelation comes when she speaks to him and asks if he is going to Araby, an oriental bazaar held in the city. She cannot go herself for the event coincides with a retreat at her convent. The boy makes a pledge. 'If I go . . . I will bring you something.'

So devotion to the idealised beloved has now become entangled with escape to the magic and luxury promised by the coming bazaar. The boy longs for the night of fulfilment with desperate impatience. But the rest of the story is another downhill rush from delirious dreams of enchantment to utter disillusionment. For though his uncle and aunt agree that he should be allowed to go, the contrariness of things conspires against him. On the crucial day his uncle is late home; a garrulous visitor calls; time passes, and not until after nine o'clock is he able to make his journey by tram across Dublin to the bazaar. He reaches his goal to find everything on the point of closing down. The stallholders have relaxed into private conversation among themselves. Finally the lights are put out. The boy senses with anguish that he has been 'driven and derided by vanity'.

The actual bazaar 'Araby' was held in Dublin from 14 to 19 May 1894 in aid of Jervis Street Hospital.

'Eveline'

With the fourth story Joyce moves from first-person presentation to third-person narration and forsakes childhood for a group of tales about what he called 'adolescence' but which we might prefer to call young manhood and young womanhood. The tale, more than any other perhaps, exemplifies what Joyce must have meant in speaking of the 'paralysis' that lies like a dead hand on the inhabitants of Dublin. It is neatly organised in presentation. Eveline Hill, a nineteen-year-old girl, sits brooding on her lot at the eleventh hour before a planned escape. Thoughts of happiness are largely in the past – or in the future. Things were better in earlier days when she had her brothers and sisters and neighbouring children to play with. But her mother is now dead, her living brothers and sisters grown up, and she has to struggle to look after two young children left in her charge and her selfish, brutal, and often drunken father. She works as a shop-assistant for seven shillings a week and has difficulty in getting money for housekeeping from her father. She is in danger from his violence; she is over-worked and tired. And now she has the opportunity to escape. She has met Frank, a young man on a visit to his home country who has seen the world as a sailor and has now settled in Buenos Aires. Her father has quarrelled with him and forbidden her to see him, so they have had to meet secretly. He has begged her to come away with him to South America and to marry him. The hope of escape is alluring. All that stands in the way is her attachment to the familiar home, her father's age and his capacity to be occasionally kind to her, and her promise to her dying mother to keep the home together. The image of her mother's life of sacrifice 'closing in final craziness' seems to represent what is in store for her here as alternative to the exhilarating prospect of life and love abroad. Eveline has already written letters of explanation of her departure to be left behind for her father and her brother. The time for that departure has come.

From the touching presentation of Eveline's psychological state Joyce moves to a final page of the story in which the girl stands at the dock gates. Frank is holding her hand, urging her to hurry. Dazed, she does not take in clearly what he is saying except that he is pressing her to follow him. The boat whistle blows. Her passage is booked. A bell rings. Frank drags at her hand. 'Come!' A kind of animal incapacity to respond holds her in its grip as she clings to the iron railing, unable to take the step, while Frank rushes away, still calling her to follow him.

It may be argued that Joyce intends the reader to assume an unspoken apprehension in Eveline's mind that she fails to clarify even to herself. Might Frank be a plausible deceiver whose talk of a Buenos Aires home is false and who will take her no further than to England on the night packet to Liverpool, and shortly afterwards abandon her? Even if Eveline is innocent of any such suspicions, the reader can scarcely fail to indulge them.

'After the Race'

This story is based on an international motor car race which took place in Ireland in July 1903. The course extended over some 350 miles through the counties around Dublin and ended in the city itself. Of the twelve cars participating, three each from France, Germany, Great Britain and the USA, only four finished, the first German, the second and third French, and the fourth British. The French, with two of their four cars completing the course, were accounted the virtual victors.

The story opens as the race ends, and focuses on the four occupants of one of the French cars, Charles Ségouin, its owner, his friend André Rivière, a French Canadian, a Hungarian named Villona, and the subject of the story, Jimmy Doyle, an Irishman. These four young men are in a hilarious mood. Jimmy Doyle is the son of a Dublin butcher who has made money, opening numerous butchers' shops, getting useful public contracts, and conveniently shedding advanced nationalistic views en route to the top. Jimmy has been educated partly in England and has even put in a term at Cambridge. Hence his cosmopolitan connections include Ségouin, who 'was reputed to own some of the biggest hotels in France'. Mr Doyle senior is only too happy to encourage such connections.

Jimmy relishes being seen in this company. Knowing how hardly the family wealth has been gained, he has hitherto enjoyed spending money without being dangerously reckless. It is gradually conveyed to the reader through Jimmy's reflections that Ségouin is about to establish a motor business in Paris, that he has talked grandly of its prospects, and that he has even done Jimmy the favour of allowing him to invest in the venture, the implication being of course that the investment involved would be a comparatively trivial fraction of the total capital. Doyle senior, sensing that money is to be made in the motor business, himself first suggested this investment.

The young Irishman, captivated by his glamorous foreign friends, is included in their night of celebration after the race. A young Englishman, Routh, joins the party, and then, after dinner, a seemingly casually encountered American, Farley. The company row out from Kingstown harbour to Farley's yacht for more drinks, food, and eventually cards. In the heady, inebriate atmosphere high stakes are laid. Jimmy is scarcely aware of what is happening as he plays his cards and signs the IOUs that his friends keep putting into his hands. He and Farley lose heavily. The story ends with Jimmy holding his feverish head in his hands as the cabin door opens and Villona announces 'Daybreak, gentleman!'

What the dawning light may mean for Jimmy in terms of financial loss and remorse for his foolishness is not said. Plainly the young Irishman has been duped. His naivety, his vanity, his desire for companionship, and of course his recklessness have cost him dearly. But over the details Joyce, as so often, leaves the reader guessing. Is Ségouin a trickster? Might a touch of Eveline's sheer animal caution have saved Jimmy from making a fool of himself?

'Two Gallants'

This is one of the saddest stories in the collection, though the pathos of it is to be inferred only obliquely, for the whole presentation is through the minds and attitudes of two insensitive, selfish young men. Both are unattractive and shallow creatures. Neither works respectably for his living. Corley is a self-satisfied fellow, listens to nobody, and talks mainly about himself. Since he is 'often to be seen walking with policemen in plain clothes, talking earnestly', it may be assumed that he is an informer. Lenehan, his admirer, is a hanger-on, cunning in joining company in a bar just at the right moment to be included in a round of drinks paid for by someone else. He is vaguely assumed to be something on the seedier side of the racing world.

As the story opens the two are walking the Dublin streets on a warm August evening. Corley is boasting of his success with girls, in particular of the recent conquest of a low-grade domestic servant who pays his tram fare on their evening jaunts to the suburbs, supplies him with cigarettes and sometimes cigars. Lenehan is all admiration, but scarcely imagines that Corley will actually 'pull it off'. Corley is confident, but the reader is temporarily left guessing as to what plot is being engineered against the poor girl. Corley's attitude to her is such that he keeps her waiting when they are due to meet, then greets her and treats her with evident casualness. Lenehan is allowed to witness their meeting this evening from a distance. Then he has to fill in his time until he meets Corley again at 10.30 to learn what has transpired.

So Lenehan tramps the streets, steps into a cheap refreshment bar for a plate of peas and a bottle of ginger beer, later runs into a couple of friends, and finally arrives at the meeting point to watch Corley say goodnight to his girl friend. He sees her go down the steps to the basement entry of the house where she works, and he sees Corley remain waiting near the house. Some minutes pass, then the girl emerges from the front door of the house, coughs to catch Corley's attention, and a few moments later is seen quickly returning within. What has happened is revealed soon afterwards when Lenehan questions Corley about the success of his evening venture. Corley opens his palm to reveal a gold sovereign.

On the surface the bare outline of the story paints a simple action of crude sponging by a merciless, self-satisfied rogue. There are, however, ambiguities and touches of symbolism that give further dimensions to the tale. For instance the two fellows pass a street harpist, plucking the strings 'heedlessly' and staring wearily at passers-by and at the sky – as if he sought admiration for his casual efforts as Corley does for his. Moreover the harp is likened to the figure of a woman with drapings that have 'fallen about her knees' and seems 'weary alike of the eyes of strangers and of her master's hands'. To reinforce the image of the harpist we are told how Lenehan, on his solitary walk, lets his fingers run along the iron railings and moves his fingers and feet to the rhythm of the melody the harpist played. This indeed is vicarious activity, second-hand music-making, tuneless and vapid. These overtones seem to associate Corley's seduction of the servant girl with the image of Ireland herself wearily abused at the careless hands of her menfolk.

Quite apart from such hints of symbolism, the story is anything but simplistic in meaning. Corley, like Lenehan, is presented physically in terms of crude caricature. But his victim, the poor girl, though she has a 'stout short muscular body' and glows with 'rude health', is no charmer. 'Her features were blunt. She had broad nostrils, a straggling mouth which lay open in a contented leer, and two projecting front teeth'. The contented leer, if nothing else, prevents the reader from seeing her in pure compassion as innocence abused. She cannot be regarded as simply the guileless victim of a rotter for she has taken the initiative in some respects. The reader may suspect that the cigarettes and cigars she has given Corley have been stolen from her employer. With this suspicion in mind, can he be absolutely certain that the gold sovereign she gives Corley has been honestly come by and really is, as one commentator puts it, 'the girl's wages for at least six or seven weeks'?

Lenehan puts in several appearances in *Ulysses*. Corley, too, is encountered again, begging money from Stephen Dedalus in the early hours in the 'Eumaeus' episode.

'The Boarding House'

In an early account of the stories in *Dubliners* Joyce linked 'The Boarding House' with 'Eveline' and 'After the Race' as stories of 'adolescence'. Later, by inserting 'The Two Gallants' among them, he modified this rather unsatisfactory classification. Perhaps the element of calculated intrigue that traps its victim may be said to be common to 'After the Race', 'Two Gallants' and 'The Boarding House'. The money motif is to be found in some measure in all three.

Mrs Mooney, who keeps the boarding house, is a determined woman. Daughter of a butcher and wife of a butcher (her father's erstwhile foreman), she has to deal firmly with a drunken husband who goes to the bad and attacks her. Obtaining a separation order, she sets herself up as keeper of a boarding house, while her husband decays into a shabby little sheriff's man. The boarding house caters temporarily for holiday-makers and for actors on tour, and also has a permanent resident population of city clerks. Mrs Mooney's offspring are a son, Jack, a tough, crude, hard-living fellow, and a daughter, Polly, nineteen years old, with a fetching way of throwing her eyes coyly upwards. Polly has been withdrawn from her post as a city typist because her no-longer-respectable father has been in the habit of seeking her out at the office. She now helps her mother and flirts restrainedly with the lodgers, until a more serious relationship develops between her and one of them, namely Bob Doran, a thirty-four or thirty-five-year-old clerk in a wine-merchant's office.

The subtlety of the story lies in the oblique manner used by Joyce to intimate that the mother is privately happy to see her daughter entangle the young man, for his prospects are satisfactory: but connivance must not be recognised as such. Similarly Polly has to play her cards in such an innocent-seeming way that she gives no evidence of understanding her mother's concealed complicity. The young man who is the victim of the tacitly agreed machinations is only dimly aware that what has happened is not entirely his own doing. But when the crisis arises and (though nothing is clearly stated) Polly apparently becomes pregnant and mother has to be told all, Bob Doran recognises that unless he makes an honest woman of the girl his job may be at stake. It is only gradually, through sharing Bob's recollections, that the reader is made aware of how thorough the female conspiracy has been. Polly has visited Bob's room late at night, perfumed, undressed for bed, in search of a light for her candle. When he came in late she has waited up for him to warm up his dinner and to keep him company, close beside him, in the sleeping house. Her mother's thoroughness has produced a strategy no less nicely calculated. When Doran is called to her room to talk things over at the crisis, he catches sight of Jack the bruiser eyeing him coldly. It is not long, therefore, before a message is sent down to Polly from her mother that Mr Doran has something to say to her. 'Once you are married you are done for', his instinct has told him in the past, but now the trap has closed upon him.

In *Ulysses* we catch sight once or twice of Bob Doran the married man on his annual drinking spree. Thoroughly drunk, he sits or lurches unsteadily about in Barney Kiernan's bar in the 'Cyclops' episode.

'A Little Cloud'

This story is much more complex in its psychological analysis and its thematic ramifications. Having read it, we are not surprised to learn that it was the last but one of the stories to be written, the last being 'The Dead'. Little Chandler is not so much small in stature as an epitome of littleness – fragile in frame, quiet of voice, reserved, fastidious, and timid. He is employed as a clerk in a legal office. The fact that he is expecting to meet again a friend who eight years ago forsook Dublin for London evokes in him at once elation and melancholy: elation because Ignatius Gallaher has become 'a brilliant figure on the London press' and has invited Chandler to meet him at a superior Dublin hotel of the sort he would not normally visit; melancholy because he sees Gallaher as a formerly shabby, shady character who has nevertheless risen like a rocket while he himself remains a comparatively penurious underling condemned to drab routine in seedy Dublin.

When Gallaher and Chandler meet, Gallaher emerges as a showy, boastful, vulgar individual, full of vanity, and patronising about the old country and its inhabitants. The meeting thus sharpens Chandler's dissatisfactions, for he sees himself as a potential poet. He privately analyses his own mental and spiritual distinctiveness and allows dreams to conjure up phrases in which English reviewers might describe the book of poems he would like to write and publish. Thus, though Joyce puts Gallaher's crude vanity under judgement, it is plain that the subtle self-obsession of the more sensitive stay-at-home is equally the object of his satire. Little Chandler is not used to drinking and the successive whiskies go to his head. Thus stimulated, he finds his sense of justice offended by the inferiority of Gallaher's talents to his own; Gallaher's cheap pride in 'tawdry journalism' contrasts with his own exalted literary ambitions.

When Chandler gets home late, having forgotten the coffee he promised to buy for his wife Annie, she is annoyed and goes out to the shop herself, leaving him to take charge of the baby. What follows is a fine instance of the way Joyce brings a tale to a revelatory conclusion. Chandler studies a photograph of his wife which reminds him of her lack of passion, rapture and voluptuous yearning. Her composure and her prettiness, like the meanness and prettiness of the furniture she has chosen, do not measure up to his sensitive tastes. He opens a volume of Byron's poems and begins to read the first poem in the volume, 'Hushed are the winds, and still the evening gloom'. ('On the Death of a Young Lady' is in fact a highly sentimental poem with hackneyed diction and imagery, written when the poet was only fourteen.) Chandler's mental preoccupations with poetry and with his own unsatisfactory lot do not marry well with the need to look after the baby in his arms. When its cries interrupt his fanciful meditations he loses his temper and shouts 'Stop!' An outbreak of uncontrollably hysterical screaming follows. It terrifies him. When Annie returns she snatches the baby from him in anger to comfort it. Little Chandler's final response is one of shame: 'tears of remorse' come to his eyes.

The tale gives us an early instance of Joyce's interest in the contrast between sentimental, self-indulgent, wishful thinking and the demands of real life, a preoccupation that he was to exploit repeatedly in later work.

A 'little cloud', no bigger than a man's hand, in the Old Testament presages the coming of rain after long famine at the behest of the prophet Elijah. Joyce's title suggests that he sees Chandler's tears of shame and remorse as perhaps the start of a new acceptance of reality on the part of the day-dreaming clerk.

'Counterparts'

This story is simple in structure and direct in its implications. If the first five tales of the collection ('The Sisters', 'An Encounter', 'Araby', 'Eveline', and 'After the Race') focus on various kinds of let-down or disillusionment which guileless, inexperienced, or gullible young people encounter, the next four ('Two Gallants', 'The Boarding

House', 'A Little Cloud', and 'Counterparts') focus on the ways in which bullying or overbearing people impose their personalities on less assertive or more vulnerable individuals. Corley exploits the servant girl ('Two Gallants'), Mrs Mooney traps her unwary lodger, Bob Doran, into marriage to her daughter ('The Boarding House'), Ignatius Gallaher patronises Little Chandler hurtfully ('A Little Cloud'), and here Mr Alleyne, a partner in the firm of solicitors, Crosbie & Alleyne, bullies his clerk-copyist Farrington to the point at which, smouldering with resentment and humiliation, he takes it out on his own little boy brutally and savagely. Between the ticking-off which Farrington receives from his overbearing boss to the beating which he gives to his terrified little son, Farrington goes through an escalating series of drinking-bouts with his cronies, having first pawned his watch to finance the revengeful dissipation. The bars are the only places where he can play the strong man and repeatedly re-tell the story of his devastating rejoinder to his furious boss.

> 'Do you think me an utter fool?' . . . almost before he was aware of it, his tongue had found a felicitous moment:
> —I don't think, sir, he said, that that's a fair question to put to me.

The rejoinder all but costs him his job. He knows he will pay for it in the office a thousand times over. But recounting it in the bars gives him a taste of the mastery which otherwise only beating his little boy can give him.

But if simple, the tale is not simplistic, morally speaking. Farrington is not an innocent victim. He is slack about his work. Many times during the day he slips out of the office for a drink. Leaving his hat on its peg, he can be assumed to be still on the premises, probably in the lavatory, but he keeps a plaid cap in his pocket to put on once he is outside the door. Moreover he is neglectful in his work. He will submit a copy of a batch of correspondence from which letters are missing. He is lazy, preoccupied mentally, even when at his desk, with the hours when he comes into his own in the bars. And he is a heavy drinker. Pawning his watch for six shillings, he spends the entire sum on his evening binge – a lot of money at the turn of the century. Farrington's glass of porter at O'Neill's costs him one penny and there were seventy-two pennies in six shillings. Joyce's representation of life in Dublin's bars contributes to the overall picture of the city's paralysis. Habitués waste time and money in hollow chaff, empty boasting, and endless rounds of drinks.

'Clay'

The story takes place on All Hallows' Eve. The title refers to a popular and ancient divination game. Various items were arranged and a blindfolded person had to choose one of them. Generally a ring was included and if a woman touched it, this was a sign that she would be married in the course of the following year. If she touched a prayer-book, it was a sign that she would go into a convent. Traditionally a piece of clay was included among the items, and if the person touched this, it was a sign that she would die. For this reason clay was naturally omitted from the prepared items in the version of the game played at nineteenth-century parties.

Maria is employed at the Dublin by Lamplight institution, a Protestant home for fallen women, which runs a laundry. Maria is a Catholic. She seems to acquire symbolic status from her name, from the fact that she is regarded as a 'peace-maker', and from her brother Joe's description of her as his 'proper mother'. Whether these vague associations with the Virgin Mary – or the Church, or Ireland – are of any significance is not clear. Moreover there are three references to her long nose and chin which all but touch when she laughs. For some critics this very emphatic repetition gives her a witch-like status and, of course, witches are abroad on All Hallows' Eve. One might read significance, too, into the fact that her purse with its silver clasp comes from Belfast – from the even then more 'British' part of Ireland – and into the quarrel between Maria's two brothers, Joe and Alphy.

The superficially simple progression of events in the story seems to call for interpretation. Maria is to have an evening out as soon as she has finished supplying tea to the women inmates. She is going to visit her brother Joe who lives with his wife and children in Drumcondra, a twenty-minute tram ride from the city centre. Maria buys a bag of mixed cakes and then, as a very special gift, a large slice of plum-cake topped with almond icing. On her tram-ride an elderly gentleman, looking like a colonel, makes space for her on the seat at his side and takes a friendly interest in what she is about and what she has in her bag. When Maria gets to her brother's house she finds that the plum-cake has disappeared from her bag. Her sister-in-law suggests that she must have left it behind in the tram. Maria recalls that the elderly gentleman confused her with his friendly chaff and attributes the loss to her confusion. The reader naturally wonders whether this perhaps British, perhaps military individual deftly purloined her cake; but Joyce gives no clear encouragement to that notion.

Various other little matters go wrong. Nuts are distributed but the nut-crackers are nowhere to be found. The neighbours' children arrange the saucers for the divination game. One of them naughtily includes a dollop of clay, and Maria touches it first. But, being blindfolded, she is not clear what has happened and, after some whispering and scuffling, she is given a second turn and this time gets the prayer-book. Finally Maria is induced to sing and chooses 'I dreamt that I dwelt in marble halls' from Balfe's *The Bohemian Girl.* In her confusion she sings the first verse twice instead of going on to the second verse, which tells how suitors sought the heroine's hand and pledged their faith to her. Whether this omission represents one more cryptic element in a sequence that seems to embody in Maria's experience the fate of her motherland is left to the reader to determine.

'A Painful Case'

Mr James Duffy lives in Chapelizod ('Isolde's chapel'), the village associated with Isolde and her romantic passion for Tristan. But Duffy is the opposite of a person who might be mastered by overpowering passion and cast off the fetters of respectability. A bachelor in middle life, he abhors 'anything which betokened physical or mental disorder'. Cautious, modest in his expectations of others, he lives 'at a little distance from his body' and mentally often refers to himself in the third person. His daily routine keeps him moving mechanically between his home, the city bank where he is a cashier, a bar at lunch-time, and a plain eating-house at dinner time. He has 'neither companions nor friends, church nor creed'.

Upon this specimen of human isolation and emotional barrenness the wife of a sea-captain impinges by accident at a concert in the Rotunda, then at a concert in Earlsfort Terrace, and then by a remarkable coincidence on a third occasion. Duffy arranges to meet her again and, such is the friendliness and seeming understanding between them, they then begin to meet regularly for walks. Duffy will have nothing underhand and insists on being taken to her home and meeting her husband. Captain Sinico is frequently away from home. He assumes that Duffy is interested in his daughter. ('He had dismissed his wife so sincerely from his gallery of pleasures that he did not suspect that anyone else would take an interest in her.') So Duffy and Mrs Sinico meet regularly. She becomes a sympathetic sounding-board for his rather pretentious theories, and for him this constitutes a sharing of 'intellectual life'. What it means for her is suddenly revealed one evening when, after his talk of 'the soul's incurable loneliness', she excitedly seizes his hand and presses it to her cheek.

Duffy is taken aback. He ceases to visit her: then arranges a meeting and a three-hour-long walk during which they agree to break off their relationship.

Four years later Duffy, safely restored to his lonely routine, reads of

Mrs Sinico's death in the newspaper. She has been knocked down by a train while crossing the line at a station. It emerges at the inquest that for the last two years she has become addicted to spirits.

At first Duffy is disgusted, feels that somehow her degradation has contaminated him, and congratulates himself on having escaped her. But Joyce traces a gradual change of attitude in him. Duffy begins to ask himself how otherwise he might have acted and whether he was himself to blame. He senses her presence on his night walk and begins to ask himself 'Why had he withheld life from her? Why had he sentenced her to death?' Seeing couples lying in Phoenix Park, furtive lovers, he suddenly recognises himself as an 'outcast from life's feast'. One person offered him love and happiness and he had sentenced her to death.

Duffy's life of ordered routine and self-containment has insulated him against emotional entanglements, cut him off from communion with others, and imprisoned him in a state of moral inertia.

'Ivy Day in the Committee Room'

Ivy Day, 6 October, is the anniversary of Parnell's death, on which day his devotees used to wear a leaf of ivy. The story may be said to lack intensity. There is nothing to match the emotional currents that are sensed in 'A Painful Case', 'Counterparts', and 'A Little Cloud'. There could not be, for by design this is a picture of sterility and inertia. Only the ivy leaves and the frequent references to Parnell give vitality to the record: for they represent a career of forceful idealism, of action and sacrifice, by the side of which Joyce's portrayal of contemporary political life in Dublin is a record of laziness, apathy, and nullity. Parnellism has evaporated in sentimentality. Joyce's title for the story is ironically evocative. It would remind the Irish reader that it was in 'Committee Room' 15 at the House of Commons that a fateful meeting challenged Parnell's right to continue his leadership.

The tale focuses on public life. No characters are subjected to the kind of inner analysis applied to Mr Duffy or Little Chandler. All are seen externally. The scene is a committee room for those campaigning for the election of Richard Tierney for the Royal Exchange ward in the municipal elections for Dublin Corporation. Tierney is the nationalist candidate, but he is no radical. Plot is non-existent. Events are insignificant. People come and go, talk and drink, activities which they seem to prefer to the rigours of street-by-street canvassing, which is what is supposed to be afoot. The most telling piece of symbolism is that the caretaker is doing his best to re-vitalise a dying fire in the grate and that the warmth it produces is mainly used to blow the corks out of stout-bottles in the absence of a corkscrew.

None of the men has force or vitality. Mr O'Connor is lazy. Joe Hynes is suspected of being a spy for the rival candidate. Mr Henchy is impatient for his drink. Father Keon flits in and out, a disgraced priest on the fringe of respectable society. Crofton belongs to the Conservative party and is not in sympathy with the others. Conversation, when it is not concerned with the next drink or with getting paid by the candidate, turns on Parnell and on the proposed visit to Ireland of King Edward VII. It seems that Dublin Corporation proposes to present the king with an address of welcome. The question whether such an act would be worthy of Parnell's followers is answered by the argument that a royal visit will be good for trade. The only event to give focus to the rather disjointed account of men frittering away time in vapid talk oiled by stout is the final recitation by Hynes of a poem in praise of Parnell. This at least brings the company to attention, reduces them to silence, and is greeted with applause. But the irony is that the poem is a piece of utter banality compounded of cheap rhetoric and worn-out poeticisms.

In a sense this story is the 'quietest' piece in the collection. There is no drama, no pain, no joy, no intensity of any kind. Yet the scalpel of the satirist cuts deeply as the record of human shallowness and self-centredness culminates in applause for a performance that exudes pretentiousness and bogus sentiment.

Joe Hynes, a journalist, reappears in *Ulysses*, reporting on Paddy Dignam's funeral in the 'Hades' episode, and leading the mourners 'round by the chief's grave'. Bloom sees him later in the newspaper office in the 'Aeolus' episode and drops a hint on matters financial, for Hynes owes him three shillings. Finally he is among the drinkers in Barney Kiernan's bar in the 'Cyclops' episode.

'A Mother'

This is the middle story of three which focus on the public life of Dublin. 'Ivy Day' focuses on its political life, 'A Mother' on its musical life, and 'Grace' on its religious life. As the title indicates, Joyce's aim is to portray another forceful mother no less determined to have her own way than Mrs Mooney ('The Boarding House') and no less thorough and ruthless in her strategy. Educated 'in a high-class convent', pale in complexion and stiff in manner, she has had to stifle any romantic inclinations and has settled for marriage to a sober bootmaker of satisfactory means. So it was that Miss Devlin became Mrs Kearney 'out of spite'. Of her two daughters the one that concerns us is the elder, Kathleen, who is a tolerably accomplished pianist. Mrs Kearney has her eye on the main chance and espouses the Irish cause when the Revival becomes fashionable, and it is nationalist acquaintances who arrange four concerts at the Antient Concert Rooms and give Kathleen a contract to play as accompanist at all four for a fee of eight guineas.

Mrs Kearney for her part goes to great expense in dressing Kathleen for the occasion and in giving away tickets, but when the first night comes the audience is pitiably small. She tackles Mr Holohan who has organised the event, criticising the mediocrity of the performers he has chosen. The second night's audience on Thursday is only slightly larger than Wednesday's and the organising committee decide to cancel Friday's performance and concentrate on further publicising Saturday's. At this point Mrs Kearney's underlying concern surfaces – her daughter's fee. 'But, of course, that doesn't alter the contract,' she says, but fails to get clarification from officials whom she tackles on the matter. They refer her to 'the Committee'.

So it is that she decides to force the organisers' hands. She takes her husband with her for the Saturday night performance, for 'though she knew the small number of his talents she appreciated his abstract value as a male'. There is a much larger audience and as the time to begin approaches Mrs Kearney tackles Mr Holohan. 'Her daughter had signed a contract for eight guineas and she would have to be paid.' Mr Holohan is evasive and refers her to another member of the committee. Thus when Mr Bell, the tenor, is ready to go on stage for the first item, his accompanist, flanked by her parents, makes no move. The audience is getting noisily restive. Mr Holohan pleads, but Mrs Kearney remains firm. 'She won't go on. She must get her eight guineas.' Amid general embarrassment the Kearneys hold their ground until eventually Mr Holohan and Mr Fitzpatrick produce four pound notes for Mrs Kearney and assure her that she will get the rest at the interval. It is four shillings less than half the agreed fee but Kathleen takes Mr Bell on stage and the concert begins. During the interval there is a good deal of hostile comment in the dressing room about the behaviour of the Kearneys. Mr Fitzpatrick and Mr Holohan tell Mrs Kearney that the remaining four guineas will be paid after the committee meeting on the following Tuesday. Also, the committee will consider the contract broken if Kathleen refuses to play in the second half of the programme. Mrs Kearney is obdurate. 'My daughter has her contract. She will get four pounds eight into her hand or a foot she won't put on that platform.' But it is clear that the committee have now taken the trouble to get hold of an understudy, and she goes on stage while Mrs Kearney defiantly calls a cab to take the family home.

One of the most entertaining tales in the collection, this story has a conventional shapeliness and the directness of its satirical humour is in strong contrast to the sophisticated subtlety of presentation employed in 'Ivy Day'.

Joyce was in fact re-working an experience of his own which occurred in August 1904 when he appeared as a soloist alongside John McCormack in the Antient Concert Rooms. Next day's *Freeman's Journal* reported: 'Mr James A. Joyce, the possessor of a sweet tenor voice, sang charmingly "The Salley Gardens", and gave a pathetic rendering of "The Croppy Boy".' But the reporter who wrote these words had left well before Joyce sang. So had the offended pianist; and her substitute was so poor that Joyce had to sit down and accompany himself for 'The Croppy Boy'.

In *Ulysses* Kathleen Kearney has become singer as well as pianist, to judge from Molly Bloom's scathing reference to 'Kathleen Kearney and her lot of squealers' in the 'Penelope' episode. And, oddly enough, her father – or certainly a Mr Kearney – has acted as guarantor for Bloom in joining the lending library. (See the 'Calypso' episode.)

'Grace'

The story of Tom Kernan is a distinctive one in the series. It is not a record of disillusionment. No one suffers a great disappointment. On the contrary, it is a record of rehabilitation. Moreover its characters are on the whole good-natured people who are performing an act of charity. No one is trying to get the better of others. Though the story turns on the public religious life of Dublin, and though its tone is often ironic at the expense of the simple faith of unlettered Dubliners, the irony is light, indeed indulgent. As a result the story may be said to have 'charm'. Dubliners here are held under compassionate scrutiny.

Tom Kernan, a tea merchant, has been drinking too much. He stumbles on the way down the stairs to the gentlemen's lavatory, where two men find him face downwards, unconscious, his mouth bleeding – it later emerges that he has bitten a piece out of his tongue. It takes three of them to carry him upstairs and lay him on the bar floor. No one seems to know him. A policeman is called. Practical help is forthcoming from a young man in a cycling suit, apparently a medical student, who forces brandy down Kernan's throat. Fortunately someone who knows Kernan appears, Mr Power. Aided by the young man, he gets Kernan into a taxi to take him home.

Mr Power, a much younger man than Kernan, has a respectable job in the offices of the Royal Irish Constabulary and he has helped Kernan, a chronic debtor, in the past. It is interesting that when he reaches Kernan's home he finds the children rougher and cruder than he expected. Mrs Kernan puts her husband to bed while Mr Power speaks of a plan to rescue him from his bad habits. Two days later Mr Power brings along two friends, Mr Cunningham and Mr M'Coy, to see the invalid. Cunningham is an elder colleague of Mr Power who, having an incurably alcoholic wife, has practical experience relevant to the present case. M'Coy's career has been a varied one, but he is now secretary to the City Coroner. The three are practising Catholics bent on recalling Kernan to his religious duties. They have to move carefully because Kernan is a Catholic only by reception on his marriage, having had a Protestant upbringing. The conspirators let Mrs Kernan into their plot. A realist, she is not optimistic about its success.

Conversation round the sick-bed elicits the news that Kernan has fallen under the disreputable influence of a Jewish money-lender, Harford. The suggestion that Kernan was only narrowly rescued from the policeman's clutches on the fatal night irritates Kernan to an outburst against the crude fellows who nowadays get into the force. When Mrs Kernan brings in a tray of stout the moment is chosen for the three visitors to refer, as if casually, to a meeting they have fixed up for Thursday night. Kernan's curiosity is stirred. They satisfy it. They are to go into retreat together. The information having been conveyed, Mr Cunningham suddenly has the bright idea that Kernan might like to join them. The friendliness of the proposal is reinforced by a good deal of talk about the social and intellectual standing of the Jesuits, one of whom, Father Purdon, is to conduct the retreat. After some tolerant observations about Catholic and Protestant divergences and similarities, the company is joined by Mr Fogarty, a grocer, who has brought a bottle of whisky for the invalid. Under its influence the conspirators warmly praise the Catholic Church and the Popes in talk which contains a fair amount of factual error (especially over Latin mottoes) and misunderstandings. In particular Mr Cunningham gives an account of the debate leading up to the declaration of Papal Infallibility which contains some inaccuracies. But the high point of Joycean irony occurs when the great faithfulness of Cardinal MacHale is exemplified in the way he strenuously opposed the new doctrine by weighty argument throughout the cardinals' debate, and yet responded to its promulgation with an immediate and mighty shout, 'Credo' (I believe). This stirring testimony to the immensity of the Church's power impresses the company. When Mrs Kernan returns she learns that her husband is to join the others at their retreat.

The scene shifts to the church. Mr Cunningham and Mr Kernan sit together, Mr M'Coy is alone behind them, and Mr Power and Mr Fogarty are behind M'Coy. They have 'settled down in the form of a quincunx'. The pattern is associated with the five wounds of the crucified Christ on his hands, feet, and in his side, and as they sit there they listen to a sermon by Father Purdon on the most taxing parable of all about the steward who reduced the debts of his master's debtors so that when he was dismissed he would not be friendless. Father

Purdon makes it a means for addressing his congregation as businessmen who believe in accurate accounting, and urges them to keep a correct moral and spiritual balance sheet with God.

The image of the five wounds hints at a symbolic structure in the story to which Joyce's brother, Stanislaus, referred specifically. The tale is shaped as a parody in miniature of the progress from hell to heaven presented in Dante's *Divine Comedy*. That the underground lavatory is a kind of hell is plain. Kernan's experience in the sick room constitutes a purgatory. The five men, bent on penitence and reform, worship in church as though in heaven.

The main characters of this story reappear in *Ulysses* with much more than passing references. Martin Cunningham, Jack Power, and Tom Kernan attend Paddy Dignam's funeral in the 'Hades' episode, where Kernan compares the Catholic rite unfavourably with the Protestant one: '*I am the resurrection and the life*. That touches a man's inmost heart.' He also turns up in the Ormond bar to indulge his addiction to gin in the 'Sirens' episode, and it is he who persuades Ben Dollard to sing 'The Croppy Boy'. Martin Cunningham and Jack Power journey to the funeral in the same carriage as Simon Dedalus and Leopold Bloom. Cunningham is again involved in good works, for he writes to Father Conmee seeking help for Dignam's orphaned son and tries to interest others in a Dignam Fund ('The Wandering Rocks'). Indeed it is because Bloom is due to meet Cunningham on this very matter that he turns up at Barney Kiernan's bar in the 'Cyclops' episode. Bloom admires Cunningham's sympathy and intelligence. He also finds Jack Power polite and friendly, though he has heard gossip that Power keeps a mistress, and on this subject Molly Bloom's thoughts are more specific in the 'Penelope' episode – 'Jack Power keeping that barmaid'. Power emerges as generous, however, for Simon Dedalus borrows two shillings from him ('The Wandering Rocks'). When he comes with Cunningham to Barney Kiernan's in the 'Cyclops' episode, the two of them are accompanied by the Crofton of 'Ivy Day'. Charlie M'Coy, missing the Dignam funeral, asks Bloom to add his name to the list of mourners for the press. Bloom understands that M'Coy, who used to work for the *Freeman*, was sacked for making off with cash for advertisements.

'The Dead'

This, much the longest story in the collection, must be accounted one of the greatest short stories in our literature. It has been compared with Conrad's *Heart of Darkness* in having the weight and density of substance appropriate to a short novel. Like the first story, 'The Sisters', it is concerned with death. As in 'Ivy Day' there broods over it the spirit of a man no longer alive. But the main substance of the story is a picture of Dublin hospitality, warm and generous, which was specifically intended by Joyce to correct the balance in his portrait of his native city.

The larger part of the action takes place at the home of the Misses Morkan on the occasion of their annual New Year party. Julia Morkan, though aged, is still the leading soprano in a Dublin church choir. Her sister Kate, now feeble, manages to give a few piano lessons to beginners at home. Their niece Mary Jane is an organist and a piano teacher with pupils from well-to-do families. Their annual party naturally involves a cross-section of the city's musical life. Attention focuses throughout on the Misses Morkans' favourite nephew Gabriel Conroy, son of their dead sister and much cherished by the aunts. It is to him they turn to supervise the carving of the goose and to deal with such inconveniences as the presence of the inebriated Freddy Malins. Moreover it is a tradition of the occasion that Gabriel makes a speech of thanks to the hostesses. A man of university education, now a language teacher, and making money too by reviewing books for the *Daily Express*, Gabriel is considered to have done well. He has married Gretta, a girl from Galway, whom his mother at first disapproved of as being 'country cute'. Gretta is shown as a direct, unselfish, and warm-hearted woman and Gabriel remains devoted to her. The couple have children who have been left for the night at their home in Monkstown, a very respectable suburb, five miles south of Dublin.

Gabriel is a highly sensitive person, anxious to behave good-naturedly, uncomfortably aware sometimes of the cultural gap between himself and his simpler relations and acquaintances, and doing his best not to appear superior or patronising. Yet, ironically enough, he finds himself rebuffed, and his solicitousness is made to seem wrong-footed. Thus when Lily, the caretaker's daughter, acting as servant, receives him and he chaffs her about possible marriage, she is curtly dismissive. Gretta meanwhile teases him publicly about his insistence that she should wear goloshes. His solicitude is a standing joke with the aunts. (The theme of protecting oneself from the cold is a pervasive one and gradually assumes symbolic significance.) Gabriel receives further rebuffs when he dances with an old university contemporary, Miss Ivors, and she chaffs him about his reviews. She is ashamed that he should write for a paper such as the *Daily Express* and calls him mockingly 'a West Briton'. Thus a further gap opens up between Gabriel and those among whom he lives. His taste for culture, for literature, for the cosmopolitan is pulling him away from those with Irish nationalist aspirations. The gap is widened when Miss Ivors suggests that he should join a party going west to the Aran islands in summer. He prefers to go to the continent and, when taunted with his lack of interest in Ireland and the Irish language, he retorts that he is sick of his own country; and this response amounts to a further rebuff. Gretta, when she hears about this altercation, is all agog to see Galway again. Thus Gretta's Galway origin relates to the developing theme of Gabriel's increasing severance from simple earthy things Irish. Miss Ivors, who has made Gabriel uncomfortable on this score, leaves the party early.

Joyce describes events at the party with masterly control, moving selectively so as to record light-hearted conversational exchanges between various guests against the background of music and dancing, to picture the richness and variety of the laden tables, and to give side glances at the current musical gossip of Dublin – a gossip which tends to look back nostalgically to the great singers of the past. Gabriel makes a speech which is at once graceful, charming, and sophisticated, a model of literary skill exercised in support of the current social roundabout of Dubliners whose heads are perhaps in the past but whose hearts are in the right place. To what extent the rhetorical clichés of the speech may be said to represent an unworthy accommodation of talent in the service of shallow sentimentalised *bonhomie* is a question Joyce leaves with the reader. The crucial thing about Gabriel is that he is himself sensitive to the element of dishonesty in the tributes he pays to aunts who 'are only two ignorant old women'. Indeed Gabriel's defect seems to be that his concern with his own self-projection – even as a generous, unselfish person – is too obsessive to be other than self-centred. At moments his sense that there is a fresher, more vital world amid the snow outside the barrier of the window panes breaks upon him. Perhaps it is his saving grace that he longs momentarily to be away from the warmth and fabricated jollity, walking alone in the wintry night.

Nevertheless within the house Gabriel is a great success. Perhaps, however, the amusing party tale he tells from the family archives should be taken as reflecting upon himself. His grandfather, a glue-boiler, had a horse, Johnny, accustomed to driving the mill by walking round and round. One day the old man, aspiring to drive out into society, put on his best clothes and harnessed Johnny to take him through the park. All went well until, reaching King Billy's statue, Johnny assumed that he was back in the mill and insisted on walking round it in circles. Whether Gabriel's cultural aspirations and consequent rise in society may be said to have brought him to the point at which he is circling slavishly round the Anglo-Irish establishment that King William represents is left to the reader to decide.

This is not the only symbolic hint of what the story is ultimately to convey of Gabriel's situation. Earlier in the evening Gabriel stared at two pictures on a wall of the Morkans' house: one of them representing the balcony scene in *Romeo and Juliet*, the other the murdered princes in the Tower. What these two pictures hint at begins to emerge with the strange turn events and talk take at the end of the party. As Gabriel is downstairs prepared to depart and waiting for Gretta, he sees her at the top of the stairs transfixed in 'grace and mystery' by a song Bartell D'Arcy is singing – singing in spite of a cold which renders him hoarse. Gretta later asks the name of the song. It is 'The Lass of Aughrim', a ballad about a seduced and forsaken girl. The image of Gretta's heightened beauty in listening to this song conspires with Gabriel's general excitement to fill him with desire for his wife as they walk away from the party. Gabriel has booked a room for the night at the Gresham Hotel in the city centre. They eventually get a cab and are taken to their room at the hotel, where Gabriel's emotional state is such that he is eager to take his wife in his arms. In fact he meets a series of rebuffs which are purely the result of his own inadequate awareness. Gretta is rather tired. She is also abstracted. Gabriel pries for reasons, and Gretta collapses on the bed in tears. Cross-questioned, she at last tells her story. The singing of 'The Lass of Aughrim' has revived memories of her first love, a boy back in Galway, Michael Furey, who used to sing the song and who really died for love of her. He had no social status, for he worked in the gasworks, but he insisted on waiting outside her bedroom window in the snow when he was seriously ill. Soon after he died. Overwhelmed by her tragic memory, Gretta sobs herself to sleep.

Gabriel is left to muse on the way a simple, poor boy has died for the sake of his wife, while he himself by comparison has played such a poor part in her life. He is conscious of the shallow artificiality of the roles he plays. He is sensitive to the ephemerality of all life, and his eyes fill with 'generous tears'. The experience has chastened him. In one sentence Joyce sums up the transformation. 'The time had come for him to set out on his journey westward.' The symbolism contrasting the vital unsophisticated Ireland of the west with the pretentious, anglicised life of the cultured metropolis attains its clearest expression. The contrasts go deep. The simple ballad of the lass of Aughrim, who is prevented from entering the betrayer's castle with the baby he has fathered, is literature rooted in the pathos of deeply felt human suffering, and as such is far removed from the finely contrived speechifying of Gabriel Conroy. The wild, romantic, Irish-speaking west beyond the dividing line of the river Shannon had an awesome fascination for sensitive easterners. It was here that Michael Furey died for love of Gretta, and it was here that Yeats's Cathleen ni Houlihan, the personification of Ireland herself, told another Michael how many an Irish patriot had died for love of her, and claimed his allegiance. The call to which Gabriel responds is a momentous one.

The main characters in 'The Dead' do not put in personal appearances in *Ulysses*, but there are passing references to some of them in thought and talk. Through Bloom's reflections in the 'Calypso' episode we learn that Molly has shown interest in what Gretta Conroy wears, and he refers to Gabriel's brother as a 'curate' in 'Nausicaa'. Bloom also recalls how Julia Morkan 'kept her voice up to the very last'; and he believes that she was actually a pupil of Michael Balfe, the composer of *The Bohemian Girl* – though Bloom is not always a reliable guide in such matters ('The Lestrygonians' episode). More interestingly perhaps we learn in *Ulysses* that Kate Morkan was Stephen Dedalus's godmother ('Ithaca' episode). There are references too to Bartell D'Arcy, who seems to have had a mild flirtation with Molly Bloom, for she remembers him 'kissing [her] on the choir stairs after [she] sang Gounod's Ave Maria' ('Penelope' episode).

A Portrait of the Artist as a Young Man

The *Portrait* is a novel about growing up. Growing up is a process in which the individual has to make a series of adjustments to the influences playing upon him in the family and the wider circle of acquaintances, and to the more public influences playing upon him in the schools he attends and the church in which he is nurtured. There are also social, cultural, and political movements alive in his environment. All these influences demand approval and co-operation. Some of them – parents, school and church, for instance – also demand obedience. The development of the individual will thus involve a series of choices. He will accept some influences and demands: he will reject others. As time passes his preferences and allegiances will change. If his environment is in any ways a strictly demanding one where non-conformity can be adopted only at great personal cost in friendship, in family approval, in career prospects, and in public respect, then the struggle will be especially acute for a person of independent or rebellious temperament who feels that the true roots of meaning and decision lie rather in his own nature and not in what society tries to impose on him. The young artist is just such an individualist. His dilemma is highlighted in Joyce's picture of his struggle against the sometimes contradictory but nevertheless powerful conformist pressures of late Victorian and early Edwardian Dublin.

The *Portrait*, however, is not a simplistic account of spirited rebellion by a young idealist, for Joyce presents Stephen Dedalus, his alter ego, in such a way that his defects are plain to see. If the environment of the young artist makes cramping demands upon him that are patently absurd, the exalted private notion of himself that he cherishes and the pretentious solemnity with which he hurls himself against conformist demands are in many respects equally absurd. This is where the subtlety of the *Portrait* resides – in the humour and irony produced by picturing a rebellious hero who gains the reader's sympathy for what he has to endure, yet who makes the reader laugh at the extravagance of some of his reactions to the people and the pressures he resists.

Joyce used to be considered a 'difficult' writer. This is because he pioneered a narrative method which gave fiction a new direction. The conventional nineteenth-century novelist's method of presentation was to arrange passages of direct narration, inner reflection, description, and dialogue in separate chunks strung together. Joyce was one of the earliest to break away from this technique. In this respect we can see his experimentation developing as we turn from *Dubliners* to the *Portrait*. Joyce moves increasingly between outer narrative and inner exploration of characters' thoughts without explanatory notation. That is to say, just as there is more restraint in peppering dialogue with notations such as 'said Mr Power' or 'he said' or 'said his wife', so too explanatory links such as 'he said to himself' or 'he thought' disappear from records of reflection. Whereas in 'The Dead' Joyce could write of Gabriel and Miss Ivors: 'Gabriel asked himself was he the cause of her abrupt departure', by the time he came to write the *Portrait* he would have have written: 'Was he the cause of her abrupt departure?', using some other device to make clear that Gabriel's thoughts are being represented. Moreover Joyce begins to interweave dialogue with narration and description so that the reader has the outer scene and what people are saying and what is passing in people's minds held before him simultaneously. This, of course, is what life is really like.

Again there is no recognisable author's voice in the *Portrait*, putting the reader in the picture or chatting with him over the heads of the characters. What all this amounts to is that the reader has to keep his wits about him, for Joyce is determined not to instruct him in an unmistakable authorial voice about the scene, the participants, their speeches, thoughts, and attitude. Still less will he clearly tell the reader what he ought to think about the characters' behaviour and assumptions. Reading Joyce, you are not in the audience with the author at your side while the drama unfolds on the stage before you. Rather you are taken on to the stage. And even this metaphor is inadequate. The reader spends his time, not in the company of an all-knowing, all-judging author, but in the company of the hero, seeing what he sees, hearing what he hears, sharing his reactions, and following him in his thoughts even when they deviate from the immediate situation and roam back over the past, muse foolishly about the future, or indulge grandiose dreams. To give vitality and convincingness to this manner of presentation Joyce adjusts the style appropriately to the succeeding stages of his hero's development. When the book opens the reader is taken into the world of the child's infancy, and impressions are recorded as they strike the child's mind. When the book closes the reader is in the world of the young man who has been stuffed with culture at the university and has grown accustomed both to the sophisticated language of philosophy and literature, and to the crude banter and backchat of student life. The style is appropriate to this point of youthful maturity. In between Joyce rings the changes on modes of presentation and varieties of stylistic idiom appropriate to boyhood, adolescence and gradual understanding of the adult world.

The *Portrait* is a very carefully constructed novel. It has five numbered chapters and each chapter contains a number of sections (sometimes three, sometimes four, sometimes five). These sections are not numbered in the text (as they are in this book) but are clearly separated by asterisks. The episodes which make up the succeeding sections are mostly shaped around crises that are milestones in the story of Stephen's development. These crises are points at which Stephen is confronted by forces and events that are taxing or hostile. Sometimes he is humiliated or frustrated. On other occasions he tastes success and victory. In all of them we can trace the moulding of the character who is to embark boldly and idealistically on his adult life at the end of the book.

Chapter 1 (Infancy and Childhood)

Section i

Stephen's memories of his infancy are given in the jumbled way in which impressions of one's earliest days tend to recur to the mind. Father's bed-time story, Stephen's first attempts to sing a song, the comforts and subsequent discomforts of wetting the bed, mother's piano-playing, and the neighbour's daughter Eileen – all these memories are recorded and, in conclusion, a memory of hiding under the table after having been naughty and provoked adult threats of what may happen to him if he does not apologise. Some of the most crucial experiences that Stephen has later build on the early taste of disillusionment after bed-wetting, the early interest in a girl, and the first insistent demands for repentance. Thus in the child's earliest memories seeds are sown of what is to follow in later life.

Section ii

The haphazard inarticulacies of babyhood are left behind. Stephen is now a little boy at school at Clongowes Wood College, County

Kildare. He is supposed to be playing football but he is preoccupied with his own thoughts. He was pushed into a ditch by a bully and in consequence is now shivering with a cold. Memories of mother and father and the cosy warmth of home contrast with the cheerlessness of school. The class goes in for a mathematics lesson but Stephen's chill prevents him from concentrating on his sums. Next they go to the refectory and a boy called Fleming notices how ill Stephen looks. Afterwards, alone in the play-room, he is cross-questioned and mocked by Wells, the bully who pushed him into the ditch. Then it is time for study and he broods meanderingly over his geography text-book. Shivering and yawning, he longs for bed, but there are prayers in chapel first before he can go up to the dormitory and climb between the cold sheets. Once there, day-dreams of the old castle buildings which are part of Clongowes, of ghosts and murders and battles associated with its history, eventually give way to sleep and real dreams. From a delicious dream of going home for Christmas and being welcomed by his mother he wakes to the reality of his own feverishness, the noises of morning, and the call to get up. Stephen can make but a feeble effort to obey and the prefect takes him off to the sick-room, where Brother Michael, the infirmarian, receives him. There is one other sick boy there. In bed Stephen broods about his sickness, imagines himself writing a letter home to his mother, wonders if he will die, and pictures his own funeral at the college. Brother Michael brings him some beef tea before leaving the infirmary for a while. Stephen chats with his fellow-invalid, and he then falls musing. Increasingly dreamy, Stephen is only half-conscious that Brother Michael has returned, bringing sensational news of Parnell's death, and the news of this significant event merges with his delirious fantasies.

Section iii

This section is virtually a short story in itself. It describes the Christmas party at Stephen's home to which he looked forward when at school, dreaming of happiness to come. There is a blazing fire in the grate and the table is spread for Christmas dinner. The party includes Mr Dedalus, Mrs Dedalus, Mrs Riordan (whom Stephen calls 'Dante') who lives with them, Uncle Charles, and a guest, Mr Casey. Mr Dedalus is a man with a lively sense of humour, a racy Irish wit, and a rich command of verbal invective which can easily annoy people. He has nationalist sympathies and is fiercely anti-clerical, resenting especially the Church's 'betrayal' of Parnell. Mr Casey shares Mr Dedalus's views in this respect. He is a nationalist who has been in gaol. An occasional visitor at the Dedaluses, he is an attractive character who has a rather winning way with children. Dante is a blindly obedient

Catholic for whom the word of the clergy is law. Her irritating dogmatism and inflexibility naturally provoke Mr Dedalus to characteristically boisterous fluency in vituperation. Mrs Dedalus, as hostess, is the would-be peacemaker.

The atmosphere is warm and friendly when the company sit down to dinner. In particular Stephen relishes the warm room and rich food after the austerities of Clongowes. But a chance piece of gossip exchanged between Mr Dedalus and Mr Casey proves to be the spark that fires the dynamite. It concerns a parish priest who has been sharply criticised by a parishioner for bringing politics into the pulpit. But priests cannot be criticised with impunity or decency, however lightly, in Dante's presence. She is outraged at the man's effrontery and says so. Mrs Dedalus tries vainly to forestall the threatening conflict, and Uncle Charles supports her. But it is of no avail. Dante persists in a provocatively sweeping defence of the clergy. Mr Dedalus and Mr Casey deeply resent the Church's part in destroying their adored idol. They cannot contain themselves. When Mr Casey repeats an anecdote about one of Parnell's last meetings at which an old woman who insulted Kitty O'Shea was spat upon in the face, there is laughter among the men and Dante is furious. Stephen himself is mystified by the venomous hostility between parties who, he knows, are equally devoted to Ireland and the Irish cause. But all restraint is laid aside. Mr Dedalus and Mr Casey lament the past betrayal of the Irish cause by the bishops, while Dante abuses Parnell and screams 'Blasphemer, Devil' at Mr Casey. The party which began so promisingly ends with Mr Casey sobbing for his 'dead king' and Dante quivering with angry delight at the way Parnell was 'crushed'.

Stephen is terrified. It is symptomatic of the way life's expectations are trampled upon that the pressures of conflict in church and state have intruded into the family circle at Christmas to turn the festival of joy and good-will into an occasion of misery and rancour.

Section iv

The last section of the first chapter takes us back to Clongowes school. Stephen is listening to excited talk by the boys about five of their number who are in disgrace. The air is alive with rumour. One report, that the fellows had stolen altar wine, especially horrifies Stephen. He is in some discomfort because a boy on a bicycle knocked him down yesterday on the cinder-path, breaking his glasses. He cannot see adequately without them. Hence, when the boys go in for a writing lesson, he sits with arms folded, having been excused work. The next lesson is Latin and Father Arnall is the teacher. He gets angry when he receives incorrect answers to his questions and makes one boy, Fleming, kneel on the floor. He is still kneeling when the hated Father

Dolan slips in, the prefect of studies, a thoroughly overbearing bully who takes delight in flogging. 'Any boys for flogging here, Father Arnall?' he asks, then, spotting Fleming, gives him six strokes of the cane on each hand. That task accomplished, he notices that Stephen is not writing, ignores Father Arnall's explanation that he has been excused, calls him out, declares him a 'lazy little schemer', and canes him fiercely on either hand, so that Stephen quivers with pain and scalding tears flow down his burning cheeks.

The punishment is something of a revelation. The doctor has forbidden him to read without glasses. The cruel injustice done to him by one who is a priest of the Church rankles. After the lesson the boys urge him to take his complaint to the rector. Stephen's imagination is stirred by the conception of himself as someone standing boldly up against tyranny like great heroes of history. He summons up his courage and makes his way to the rector's room. Father Conmee, the rector, receives him kindly but tries to smooth things over by suggesting that Father Dolan must have made a mistake. Stephen courageously resists the suggestion, and the rector promises to have a word with Father Dolan himself. Stephen is full of gratitude. When he returns to his mates, they are thrilled by his account of what has happened and they lift him up in triumph.

Section i ended with little Stephen under a table, being threatened with horrors if he will not apologise for his naughtiness; Section ii ended with Stephen delirious in the sick-room, experiencing a strangely prophetic dream of Parnell's death and the grief it causes; Section iii ended with a Christmas party thrown into a chaos of anger and bitterness. These negative crises are now to some extent compensated for, in that Section iv ends with Stephen tasting triumph and success, having challenged the powers-that-be after a gross injustice and been vindicated.

Chapter 2 (Boyhood and Adolescence)

Section i

Stephen is back home again in Blackrock. It is the summer holidays. He spends a good deal of time with Uncle Charles who takes him shopping. Another old man, Mike Flynn, joins them and he trains and times Stephen as he runs round the racing track in the park. These fading, bumbling adult companions seem to represent the influence of what is lifeless in Dublin. Uncle Charles fills himself with tobacco smoke, hums sentimental songs, and prays from a tattered prayer-book, while Mike Flynn is a flabby, decayed old man soon to be taken into hospital. Moreover at weekends Stephen is taken for long walks in the countryside around Dublin by his father and grand-uncle, and talk tends to turn on Irish politics and family affairs. Among other activities Stephen founds a gang with a boy, Aubrey Mills, and the two of them are given rides in the milk-cart to the milkman's farm at Carrickmines. Here they are allowed to ride the horse around the field.

In more than one sense Stephen is at this point going round in circles. He runs round the race-track, circles Dublin in weekend walks, accompanies the milkman on his milk-round, and rides his horse round the field. He can fitfully indulge the dream of spending his life delivering milk to clean cottages and well-lit town-houses, and this dream (since the cow is symbolic of Ireland) represents an idealistic picture of settling down and merging in the country's life. We are reminded, however, that the milk trade involves not just calling at rural homesteads but wading through farm-yards deep in dung and filth. (Going round in circles is no fit occupation for the future artist. We recall Gabriel Conroy's story of the family horse 'Johnny' in 'The Dead'.)

Stephen's aspirations at this stage are in fact turning away from the real world of contemporary Dublin. He reads *The Count of Monte Cristo* in the evenings, retreating to a fantasy world where the image of Mercedes, the heroine of the story, exercises a disturbing fascination on him, stirring in him strange restlessness and ambition. The contrast between the real world of the boy's day-to-day life and the ideal world of his youthful imagining is all the sharper because in this chapter we receive hints of a deteriorating situation at home. Stephen's father is in financial difficulties, and for this reason Stephen will not be able to go back to Clongowes.

Section ii

The family moves from Blackrock, a resort five miles south of Dublin on the coast, to the city itself. The removal is a sad affair. Plainly the family fortunes are declining. The new home is bare and cheerless. Meanwhile Mr Dedalus begins to emerge as an irresponsible household head more given to talk than to work, who blames his misfortunes on imaginary enemies. Stephen becomes something of a loner, exploring the city in detail. Foreign shipping in the docks revives romantic dreams of Mercedes in the city of Marseilles. His mother takes him to visit various relatives but he maintains a bitter taciturnity, angry with his own moodiness and with the squalid world around him. There is a crucial intrusion of the romantic world upon the real world one night when he attends a party at Harold's Cross and finds himself disturbed by the exciting glances of a girl, Emma Clery. After the party is over the two go out together, as he is to take the last tram home. They stand together on the tram steps and she seems to invite him to take hold of her and kiss her, but he cannot respond and is angry with himself for his failure. Next day he decides to write a poem to her. So if the ideal world as figured in literature seemed about to impinge on the real world on the tram steps, the real world is dragged back into the ideal world as Stephen turns his practical failure into material for literature. It is plain that the verses are remote indeed from the living experience. And when they are written Stephen goes off to stare at himself in the mirror. The young poet of love is more interested in himself as poet and lover than in the girl who is supposed to be his inspiration.

One evening Stephen learns that Mr Dedalus has met Father Conmee and that as a result Stephen and his brother are to have free places at Belvedere College, the Jesuit day school in Dublin. Mr Dedalus's loose chatter also delivers what plainly must be a shocking revelation to Stephen. He tells amusingly how Father Conmee and Father Dolan together laughed uproariously over Stephen's protest at the unjust caning at Clongowes. The youthful triumph of integrity over adult injustice now looks hollow indeed.

Section iii

Two years have passed. Stephen, now a leading senior boy at Belvedere, has a main part in a school play – that of an eccentric schoolmaster. Boys urge him to take the opportunity of mimicking the rector in acting the part. These, however, are external things, and Stephen's inner life is in turmoil. The decaying family fortunes and the fact that his fees are excused throw a shadow over his standing in the eyes of his school-fellows and embarrass him. Moreover he has had brushes with authority and with received opinion in claiming greatness for the wicked poet Byron and in making a heretical statement in an English essay. Subsequent demands that he should retract his errors are in line with the childhood experience of being required to apologise. Stephen is beginning to question the voice of authority. Threaded through the web of his inner life just now is the thought of Emma, who is to come with his parents to watch him in the school play. This thought gives him confidence and zeal which enable him to give a convincing performance on stage. Then comes another great let-down. He rushes from the theatre in excited anticipation only to discover that after all Emma is not there with his family. His pride and hope crushed, he dashes wildly away without aim or reason till he finds himself in a seedy corner of the city.

Section iv

Stephen is taken by his father to Cork where Mr Dedalus was brought up. He still has property there which is to be auctioned, heavily mortgaged as it is. The two take the night train from Dublin and end the hours of darkness in a hotel bedroom in Cork. In the morning, after breakfast, Stephen tags on behind his father who is bent on making a sentimental return visit to his old haunts, for Mr Dedalus had been a student at Queen's College. Surveying the desk in a lecture room where Mr Dedalus carved his initials long ago, Stephen is shocked to find the word 'Foetus' repeatedly carved there. But this is only one aspect of a totally disillusioning experience for Stephen. His father's irresponsible attitude, his sentimental nostalgia, his cliché-ridden chatter which is supposed to pass for good advice from one generation to the next, the ease with which he is flattered by an obsequious college servant, and the cheap way in which he flirts with barmaids and wastes time and money in shallow self-centred gossip with old cronies in bars – all this snaps what bond there has been between father and son. Stephen is sadly aware that he lacks any sense of youth's pleasures and companionships to match the Cork experiences that his father recalls. Childhood has slipped away. Indeed he feels older than his father, and the outer world seems remote and unreal as a sense of life's melancholy and meaninglessness overtakes him: the most vital force within him seems to be that of lust.

Section v

Stephen has won prize money for an essay and, as the section opens, his father takes him to the bank to cash the cheque. The money gives Stephen the opportunity to begin a spending spree by taking the family out to dinner. Then he orders groceries and expensive food-stuffs, and takes the family repeatedly to the theatre. He also buys presents, starts to overhaul his room, and indeed plans a reorganisation of the household with himself as banker. When the money runs out he recognises the futility of trying to resist the flood of sordidness overwhelming the family. His efforts have not restored family relationships in the least. He is still isolated and troubled by turbulent sexual longings. There is an idealistic element in his sexual hunger nourished by his experience of romantic novels and plays. There is also a restless adolescent urge that leads him to transmute idealistic reveries of love into sinful mental abandonment to animal lust. In this state of mind he roams Dublin's streets and wanders one night into the brothel area where vividly dressed and perfumed women move between the lighted entrance halls of houses. A prostitute accosts him, laying her hand on his arm, and the scene changes to her bedroom where, taken into her arms, Stephen feels a sudden access of self-confidence and inner power.

In the second chapter Section i ended with the collapse of the family fortunes and Stephen's retreat into inner self-dramatisation in search of the feminine ideal. The episodes of Section ii culminated in his inert failure to turn his young love for Emma into a real relationship and the let-down of learning that his noble protest at Clongowes was a great joke in the adult world. The events of Section iii gave him success in the imaginative world of dramatic self-projection and failure again to transpose his success to real life in his relations with Emma. The visit to Cork in Section iv left Stephen totally disillusioned with his father and isolated in restless inner turmoil. Once again the last section of the chapter has compensated for the sequence of let-downs by giving Stephen a taste of self-assurance in the arms of a prostitute. But will this 'success' be any more valid or permanent than his victory over injustice at the end of Chapter 1?

Chapter 3 (Repentance)

Section i

Stephen is at school, supposed to be studying in a mathematics lesson, but mentally preoccupied with his now seemingly regular night-life in the brothel area. He realises that he is guilty of mortal sin but is too proud to repent and feels superior to simple souls who do. Even so he continues to play his ceremonial part in the offices of the sodality of the Blessed Virgin Mary. Indeed the image of the Virgin Mary appeals especially to him with the savour of alluring femininity. After the mathematics lesson religious instruction by the rector is to follow. Boys suggest that Stephen should indulge in his practice of diverting the rector from his teaching by asking questions on over-subtilised niceties of doctrine. But when the rector comes in, he does not follow his usual practice. Instead he has a special announcement to make. There is to be a three-day retreat with arrangements for confessions and a general college communion. It is in honour of the school's patron, St Francis Xavier. The rector recalls St Francis's achievements as a young nobleman who threw himself selflessly into missionary work and whose faith won many souls for God. St Francis still prays in heaven for those troubled by grief or those in grave need of repentance. The rector's penetrating gaze, as he makes this point, stabs Stephen to the heart.

Section ii

Stephen is sitting in chapel listening to the first retreat address given by Father Arnall who, we remember, taught him at Clongowes and therefore is associated in his mind with the days of his childhood innocence. Father Arnall explains that a retreat involves withdrawal from day-to-day life in order to concentrate on spiritual matters. His addresses will deal with the Four Last Things; death, judgement, hell, and heaven. The boys must recall that their sole purpose in life is to do God's will and save their souls. Those who keep the Four Last Things in mind will live well, die well, and find their reward in heaven. After this first day of retreat Stephen goes home plunged in gloom and despair, revolted by his bestial sinfulness.

Next day Father Arnall preaches on death and judgement which put an end to the sinner's wickedness and his neglect of God's commandments. Each human soul will be judged and then, when Christ returns to earth, the whole human race will be judged and the wicked cast into hell. Sooner or later everyone must die, but death is fearsome only to sinners: to the righteous it brings no terrors at all. After this sermon Stephen is filled with fear and shame. The sordid details of his orgies stink all the more foully because of the purity and innocence of Emma, whose image he has mentally brutalised with lust. Yet God and the Virgin Mary are now inaccessibly remote: the only way he can hope to repent is through Emma. He pictures her at his side, the two of them hand in hand, being forgiven and blessed by a sympathetic Virgin Mary.

Father Arnall now preaches on hell. He tells how the archangel Lucifer rebelled against God through the sin of pride, declaring *Non serviam*, 'I will not serve'. Thus he and his followers were cast from heaven into hell. When God created Adam and Eve and gave them the Garden of Eden to dwell in, he imposed only one condition – that they should not eat of the forbidden tree. Satan tempted them to disobedience. They ate the forbidden fruit and were banished from Eden into the world of toil and suffering. When God in his mercy sent his only Son to be born of a pure virgin and to redeem mankind, he was crucified like a criminal. Yet Christ founded his Church so that by grace made available in the sacraments men and women might still find eternal life.

Father Arnall then delivers a lengthy account of the pains of hell which the damned will endure. He piles up imagery of fire and brimstone, filth and stench, rot and putridity, scorching torment and screaming agony. The verbal orgy of blood-curdling rhetoric leaves Stephen shaking, convinced that every word is meant for him. His brain simmers and bubbles. Only the voices of other boys reassure him that he is still alive. So there is still time for repentance. But an announcement that confessions are now being heard in chapel chills him. He feels that his shame must be uncovered elsewhere.

Back in chapel Father Arnall, seemingly forgetful that the fourth of the Last Things is heaven, returns with renewed vigour to the subject of hell. He has dealt with its physical torments. Now he must deal with its spiritual torments. And he does so systematically and exhaustively under fives heads: (1) pain of loss in being alienated from God, (2) pain of conscience in bitter recollection of past pleasure, and remorse for the hideousness of past sins and for lost opportunities for repentance, (3) pain of 'extension' in that earth's separate torments can now all be experienced simultaneously, (4) pain of intensity in that there is neither possible relief from suffering nor possible inurement to it, and (5) the eternity of pain. This punishment is what a just God accords to those who die in mortal sin. The severity of it can surprise only those who fail to grasp the true hideousness of even one sin. A single sin brought down Lucifer and a single sin drove Adam and Eve from Eden. Christ came to earth to suffer and die in order to save us, and therefore every sin renews the wounding of Christ. Father Arnall ends with a personal appeal to any of the boys who have fallen from grace. No matter how foul the sins, repentance will earn forgiveness. Finally he leads them in a prayer of contrition. Stephen cannot move his tongue, but he prays silently in his heart.

Section iii

That evening after dinner Stephen goes up to his room in terror. He fears that death may overtake him, that fiends might claim him, and there are faces about his head and voices in his ears. In his room he kneels, prays feebly, then crawls into bed where horror of his filthy sins produces a delirious nightmare. Bestial images of lust finally send him jumping out of bed to vomit. Afterwards a paragraph by Cardinal Newman in lyrical praise of the Virgin Mary comes to mind: he weeps for his lost innocence and determines to confess.

So he leaves the house and walks the dark streets, pondering his own sinfulness, disgusted and mystified by the ease with which men's sexual nature can betray them. Even frowsy-looking girls in the streets probably have a radiance in God's eyes that his sinfulness denies him. He asks an old woman if there is a chapel nearby and she directs him to one.

Inside the chapel he kneels among those waiting to confess and prays to be given a humility like theirs. One by one they go up to the confessional box. Stephen realises that there is still time to escape the shame of saying what he has done, but he resists the temptation, takes his turn in the confessional, and recounts his sins. The priest is gentle but implores him to give up his wickedness. Stephen hears the words of absolution with tears in his eyes. He walks home conscious that his soul is once more fair and holy. Happiness overwhelms him and next day, when he receives communion, he tastes an ecstasy of joy.

The pattern of this chapter follows that of the first two. The climactic moments in the succeeding episodes are experiences of fear, shame, guilt, self-disgust, and terrifying delirium, but the concluding climax of the last section cancels out these negative experiences in an experience of blissful restoration to peace and virtue. Joyce's irony is powerful, however. Although Father Arnall's preaching begins calmly and reasonably and indeed conveys a sincere appeal to his congregation, his account of the horrors of hell escalates into something grotesque. Brains boil in skulls, entrails turn to red-hot pulp. The verbal excesses indeed constitute a burlesque. Yet Stephen's response is almost equally extravagant. Whether he is dwelling on his own state of filthy sinfulness or picturing himself in sentimentalised penitence, the self-projection is dramatised into burlesque. Such is the young artist's nature. He exaggerates alike his own wickedness and his attempts at humility and contrition. There is of course an element of true sincerity in both the priest's exhortations and the penitent's response, but it is exaggerated into caricature.

Chapter 4 (Reformation and a new 'Conversion')

Section i

After absolution Stephen sets about his spiritual and moral reformation with a thoroughness which is at once touching and comic. He subjects himself to a rigorous routine of self-discipline, allotting to each day of the week a special focus for his devotions. Each morning begins with private prayer and attendance at mass, and he divides the day up into periods of prayer for souls in purgatory. He carries rosary beads and recites cycles of prayer for strengthening in faith, hope, and charity. On successive days of the week he prays for the seven gifts of the Holy Spirit one by one in order to counter the defilement of the seven deadly sins. Clearly he is now attempting to live on an ideal level in religious devotion as he earlier tried to live on an ideal level through romantic literature. In fact he drifts so far from reality that he specially values the doctrine of the Trinity because he cannot make sense of it, and conceives God's love only in vague abstract terms as a sense of divine meaning permeating creation. He mortifies his senses by such artificial devices as forcing himself to smell unpleasant odours and leaving his face and neck uncomfortably undried after washing. He is conscious of difficulty in attaining real communion with other people but experiences fervour through meditation on religious literature. He finds some satisfaction in his reformed life, but plainly his rarefied practices are no more an experience of real love than was his literary idealisation of Emma Clery. Such practices have lacked roots in physical human relationships, just as his physical relationships with prostitutes have been removed from the experience of real love.

Section ii

Stephen has been called for an interview with the director of studies. After beating about the bush in ostensibly casual conversation, the director comes round to the point and asks whether Stephen has ever considered vocation to the priesthood. Stephen's thoughts during the director's chatter have been unduly stirred by a chance reference to women's skirts, and have dwelt too both on his debt to the Jesuits and on his occasional doubts about their judgement. Now he listens intently as the director declares what an honour God bestows in calling a man to the priesthood, and proclaims priestly authority as higher than any earthly authority. In fact Stephen has often pictured himself in the priesthood, lured by the power it exercises. He recalls these dreams of the priestly state as he leaves the director's room and goes out into the street. But he is brought back to solid earth by the sight of four young men who stride swingingly along the street with linked arms to the sound of a concertina. By comparison the face of the director is a 'mirthless mask'. Stephen realises that his own pride cannot be accommodated in the order of the priesthood, for his destiny is to stand apart from others. He cannot tolerate the implicit threat to his freedom that the priestly life would involve. So he makes his way home, smiling to himself at the oddities and disorders of the alternative life he has chosen. Back home, the table is littered with the unappetising remains of tea. His brothers and sisters are talking facetiously of yet one more family removal to escape an irate and unpaid landlord, and then they burst into song. Mentally Stephen dwells on the universal weariness and melancholy of the human lot.

Section iii

Stephen has been pacing about the street for an hour while his father makes enquiries about a university place for him. His mother is hostile to the idea, but Stephen sees it as a way of breaking through to the realisation of his destiny. Walking away, he makes for the shore and, crossing the wooden bridge to the island called 'The Bull', he encounters a group of Christian Brothers coming the other way. They are a humble, pious, and charitable order, and the fact that he is going in the opposite direction from them is significant. They are going back to the tired city; his face is turned towards the sea. He recognises now the truth that it is only in the magic of words that he can harmonise the outer scene and his inner emotional life. Bantering voices of student friends are heard nearby, mocking his name, but he sees himself as a fit successor to his namesake Daedalus, for he too is an adventurous fabricator who will soar to a new life of artistic creativity. The idea excites him. Taking off his shoes and stockings, he climbs down on to the sand. He feels that he can now shed all the shames of his boyhood, for he is aware that he is alone and young and wild in heart. At this point he catches sight of a girl standing in midstream, staring out to sea, her legs and thighs bared. She has a wonderful girlish beauty and she now looks lingeringly towards him. She is the perfect image of the new life that is calling him. 'Heavenly God!' he exclaims, for this is a different kind of 'conversion'. After the negative retreat sermons he withdrew trembling into the 'cave' of his bedroom to brood on desolation and filth. After this positive revelation he strides trembling over the sands to 'greet the advent' of his new life.

This chapter is structurally the pivot of the whole book, for it is the chapter of decision. It concludes, like the previous chapters, with a climax of release and fulfilment. In turning his back on the suggested call to the priesthood, as offering only servitude and sterility, Stephen opts for an alternative vocation to the service of life and beauty in self-dedication to all that is symbolised in the figure of the wading girl. This vision of the girl not only counter-balances all previous experiences of humiliation and frustration, it also transcends the previous fulfilments which have proved each in turn to be hollow and ephemeral.

Chapter 5 (Student Days)

Section i

Stephen is now a university student. We see him eating breakfast in the now squalid home where the family is reduced to pawning articles of clothing. He is already late for his lectures and when angry shouts are heard from his father upstairs he slips out by the back door. On his morning walk across Dublin he has grown accustomed to allowing fanciful literary associations to be linked with his surroundings. The contrast between the reality of the Dublin streets and the bookish romanticism which preoccupies Stephen's thinking provides one more instance of his failure to break through from cerebral sentimentality to real human contact. He also broods on his fellow students, notably Cranly, his confidant, who receives his 'confessions' with priestlike unresponsiveness, and Davin, a student from a peasant background who is a loyal Catholic and a fierce nationalist and who has told him how once, when he was returning through the countryside late at night, a peasant woman invited him to her bed. (Perhaps we may assume him to represent therefore what Irish womanhood craves for.)

Reaching University College, Stephen goes into the physics lecture theatre where he finds the Dean of Studies trying to light a fire. Stephen answers his friendly questions in a clever-clever, half-serious manner for he thinks him an insipid, uninspired fellow, though he concedes that he is a decent sort. The physics professor comes in and delivers his lecture against an undertone of mocking student backchat. After the lecture Stephen finds a cluster of students in the entrance hall where MacCann, a political progessivist, is collecting signatures in support of an international appeal for peace initiated by the Czar. Stephen resists MacCann's attempts to involve him. MacCann calls Stephen a reactionary and Stephen mocks MacCann's photograph of the Czar as a 'bogus Jesus'. Plainly Stephen's tendency to score cleverly off all who tackle him rests on an assumed superiority which is no recipe for popularity. 'You're a born sneerer, Stevie,' says his friend Davin who wants him to throw in his lot with the Irish movement. But Stephen dropped out of the Irish language class when he saw Father Moran, the instructor, flirting with Emma. He regards political and religious causes as crippling obligations imposed on the present by the past.

So it is that Stephen goes off with Lynch, a tough, muscular fellow, and as they walk Stephen propounds his aesthetic theory with the maximum seriousness. Although Lynch periodically interjects a burst of crude banter, Stephen solemnly continues his exposition.

He first distinguishes between pity which joins the observer's mind with the sufferer and terror which joins it with the cause of suffering. Calamitous accidents are not truly tragic. Tragic emotion is static. By contrast, for instance, pornography and moralising arouse feelings of desire or loathing which are kinetic. A work of art embodies an image of beauty in some medium. The artist arranges what appeals to the senses or the mind with an aesthetic intent. The beautiful is what can be pleasurably apprehended by the senses or the mind, and it has to be received statically in order to satisfy and not to stir feelings of desire or loathing, as the moral element does. Truth satisfies the intellect while beauty satisfies the imagination.

The fact that different races admire different types of female beauty shows that beauty involves 'relations of the sensible' which are detected through different forms by different people. Aquinas declared the three needful constituents of beauty to be wholeness, harmony, and radiance. Wholeness sets a thing apart from everything else as a single entity. Harmony is the unity of various parts in the whole. Radiance is the quality that makes a thing itself and nothing else. In artistic appreciation the mind is seized by the wholeness, fascinated by the harmony, and enchanted by the radiance.

There are three forms of art – the lyrical, which is the direct expression of emotion, the epical, in which the artist projects the centre of emotional gravity outside himself so that his personality passes into the narration itself, and the dramatic, in which the artist's statement is impersonalised and vitality inheres in the characters themselves. Thus the artist, like God, becomes transcendently detached from his creation.

The propounding of this theory is the most substantial declaration in the book after the retreat sermons of Father Arnall. The two pronouncements match each other in rhetorical solemnity if not fully in rhetorical exuberance. In each case the speaker seems to be carried away by the force of his own conviction, the attachment to his own logic, and the crusading fervour of his zeal. Joyce's irony makes clear the way Father Arnall's rhetoric lifted him out of the area of simple commonsense and of contact with mundane human life. He seems to intend to pass the same judgement on Stephen's rhetorical theorising. For as the disquisition on beauty ends, Emma is seen, and thus living beauty impinges on the mind that has been theorising about beauty. And Stephen's first response is to feel bitterness and mistrust. Then, for a moment, he questions himself more healthily. Has he perhaps misjudged her? Might she, after all, have a heart 'simple and wilful as a bird's heart'? Plainly the question, thus posed and then romantically elaborated, once more takes Stephen out of touch with the living human reality into a world of poeticised reflection.

Section ii

In mood and tone this section takes up where the last section left off. It is next morning and Stephen wakes up in a state of enchantment and poetic inspiration. The image of Emma's 'strange wilful heart', burning rose-like and setting the world alight, fuses in his mind with the rhythmic lilt of a villanelle, and lines frame themselves on his lips. He tears open a cigarette packet and begins to write his poem on the back. Memories of Emma are evoked, snatches of conversation recollected, and then comes the memory of what turned Stephen against her – the scene at the Irish class which he left in resentment because he saw her flirting foolishly with Father Moran, the language tutor. Stephen recognises, however, that even his resentment is a kind of homage. Emma, like Ireland, turns from her true lover to whisper her confession to a priest of the Church instead of to a priest of the imagination like himself. For his own calling is a vocation to a poetic priesthood which transubstantiates the bread of daily experience into the divine body of eternal life. Thus imagery of the mass is utilised in a poem of worship and prayer to the idealised beloved.

Stephen recalls that he last wrote a poem to Emma ten years ago after the memorable parting on the tram. He decides not to send her the poem, but he abandons himself to a day-dream in which she responds to him voluptuously. Clearly this episode simply inflates the experience of ten years back when instead of making a living human approach to Emma, Stephen turned his romantic aspirations into the stuff of highly idealised poetry. The villanelle is a contrived verse form of five three-lined stanzas and a final four-lined one that uses only two rhymes throughout, and Stephen's poem proves to be rather pretentious. There is a good deal of rich metaphor and rhetoric about uplifted hands and eucharistic praise, but no humanly realised presence of a living girl. The poem is a cerebral self-indulgence rather than an emotional communication. It results in a private orgy of sex-in-the-head. It is notable that Emma's name is never mentioned in this episode which brings to a climax all Stephen's admiration of her beauty and longing for her.

Section iii

Stephen is standing on the steps of the library, brooding. Birds are crying and circling above him. Lines from Yeats's *The Countess Cathleen* come to his mind, and he dwells on the crude philistinism of the Dublin students who greeted the play with boos and catcalls for its supposed heresy and criticism of Ireland. The cultural alienation he feels from his homeland is one of the things that are driving him away. He goes into the library, finds Cranly, and takes him outside to join a group of students under the colonnade. Amid the banter and the backchat Stephen sees Cranly raise his hat. Stephen turns and sees that Emma is coming out of the library; she bows at Cranly's greeting while ignoring him. Moved inwardly, Stephen walks away from the others. Once more the sight of Emma has stirred inner excitement, but once more the emotion flows into literary and erotic reverie. Indeed he comes to the conclusion that he must dismiss her from his thoughts, and he rejoins the group of students, who embark on a half-serious discussion about the Church's teaching on the fate of unbaptised children.

At last Stephen drags Cranly away for the walk and the private talk he wants to have with him. He tells of a new crisis at home. His mother has pleaded with him tearfully to go to confession and Easter communion, and he has refused. Cranly questions him about his religious position, and about his father and mother, discovering what a wastrel Mr Dedalus is and how his wife has suffered. Then he delivers a sober judgement that a mother's love is more real than abstract ideas, and that Stephen ought to accommodate Mrs Dedalus. When Cranly probes further, Stephen concedes that he cannot take the sacrament idly because he is not at all sure that the mass is bogus.

Their walk takes the two friends out into the suburbs. Stephen reveals his intention to go away. Cranly argues that it is unnecessary for him to go merely on account of his rebellion against the Church, for many Catholics share his reservations. But Stephen sums up his attitude solemnly. 'I will not serve that in which I no longer believe, whether it call itself my home, my fatherland, or my church; and I will try to express myself in some mode of life or art as freely as I can and as wholly as I can, using for my defence the only arms I allow myself to use – silence, exile, and cunning.' Stephen finally rejects by silence Cranly's offer of life-long friendship. Thus one more link binding Stephen to his homeland is snapped.

Section iv

This final section consists of scraps from Stephen's journal for his last five weeks in Dublin. They touch briefly on various relationships with student friends, with his mother, and with Emma. The references to Emma are short and sketchy like all the rest. On 23 March he notes that he has not seen her and that perhaps she is ill. On 24 March he notes that she is apparently still not out and about, and he asks himself whether he is worried about her health. On 2 April he catches sight of her in a café. On 6 April he wonders whether she remembers the past as he does. There are further references to her on 6 April and, finally, on 15 April when he records meeting her face to face in the street. The reader gathers from the detached jottings that she tried to be friendly, but he responded confusingly. However he admits that he 'liked her today . . . and it seems a new feeling to me'. But next day romantic jottings voice the call of distant regions and of those who have broken away. A jotting for 26 April records his preparation for departure. 'Welcome, O life! I go to encounter for the millionth time the reality of experience and to forge in the smithy of my soul the uncreated conscience of my race.'

The pretentious claims which the young artist makes for himself on his departure contrast with the rather chilling dissection of his friends' characters as he prepares to leave them. Indeed in these jottings friends are scarcely treated as human beings evoking a human response. They become rather material for self-consciously precious penmanship.

Connection with *Ulysses*

Ulysses takes up the story of Stephen Dedalus some months after his departure from Dublin for Paris, when he has been called back home on account of his mother's terminal illness. The young Stephen pictured in the *Portrait* has an over-cerebral attitude to human life and human beings, and so, of course, has the Stephen Dedalus of *Ulysses*. Indeed a notable theme of the later book is Stephen's first experience of deeper sympathy with others which is brought about by his contact with Leopold Bloom.

Simon Dedalus, Stephen's father, reappears at various points in *Ulysses*. He goes to Paddy Dignam's funeral in the 'Hades' episode.

He is among the men chattering in the newspaper office in the 'Aeolus' episode. He is pestered in the street for cash by one of his neglected hungry daughters in the 'Wandering Rocks' episode. And in the 'Sirens' episode we see him flirting with a barmaid in the Ormond Hotel, and then singing the aria 'M'appari' from Flotow's *Martha* so lyrically and feelingly that Bloom is stirred to marvel at him: 'Glorious tone he has still . . . Silly man! Could have made oceans of money . . . Wore out his wife, now sings.' We also catch sight in the 'Wandering Rocks' episode of some of Stephen's sisters, Boody, Dilly, Katey, and Maggy, struggling in their mean home to feed themselves on bread and pea-soup begged from the nuns. And we pick up here and there a few tit-bits about Mrs Riordan ('Dante') who lived with the Dedaluses until December 1891, then moved into the City Arms hotel, where Leopold Bloom used to visit her and sometimes push her about in her bath-chair, hoping, according to his wife Molly, that she might leave him something ('Penelope' episode).

Father Conmee is given pride of place in the 'Wandering Rocks' episode as representative of Dublin churchmen. His progress on an errand of mercy is traced across Dublin. Of Stephen's student friends in the *Portrait* there are only brief mentions of Cranly and Temple, but Lynch is among student revellers in the Maternity Hospital in the 'Oxen of the Sun' episode, and it is he who accompanies Stephen to the brothel in the 'Circe' episode, where he is represented as a betrayer.

Stephen Hero

The surviving manuscript of *Stephen Hero* covers the period of Stephen's life as a student. The material is therefore contemporaneous with events in Chapter 5 of the *Portrait*. In fact the manuscript opens with an account of Stephen's late arrival at college one morning where he finds Father Butt lighting a fire in the grate of the physics theatre, as the Dean does in Chapter 5, Section i, of the *Portrait*. There are some 230 pages of print covering the period represented by the last ninety pages of the *Portrait*.

It is not surprising that Joyce failed to find a publisher for *Stephen Hero*. It reads like the raw material for a novel rather than a finished product. This does not mean that it is carelessly written: on the contrary it is polished in style. But it is over-documented in detail and the episodes succeed one another without conveying any sense that they have been subjected to the shaping process, let alone the pruning process, to which Joyce subjected his material in the *Portrait*. Moreover, narrative presentation is much more conventional than in the *Portrait*. The quick shifts from external description to inner reflection, from actual dialogue to recollected scene or dialogue, are not present. The method is closer to that of *Dubliners* than to that of the *Portrait*, though the compression and 'scrupulous meanness' of style found in *Dubliners* are not evident. In narration, in description, and in reflection the text of *Stephen Hero* is more direct and explicit than that of the *Portrait*. It is also more detailed and less selective. There are pages of description of Stephen's development which in the *Portrait* would be capsulated in brief dramatic vignettes. Thus *Stephen Hero* is a rather diffuse objective record whose interest for the reader of the *Portrait* lies largely in the way it fills out his knowledge of a background that is sometimes too sketchily hinted at in the later book.

For instance, Stephen's home life is presented in greater detail in *Stephen Hero*. Maurice, Stephen's brother, comes to life as a companion to Stephen in many of his pedestrian wanderings around Dublin, and as a foil to him at home. The home situation is more explicitly described. Mr Dedalus is as abusive, irresponsible, and tyrannical as one might expect. 'He knew that his ruin was his own handiwork but he had talked himself into believing that it was the handiwork of others.' He is given to prolonged and repetitious tirades of vengefulness. He detests his wife's family, but his wife is a model of duty. He is all the more irritated by 'her dutiful symbolism'. Mr Dedalus clings to the hope that his clever son is going to retrieve the family fortunes, but Stephen's failure to work hard at his studies and to conform to a tolerable degree to the powers-that-be threatens all his hopes. Instead of accommodating himself to the Jesuits who would be only too ready to help him to get a good job with a salary that could retrieve the family's fortunes, Stephen entertains a series of strange ideas that wreck his prospects. The underlying pathos of Mr Dedalus's disappointment resounds through his vituperation.

Mrs Dedalus, too, is far more clearly pictured in *Stephen Hero* than in the *Portrait*. Her relationship with Stephen is such that he asks her to listen to a paper he has written, and she discusses it with him afterwards. And when the clash comes over his refusal to make his communion, it is fully recorded in direct conversation between mother and son. Thus Mrs Dedalus comes forward from the misty shadows that seem to envelop her as a personality in the *Portrait*. Moreover, there is one family crisis described here in touching detail – the death of Stephen's sister, Isabella. (In reality the description relates to the death of Joyce's younger brother, George.) She arrives home ill from her convent school, is put to bed, and gradually wastes away. The doctor orders special foods for her when poor Mrs Dedalus can scarcely afford to keep the family fed on the cheapest and simplest diet. The description of Isabella's last days and of her death is powerful, and Joyce's analysis of Stephen's reactions to the tragedy is subtle and moving. One can only assume that Joyce felt this event would distract from the emphatic focus on Stephen's personal development in the world outside the family if it were included in the *Portrait*. The omission suggests a deliberate attempt to take the spotlight off Stephen's basic human contacts in the home. (The description of Isabella's funeral, however, became the basis for the full-scale account of Paddy Dignam's funeral in the 'Hades' episode of *Ulysses*.)

The relationship with Emma Clery is much more fully presented than in the *Portrait*. Here Stephen is a regular visitor at a house in Donnybrook belonging to Mr Daniel, who has several daughters and who entertains likely young students on Sunday evenings. Stephen is in demand here to play and sing. Two things lure him to keep up his visits: the unpleasantness of his own home, and the attractions of a young lady, Miss Clery. He makes enquiries about her and discovers that she has nationalist leanings and goes to an Irish language class. (In this respect she is like Miss Ivors in 'The Dead' in *Dubliners*.) He decides to join the class, much to the surprise of his friend Madden, whose nationalist enthusiasms he has mocked. (Madden, who appears again in *Ulysses*, is the equivalent of Davin in the *Portrait*. Both characters were based on Joyce's friend George Clancy, a fellow-student at University College who was later to be killed by the Black and Tans when he was Mayor of Limerick.) Details of the Irish class fill out a documentary background that is thin by comparison in the *Portrait*. The class is taken by a Mr Hughes. As well as weekly classes on Wednesdays there are meetings on Fridays which are public. Stephen attends these with Emma, and it is at one of them that he sees her responding to the gentle flirtatiousness of Father Moran. Stephen is in the habit of seeing her home after these gatherings, and he is annoyed by her failure to grant him exclusive proprietorship, by her sometimes harsh criticisms of the Daniel girls, and by the banality of much of her talk. Nevertheless there are times when the two of them are attracted to each other. Stephen, however, ceases to visit the Daniels' household and, much later in the book, Emma meets him by chance, questions him about his growing reputation for harbouring strange ideas, and presses him to return to the Daniels' house next Sunday. He does so and is once more affected by the sheer repose of spirit which her beauty seems to offer him. But Emma goes away to the Isles of Aran with a Gaelic party in the summer vacation (like Miss Ivors again), and Stephen is left alone.

One night just before Christmas Stephen runs into Emma again, looking fetching and inviting. They walk together towards her home. He is very conscious of the warmth of her body and once more, before they part, she seems to be offering a degree of responsiveness which he does not answer. The state of his feelings is made evident soon afterwards. In the middle of a tutorial in Italian he catches sight of her through the tutor's window, begs suddenly to be excused and, on the spur of the moment, darts from the building and chases her until he catches up with her. She is naturally astonished. Stephen's impulsiveness and his desire to break through all artifice have produced a rash resolution to bring things to a head with her. You are young and I am young, he tells her. I want to hold you in my arms. 'I thought I would run after you and say to you . . . Just to live one night together, Emma, and then say goodbye in the morning and never to see each other again! There is no such thing as love in the world: only people are young . . .'

Not surprisingly, Emma is deeply offended. Next time she sees him in the street she ignores him. Stephen anathemises her as 'deceptive and cowardly'. Later, one evening, Emma passes Cranly and Stephen who are in conversation. Cranly raises his hat, Stephen follows suit. Emma bows politely across Stephen to Cranly. In the *Portrait* this little episode is enacted without the background facts which give it such point in *Stephen Hero*.

Another theme of the *Portrait* which is presented in greater detail here is that of Stephen's intellectual development. Early in the book Joyce writes: 'It must be said simply and at once that at this time Stephen suffered the most enduring influence of his life', and goes on to tell how he discovered the plays of Ibsen. Stephen's advocacy of Ibsen, at the time largely unknown in Ireland, gains him the reputation of espousing dangerous atheistical new thinking. He is invited to deliver a paper at a meeting of the Literary and Historical Society. He chooses the topic 'Drama and Life', and in working on the essay he takes care 'to ensure in it a maximum of explosive force'. He regards the essay as an opportunity 'to define his own position for himself'. He regards his essay as 'applied Aquinas', but he assaults the idea that 'the end of art is to instruct, to elevate, and to amuse'. The implicit superiority of the artist to prohibitions in terms of creed or moral purpose is clearly out of key with the educational situation in a Jesuit-dominated culture. Stephen's widening of the scope of the essay leads him to change the title from 'Drama and Life' to 'Art and Life'. It is interesting that Stephen seeks appreciation of his essay at home. When his mother fails to show interest in it, he actually asks her 'point-blank should she like him to read out his essay' and naturally she then agrees. She finds it difficult, but Stephen tries to elucidate and even lends her some of Ibsen's plays to read. Father too is drawn in – with a good deal of comic irony on Joyce's part in recording the discussion of the matter.

However, Stephen is horrified to learn that it is customary for the Auditor (McCann) to submit papers to the President for scrutiny before delivery, and it soon emerges that Dr Dillon has vetoed it. In high indignation he seeks out the President, challenges him, answers his criticisms point by point, and does so with such earnestness and fervour that the President pays tribute to the thoroughness of his theory. So the paper is delivered after all and, in the discussion that follows, it is roundly attacked as 'a clever presentation of vicious principles in the guise of artistic theories' and a menace to the moral welfare of the Irish people. When this episode is set beside another, later in the book, in which Stephen attends an inaugural address to the debating society by the new Auditor, Mr Moynihan, the basis of Stephen's rebellion against the Church becomes clearer. For on this latter occasion a defence of the Church as the only instrument for ameliorating the lot of the working classes is heard with respectful approval, and the clichés in the address are corroborated in the speeches that follow. Thus the reader gets a much more detailed picture of what lies behind Stephen's rebellion: the accounts of these two debates, alongside the quoted conversations with his mother about the validity of Christian doctrines, and the much more explicit analysis of Stephen's own trains of thought, together form a record which in the *Portrait* is presented in vivid impressionistic strokes rather than in lucidly explicated sequence. Not that *Stephen Hero* is fuller and more detailed at all points in this respect. For instance Stephen's theory of beauty expounded in detail to Lynch in the *Portrait* is given in a brief summary to Cranly in *Stephen Hero*. The desire to use Stephen's declaration of artistic doctrine as a full-scale structural counterbalance in logical and rhetorical impact to the lengthy retreat sermons must be assumed to lie behind this change.

The more sophisticated narrative presentation and the omission of inessentials makes the *Portrait* a great work of art where *Stephen Hero* remains a heap of raw material. The sharpening of the edges produced by economy in the *Portrait* leaves *Stephen Hero* looking like a flabby piece of work, for all the polish of its style. Moreover the careful interweaving of thematic material in the *Portrait* and the construction of the whole around successive crises gives the later work an impact that is unforgettable. Once the shape and structure of the *Portrait* are grasped every episode in the book falls into place. By comparison *Stephen Hero* is unorganised. It remains valuable for the light it throws on Joyce's way of working up his material.* And the reader of Joyce will be constantly delighted at the unsuspected revelations it offers – such as Cranly's observation on Emma: 'Only she's so flamin' fat.'

*In *Stephen Hero* Joyce used the spelling 'Daedalus', which he later abandoned.

Exiles

Joyce's *Exiles*, a three-act play written between the *Portrait* and *Ulysses*, stands in strange contrast to both. It uses autobiographical material as fully as do the *Portrait* and *Ulysses*, but without subjecting it to the distancing process which produces the irony and humour of the great works. That is not the only difference. Joyce's great works are rich in the sights and sounds, the personalities and institutions of Dublin. Some characters in the *Portrait* may be but mistily or sketchily realised, but they all inhabit a world of street or church, school or college, that is powerfully present to the reader's mind. This vivid realisation of an active, living world is lacking in *Exiles*. The play is autobiographical rather in the sense that it explores analytically the dilemmas of Joyce's inner life, particularly the complex emotional cross-currents involved in his rejection of Ireland and in his love for Nora. This material, treated with great seriousness and frankness, is too close to Joyce's own heart for him to project it with clarity, let alone with objectivity or detachment. Joyce's very honesty in self-exploration perhaps prevented him from achieving the sharpness of outline in character and action which gives a play dramatic impact.

Act 1

The scene is set in the Dublin suburbs in the summer of 1912. Richard Rowan, a writer, has returned home from nine years' exile with his wife Bertha and his little boy Archie. It emerges that Richard had shaken the dust of his homeland from his feet. Its spirit appears to have been represented in his mother, a faithful Catholic, with whom he quarelled and who has died without reconciliation. Richard eloped before marriage with Bertha, a simple girl, causing a scandal by this as well as by his individualistic rebellion against conventional attitudes. References to a 'smiling handsome father' who, by contrast with the mother, indulged young Richard, then fourteen years old, even from his death-bed suggest the basis of dichotomies present in Richard's own nature. As the play opens Richard is visited by Beatrice Justice, a music teacher who gives Archie lessons and who has been away in southern Ireland for twelve days. During his long absence abroad Richard has carried on a lengthy correspondence with Beatrice about his work, and it appears that she has been an inspiration and has left her mark on what he has written. In short she offers that intellectual sympathy and understanding which Bertha is not equipped to provide. The relationship with Beatrice is complicated by the fact that she is closely associated with her cousin Robert Hands, Richard's own best friend, but a foil to Richard in that Robert is a journalist who has done well for himself at home (like Gabriel Conroy in 'The Dead' in *Dubliners*).

The dialogue between Richard and others has intensity of emotional suggestiveness, but skates subtly around the peripheries of clarification. The text is littered with question marks and with sentences that tail off, uncompleted, into blanks weighed down with unguessable clues which the reader feels would be important if only he could grasp them. Thus what emerges of the relationship between Richard and Beatrice suggests a commitment in love that is unrealisable, not simply because of Richard's prior tie to Bertha, but by virtue of a peculiar shared capacity to wound each other rather than to give themselves. Nevertheless Beatrice's idealised persona hovers mysteriously, if chastely, over the aspirations of the hero as does Dante's heroine, Beatrice, in the *Divine Comedy*.

The play is for the most part a sequence of duologues, punctuated by passages in which three characters are present while the transition is effected between one duologue and the next. Thus, for instance, Robert arrives and Richard leaves. Then Bertha arrives and Beatrice leaves. The interview between Bertha and Robert has its element of surprise. Robert is plainly quite conventionally in love with Bertha and has been pressing his claim. He plays the philanderer effectively and Bertha responds with a strangely permissive simplicity, allowing herself to be embraced and kissed. Robert invites her to come in the evening between 8 and 9 to an address he gives her. When Richard returns Robert reveals that he is working hard on his friend's behalf to get him well placed in Dublin. He has seen the Vice-Chancellor about a university chair (in Romance literature). The Vice-Chancellor will support Richard in senate while Robert acclaims him in the press. Richard is moodily enigmatic in response to this news – as he tends to be in response to everything. When Richard and Robert are left alone together it emerges that they shared a house in their youth in which they conducted their amorous adventures, and there is a hint that they were rivals for Bertha's affection. Robert conveys to Richard an invitation to dinner at the Vice-Chancellor's. He is to go at about 8 p.m. Robert adds, 'I shall look in about ten. So you can have an hour or so to yourselves first.'

However, when Bertha and Richard are alone together Bertha, seemingly according to plan, tells her husband everything that has happened between herself and Robert, answering Richard's enquiries in detail. The address she is asked to visit is the very cottage which Richard and Robert shared, the seat and symbol of their friendship. Bertha shows some resistance to the way she is being used and the advantage that is being taken of her simplicity; while Richard insists that she has complete liberty in all respects. Bertha suspects that

Richard merely seeks liberty for himself to make love to Beatrice. Determined to stir Richard, she urges him to forbid her to go and keep the appointment with Robert in the evening, but he refuses. It is plain that Bertha's love for Richard is unquestionable, but his enigmatic treatment of her worries her deeply.

Act 2

The second act takes us to Robert's cottage where he is plainly waiting for Bertha, playing the piano, then perfuming the room. When there is a knock on the door he exclaims 'Bertha' and rushes to let her in. But the visitor is Richard. He tackles Robert straightaway, revealing that Bertha has told him all, indeed that she has kept him informed of the relationship stage by stage. Robert thinks he has been tested by Richard and experimented on by Bertha. Richard speaks as though it is only the secrecy and deception practised by his old friend that have upset him. Robert is astonished and disturbed that Richard does not play the usual part of the jealous husband and the outraged friend. He talks in the accustomed conventionalities – of regret, remorse, apology for the way passion has overcome him, and gratitude that discovery has come early enough to save him from the ultimate betrayal. Richard, by contrast, talks mysteriously, at some points all but suggesting that Bertha may need the two of them. He refuses to speak the language of guilt and innocence. Rather he suggests that love for Bertha unites the two of them in brotherhood, indeed he confesses that he has felt secret longings to be betrayed by his best friend. He sees the present crisis as a 'battle of both our souls . . . A battle of your soul against the spectre of fidelity, of mine against the spectre of friendship'. 'All life,' he adds, 'is a conquest, the victory of human passion over the commandments of cowardice . . . Have you the courage?' His exhortation to Robert is that he must free himself. When Bertha's knock is heard at the door Robert implores Richard desperately, 'Let me go. It is over. She is yours. Keep her and forgive me, both of you.' But Richard replies, 'I will not live on your generosity. You have asked her to meet you here tonight and alone. Solve the question between you.'

Robert slips out into the garden as Bertha comes in. At first she seems relieved that Richard is here, for it suggests that he can be jealous like other men. Nevertheless she is worried about the shameful way in which she has treated Robert, and she resents being treated as Richard's tool. Plainly she wants him to defend her against Robert. But he refuses to play that part. Indeed, 'You may be his and mine . . . I cannot hate him since his arms have been around you.' So he leaves her, and Robert comes back. There is embarrassment at first. Then as the atmosphere changes and Robert talks ironically and mockingly of the preparations he had made to receive her as 'Love's Labour Lost', Bertha suddenly takes fright, seemingly at the thought that adultery might be in the air. 'Promise me, Robert, not to think of such a thing.' He gives his promise. Bertha then tries to excuse her behaviour. She was hurt that, while she told Richard everything, Robert showed no interest in whether Richard knew or not. In short he treated her as though 'like the other women' she would be a natural deceiver. Robert can still scarcely credit that Bertha has reported every detail of their encounters. When Bertha begins to speak of its being time for her to go, Robert begins to play the part of the accomplished wooer, and uses Richard's vocabulary of deliverance from bonds in the act. 'Every chain but one he has broken and that one we are to break, Bertha . . . you and I.' Bertha is rising to go, but Robert detains her fondly as the curtain falls, leaving the audience uncertain whether she will yield to him or not.

Act 3

We are at Richard's house next morning. Bertha, wearing a dressing-gown, looks pale and drawn. After an episode involving Brigid, the servant, and Archie, the little boy, Beatrice arrives, excited by an article in the morning paper headed 'A Distinguished Irishman'. It is Robert's tribute to Richard, seemingly written overnight. But Beatrice is worried because, having written the article, Robert has apparently spent the rest of the night packing to go away. In talking together of Richard, Bertha probes Beatrice about her relationship with him. When Richard comes through the room on his way to his study, Beatrice shows him Robert's article but his response is enigmatic. When Beatrice goes, Bertha tries to get Richard to ask about what she did at Robert's. 'I will tell you if you ask me,' she says. 'You will tell me. But I will never know,' he replies. She is angry that he left her there. 'If you loved me or if you knew what love was you would not have left me. For your own sake you urged me to it . . . To have it always to throw against me. To make me humble before you, as you always did . . .' She calls him a 'Woman-killer' who has made both Beatrice and herself unhappy. It is plain that she seeks a loving and possessive response from him while he continues to talk about her being free.

Richard goes into his study and Robert arrives. Bertha urges him not to go away. 'He will believe that you are going away because you are afraid to face him after last night.' Robert presses Bertha about what he must say to Richard. 'Were you mine in that sacred night of love? Or have I dreamed it?' he asks. 'You dreamed that I was yours last night', Bertha replies. So when Richard comes in Robert says, 'I failed, Richard . . . I failed. She is yours, as she was nine years ago, when you met her first.' Robert claims that he spent the night first at the Vice-Chancellor's, then at his office working on the article, then at a night-club, then with a prostitute, and finally packing his valise. When he has left there is a final episode between Bertha and Richard. She protests her unbroken fidelity, sits at his feet, seizes his hand, and speaks of their life of love together. 'I have a deep, deep wound of doubt in my soul,' Richard concedes. But he does not wish to be cured of the wound. 'It is not in the darkness of belief that I desire you. But in restless living wounding doubt.'

On this enigmatic note the enigmatic play ends. The reader may decide for himself whether there was adultery between Robert and Bertha. Perhaps a defect of the play is that a director might produce it in such a way – or actors might speak crucial lines in such a way – as to convey that the two have tacitly agreed at last to deceive Richard, or that they remain innocent. For instance Robert's question 'Were you mine in that sacred night of love? Or have I dreamed it?' might be asked as a piece of romantic rhetoric or as another way of asking: 'What story are we going to tell Richard?'

Ulysses

Ulysses was divided by Joyce into three numbered books and eighteen unnumbered episodes. In the book itself he did not use any titles for either the books or the episodes. However, when discussing the book or when writing letters about it Joyce used titles for the episodes which are derived from the narrative parallels between his epic and Homer's *Odyssey*. Critics have naturally found it convenient to use these titles in referring to *Ulysses*, and they are used here. For convenience too in this present Handbook the three books are given the titles 'The Search', 'The Wanderings', and 'The Homecoming'. The first book, containing three episodes, concentrates on Stephen Dedalus. In Homer Odysseus's son Telemachus goes in search of his long-lost father. Here Stephen Dedalus is in search of 'fatherhood', having cast off (at the end of the *Portrait*) allegiances to home, fatherland, and church. The second and largest book contains twelve episodes. It tracks the wanderings and adventures of Leopold Bloom as the *Odyssey* tracks the wanderings of Odysseus. Bloom, like Odysseus, is suffering from separation from his wife, not because there are physical 'seas between' them, but because they drifted apart, mentally and sexually, after the death of their baby son Rudy ten years ago, and because Molly has taken a lover. The third book, like the first, contains three episodes. It brings Stephen and Bloom together at

Bloom's home where Molly Bloom is already in bed. It brings a great, and to some extent hopeful, clarification of the aspirations of all three of them.

Book I ('The Search')

Episode 1: Telemachus

The opening episode introduces us to Stephen Dedalus at the beginning of the day of 16 June in 1904. Like Joyce himself, Stephen left Ireland at the end of the *Portrait* for Paris, but he was called home some months later by a telegram, 'Mother dying come home Father'. The factual basis for the settings of the first two episodes is that Joyce stayed briefly with Oliver St John Gogarty in the Martello tower on the coast at Sandycove and that he taught for a time at a private school in Dalkey. The reader must not assume, however, that the presentation of Stephen's character, activities, and relationships is an accurate record of Joyce's own, still less that other characters in the book always fairly represent the actual persons who played comparable roles in Joyce's life. Joyce is sometimes at least as hard on other people as he is on himself.

It is morning. Buck Mulligan, a self-confident, boisterous, flippant medical student comes up on to the roof of the Martello tower, overlooking Dublin bay. He has shaving equipment in his hands and is performing a mock rite as though he were a priest celebrating mass and the shaving bowl were his chalice. (The reader who is interested in symbolism will notice that since soapy water is the hygienic safeguard of our civilisation, the parallel with the mass is something more than an amusing parody.) Stephen, a more reserved, intense, and thoughtful young man, watches his friend's performance. He is worried about the presence of an English guest, Haines, who raved frighteningly overnight in a hysterical nightmare – apparently about an encounter with a black panther. Chaffing Stephen, Mulligan rebukes him for having refused to pray at the bedside of his dying mother, and memories of the death-bed scene recur to Stephen during this episode, as they do at other crucial points of the book. This act of disobedience at his mother's death-bed is symptomatic of the young artist's rebellion against constraints defined at the end of the *Portrait*. Mulligan mocks Stephen mercilessly, but he appreciates his sharp, razor-like wit: indeed he urges him to exploit his cleverness to touch their admiring English guest for money. Stephen, however, is seriously offended by the flippant way Mulligan has referred to Mrs Dedalus's death, for he is haunted by a dream in which she returns, ghostlike, to rebuke his impiety. Mulligan and Stephen go down into the tower to join Haines for breakfast. The milkwoman arrives just in time. While Mulligan teases her, Stephen sees her as a symbol of poor old Ireland, serving milk to her conqueror. Haines, an English enthusiast for the Gaelic movement, tries out his Irish on her, but, ironically enough, she cannot understand it.

The most cheerful prospect this morning, so far as Mulligan is concerned, is that it is pay-day for Stephen who is working as a school-teacher in Dalkey. He foresees a night's drinking at Stephen's expense. Haines is Stephen's admirer. 'I intend to make a collection of your sayings if you will let me,' he says. But Stephen refuses to follow Mulligan's advice and play up to this convenient admiration for the sake of profit, and he is coolly enigmatic in response. As the three of them leave the tower Haines presses Stephen to expound his theory of *Hamlet*, but Mulligan's comic horror of such seriousness pushes the subject out of the way. (In fact we are to hear Stephen expound it in full in the 'Scylla and Charybdis' episode.) 'I read a theological interpretation of it somewhere . . . The Father and the Son idea,' Haines suggests, and Mulligan replies with three verses from his blasphemous 'Ballad of Joking Jesus'. The theme of fatherhood and sonship is thus in the air, if frivolously, from the start of the book. Meanwhile Stephen's brooding turns at times on the dual subservience of Ireland to 'the imperial British state' represented by Haines (whose silver cigarette case has a green stone set in it, like Ireland, the 'Emerald Isle', ornamenting the British empire), and to the Roman Catholic Church.

The three of them reach the cliffs and make their way down to the creek [an inlet of the sea]. Here there is a male preserve, the 'Forty-Foot' bathing place where men bathe in the nude. Mulligan undresses and dives in, having first prevailed on Stephen to leave the tower key with him and to lend him twopence for two pints of beer. In reality Joyce was more likely to sponge on Gogarty than vice versa, but here Stephen is the one whose hospitality is being abused, and the handing over of the key is a symbolic act. In parting, however, he agrees to meet Mulligan at the Ship Inn at 12.30. Stephen's brooding throughout the episode pictures Mulligan as something of a tempter who would lure him to put his artistic talent at the service of the establishment, and as a usurper who has taken over his refuge. Symbolism corroborates this reading. The first view of Mulligan shows him with a yellow dressing-gown floating behind him on the morning air like a diabolical tail. If further hint of what he stands for is needed, his shaking face is 'equine in its length' and his light brown hair is 'grained and hued like pale oak'. The symbolism of the Wooden Horse by means of which Troy was betrayed is with us already. Stephen dramatises his role as a wanderer who has nowhere to lay his head. 'I will not sleep here tonight,' he says cryptically. 'Home also I cannot go.' The family home is insupportable. The temporary haven has been usurped. He is as much in need of fatherhood as Telemachus was when he set out to search for the lost wanderer, Ulysses.

There is a certain parallelism between the three episodes of Book I and the three episodes of Book III, which focus respectively on the day's beginning and its ending. Thus this first early morning episode is written in a fresh, crisp narrative style, while Episode 16 ('Eumaeus'), in which the action takes place in the early hours, is written in a wearily drifting and inconclusive narrative style. The two styles have been labelled 'Narrative young' and 'Narrative old'.

Episode 2: Nestor

We find Stephen taking a class at the Dalkey school. He is apparently giving a lesson in ancient history. The subject is Pyrrhus, King of Epirus, who wanted to emulate Alexander the Great and rule over Macedon. He did not achieve his aim. He fought against the Romans at Tarentum, Heracles, and Asculum. His victory at Heracles was so costly that the expression 'a Pyrrhic victory' has come to mean a victory that is scarcely worth having. Stephen is interested in him as the frustrated leader of a chosen people, standing (as we shall see later) side by side with for instance Moses or Parnell – both of whom only reached a point at which the Promised Land could be viewed at a distance. (And that is to be the fate of our Jewish hero, Leopold Bloom.) After history there is a poetry lesson. One of the boys recites Milton's *Lycidas*. There was talk of a man drowned in the sea in the last episode and Milton's poem is an elegy on a friend drowned at sea, which pictures his ultimate resurrection. Stephen finally dispatches his class with a riddle about a fox burying his grandmother under a hollybush. It brings Stephen's mind back to his mother's end. Thus imagery of death – and possible resurrection – accumulates.

The boys go out on to the field to play football while Stephen goes to the headmaster's room to collect his pay. Mr Deasy is an Ulsterman. His room gives off the flavour of a conventional supporter of the British establishment. There is even a portrait of King Edward VII as Prince of Wales over the mantelpiece. Elsewhere around the walls are pictures of framed race-horses. Mr Deasy's talk is full of worldly common sense. Prudent and careful, he keeps pound notes neatly in a pocket-book and his coins in a little savings-box with separate compartments for sovereigns, half-crowns, shillings, and sixpences. He gives friendly advice to Stephen about looking after his money and admonishes him on the need to save. He declares admiringly that the Englishman's proudest boast is 'I paid my way'. Stephen, recalling the tale of his debts, cannot make the claim.

Stephen's literary connections are known to Mr Deasy, and the headmaster therefore seeks his help in getting a letter he has written into print in the Dublin press. It is on the controversial topic of foot-and-mouth disease. Deasy's letter is not given in full, but the snippets quoted show that in style it is a collection of journalistic clichés and in substance it urges more drastic action against the spread of the disease. In warming to his theme, Mr Deasy hints at the corruptions and intrigue of public life and, corroborating a line taken by the Englishman Haines in Episode 1, he complains that 'England is in the hands of the Jews'. The Jews, Mr Deasy adds, 'sinned against the light . . . And that is why they are wanderers on the earth to this day.' The anti-semitic theme has special significance because Leopold Bloom, the hero of *Ulysses*, is a Jew, is made to feel something of an outsider, and on this particular day is a wanderer about Dublin's streets. Deasy also lays blame for many troubles on women. It was Helen, wife of Menelaus, whose infidelity with the Trojan prince Paris sparked off the siege of Troy. It was the faithless wife Devorgilla who brought about the first English invasion of Ireland. (Mr Deasy, at whom Joyce pokes a good deal of quiet fun, mixes up the names of Devorgilla's husband, O'Rourke, and her lover, Macmurrough, who gained Henry II's support for his cause.) Parnell too was brought low by a woman. This theme of the unfaithful wife again foreshadows the story of Leopold Bloom and his wife Molly.

Stephen leaves Deasy, carrying off his letter with the intention of trying to get it published in either the *Evening Telegraph* or the *Irish Homestead.* The final sally from Mr Deasy is that Ireland is the only country that never persecuted the Jews because, wisely, 'she never let them in'. And the exclusion of the Jew from assimilation by the Irish (not to mention the exclusion of a particular Jew from full sexual acceptance at home) is another significant theme in the book.

In seeking news of his father Homer's Telemachus goes to consult Nestor, the old warrior renowned for his wisdom who had taken part in the siege of Troy. This episode is labelled 'Nestor' because Mr Deasy too talks of himself as an old campaigner and takes it upon himself to give gratuitous advice to Stephen.

The parallelism between the first book and the third book is sustained in that the pedagogical method of this second episode of Book I is matched by an encyclopaedic method adopted in Episode 17, the second episode of Book III. The proponderance of a question-and-answer technique at the beginning of this episode is more than matched by the unbroken question-and-answer technique adopted in Episode 17 ('Ithaca'). The two styles have been labelled 'Catechism (personal)' and 'Catechism (impersonal)'.

Episode 3: Proteus

This episode is certainly the most difficult in the book. It consists largely of Stephen's musings as he walks on Sandymount strand. He is brooding on the mystery of things, on philosophical doctrines which have been invented to explain our strange relationship to our own environment (such as those of Aristotle and Bishop Berkeley), and on what he sees about him. Concrete experiences of his senses launch him into abstract theorising. Thus he reflects on his physical relationship to the ground under his feet. The sight of two midwives extends his reflection to the origins of human life, to the universal mother Eve, and to his own parents. Wondering whether to call on his uncle Richie (his mother's brother) and Aunt Sara, he gives us a mental vignette of their home life, and incidentally an echo of how Simon Dedalus speaks of his detested in-laws. Then he recalls the youthful vanity of his schooldays in self-posturing as an imaginary artist-prodigy. By this time he has inadvertently passed the way to Aunt Sara's, and memories of France succeed – of exiled Irish patriots he met in Paris, and of how his hopes for great things abroad were dashed by the arrival of the telegram, 'Mother dying come home Father'. The green bowl of sea in Dublin Bay has already reminded him in Episode 1 of the bowl of mucus at his dying mother's bedside, and the theme of exiled revolutionaries in Paris, loveless and landless, runs alongside the theme of his own isolation. Turning and looking south towards the Martello tower, he repeats to himself his determination not to return.

A dog disturbs his train of thought, and he reflects that he is really on the beach where Norse marauders first landed in the eighth century to found the city. Historical reflection turns to Pretenders seemingly because Mulligan is conceived as one. But Stephen cannot forget that Mulligan has bravely saved men from drowning and that he himself shrinks from water. He sees some cockle-pickers, the owners of the dog, and its 'redpanting' tongue brings back the image of the fox burying its grandmother. The theme of the animal rooting in the ground then brings back the memory of the black panther of Haines's nightmare. This is a recurring theme. Here it triggers off the memory of Stephen's own dream last night in which he encountered an oriental stranger who tempted him with a luscious melon and invited him in with a red-carpeted welcome. This imagery foreshadows Stephen's climactic meeting with Bloom which answers in a peculiar way his search for lost fatherhood.

Stephen's train of thought grows denser and its articulation more fragmentary, but through the aggregation of images it is clear that his poetic inspiration is stimulated and potent phrases begin to course through his mind. Seeking a piece of paper so that he can jot down the inspired lines before they fade, he tears a strip off Mr Deasy's letter and begins to scribble words on it, using a rock as a table. The phrases we read here indicate a poem about a lover coming to meet his beloved, but we are given an actual quotation only in the 'Aeolus' episode. The textual congestion increases as Stephen is stimulated by the creative mood, and as he takes up his ashplant to proceed on his way. But among the medley of images a group stands out, evoked by a sudden clouding over of the sky – the thought of the darkness when Christ was on the cross, the thought of thunder and lightning and the fall of the bright angel Lucifer from heaven. (The latter image takes us back to the retreat sermons in the *Portrait*.) The episode closes with a significant moment at which Stephen suddenly feels that there may be someone behind him and, looking around, he sees out at sea a threemaster with its upright crosstrees, faintly suggestive of the Trinity and of the Crucifixion.

In Homer Menelaus tells Telemachus how he encountered the sea-god Proteus whose ever-changing shape made it all but impossible to pin him down and question him about Odysseus's wanderings. But he was successful in the end, and it is plain from Stephen's words as he finally frames his own thoughts in the words of a poem ('Here. Put a pin in that chap, will you?'), that getting something definite, verbally, out of the shifting mixture of fragmentary thoughts about the nature of things is like dealing with a slippery Proteus.

The stylistic parallel between this third episode of Book I and the third episode of Book III (the final episode of the book) is obvious. Both are monologues. The style here of course represents the flow of thought in the mind of Stephen, a young intellectual, whereas the style in the balancing final episode ('Penelope') represents the flow of thought in an altogether less sophisticated, less cerebral person, and a woman too. Moreover the thinking in 'Proteus' is alert, fast-moving, and often sharp-edged, as befits a philosophically minded young man taking a morning walk, while the thinking in 'Penelope' is that of a tired, emotionally strained woman caught between sleep and waking in the middle of the night.

The three episodes of this first book are much concerned with beginnings – 'Telemachus' with the beginning of the June day for Stephen Dedalus, 'Nestor' with the beginning of life's span in the school class-room, with lessons on the history of our civilisation, and with talk of the history of Ireland, and 'Proteus' with the origin of life and the roots of all being. From surveying the sweep of history thought settles down to focus on the individual artist's moment of creativity. The whole of Book I may be said to prepare for the 'beginning' of the epic in Book II.

Book II ('The Wanderings')

Episode 4: Calypso

Book I focuses on Stephen Dedalus. He is a young intellectual, the 'brains' of the group of characters with whom the epic is mainly concerned. Consequently when Joyce represents his trains of thought the text tends to be difficult. But when we reach Book II and begin to focus on Leopold Bloom (the 'bread' rather than the 'brains' of the group) we find a very human figure with whose attitudes and thought-processes we can readily sympathise. (The reader will later discover that Molly Bloom and 'Blazes' Boylan represent the 'blood' and the 'brawn'.) In so far as Bloom does attempt to tackle the sphere of culture and science or philosophy in his thoughts, he tends to get things wrong. Bloom, we learn later, is thirty-eight years old. He is a canvasser for advertisements working on a free-lance basis. Whereas Stephen began his day in a world of cerebral wit, Bloom begins his day with his mind on food. He comes downstairs, prepares some bread and butter for his wife, Molly, then pours out a saucer of milk for the cat. Bloom thinks he will go and buy some kidneys for breakfast, but first he checks up from the hall that Molly does not want anything of the kind. 'Mn', she replies, which he takes for 'No'. Through Bloom's reflections we learn that Molly (properly 'Marion') hails from Gibraltar and that her father was a military man who made a corner in stamps.

Bloom takes down his hat and leaves the house. It promises to be a warm day and he is wearing black clothes, not the most comfortable of wear. They give him the appearance of the dark oriental stranger of whom Stephen dreamed, indeed of the 'black panther' of whom Haines dreamed. Bloom's own day-dreams today tend to take him to the east, which is not surprising since he is a Jew. Passing Larry O'Rourke's bar he greets O'Rourke, but his destination is Dlugacz's the butcher's shop, where he takes a page from a pile of cut sheets of newspaper used for parcelling up meat, and as he walks back home with his kidneys he studies something that caught his eye on the piece of newspaper. It is an advertisement from a German company that is planning to plant citrus groves in Israel and seeks shareholders. The name of the company, 'Agendath Netaim' (Hebrew for 'Plantations Association') is to stick in his mind. It represents the lure of the fruit-laden east with its luscious promise of abundance – a lure which is to be associated later with his hunger for his wife's voluptuous charms. But when a cloud covers the sun (the same cloud that changed Stephen's thinking), Bloom begins to brood more solemnly on images of the Dead Sea, the wandering, captive peoples of Israel, and general desolation.

When he reaches home again at 7 Eccles Street, Bloom finds two letters and a card on the doormat. The handwriting on one of the letters addressed to his wife is enough to disturb him as he goes into the bedroom and hands it to Molly. She glances quickly at it and then tucks it under her pillow. The card is from their daughter Milly, acknowledging the receipt of a parcel. The second letter is also from her. Having raised the blind to let the light in, Bloom goes downstairs again to make the tea and fry the kidneys. Coming back with Molly's breakfast on a tray and observing the torn envelope half-hidden under the pillow, he asks whom the letter came from. It was from Boylan, Molly's impresario who arranges recitals for her, for she is a singer, and there is a series of engagements in the wind. He will be 'bringing the programme' this afternoon.

The glimpse we get of the Blooms' home life is as packed with solid things as Stephen's world was packed with mental furniture – Molly's ample body, the bedclothes, her underwear, and the library book she has been reading, *Ruby, the Pride of the Ring* by Paul de Kock, who goes in for a fair share of sex and violence. But a smell of burning sends Bloom rushing downstairs again to rescue the kidneys. While he eats them he reads the letter from Milly, now working at Mullingar. Since it was her fifteenth birthday yesterday Bloom's thoughts naturally go back to her birth and there is the first of many sad recalls of his son Rudy who died after a few days of life and would now be eleven, had he lived. Milly is at a difficult age and Bloom has slight apprehensions about whether she can look after herself. She has mentioned one of Boylan's songs in her letter and it brings the image of Boylan to mind, who wormed his way into their lives as a 'friend of the family'.

Following a call of nature, he picks up an old number of *Titbits* and goes out of the back door to the privy in the garden. Seated on the stool, he reads in the paper of one Philip Beaufoy who has won the prize for his story 'Matcham's Masterstroke', about the masterstroke by which Matcham won his 'laughing witch'. The item reminds Bloom that he once fancied his prospects of writing this kind of material. But the fate of Beaufoy's story is to be torn and used as Bloom's toilet paper (rather as Mr Deasy's letter was torn and used for a different kind of productive work by Stephen). When he leaves the privy, the bells of St George's church strike the hour, reminding him of poor Paddy Dignam whose funeral he is to attend during the morning.

The connection with Homer in this episode is that the goddess Calypso held Odysseus captive for seven years by her amorous arts. The gods eventually order his release. Bloom himself is certainly bound in amorous captivity by his loving dependence upon Molly, from whom he sets out on his day's wanderings at this point.

Episode 5: The Lotus Eaters

Homer's Ulysses has great difficulty in dragging his men back to ship after they have landed among the lotus-eaters, for they have been fed on the drug which reduces them to inertia so completely that they forget their homes and long only to stay where they are. Joyce's hero is here walking in the city, idly pensive, inertly receptive to impressions from the world around him, many of which involve imagery of intoxicated self-abandonment.

Bloom takes a somewhat circuitous route to his first destination, the post office in Westland Row, no doubt because of the furtive and rather underhand nature of his mission. For it is here that he has a post restante address under a false name, 'Henry Flower Esq., c/o P.O. Westland Row City'. He is going to present his false visiting card to the postmistress and collect whatever mail may be awaiting him. Sure enough there is a letter which he slips into his side pocket. Out in the street he goes rather guiltily through the process of tearing open the envelope with one hand in his pocket, pulling out the letter, and crumpling up the envelope. His curiosity is stirred by the fact that he can feel something pinned to the letter, but at that moment he encounters an acquaintance, C. P. M'Coy ('Charlie'), a clerk in the Midland Railway. We met him in 'Grace' (*Dubliners*) where he played his part in the mission to reform Tom Kernan, and we learned then of his gambit for obtaining money from well-wishers by telling them that his wife Fanny (who has pretensions as a singer) would be able to fulfil engagements in the country if only he could lay hold of the money to equip her with the necessary portmanteau and valises. After polite exchanges about the sad death of Paddy Dignam, Bloom scents the approach of the valise trick when M'Coy says 'My missus has just got an engagement. At least it's not settled yet', so Bloom quickly turns the conversation to his own wife's very impressive engagement to sing 'at a swagger affair in the Ulster Hall, Belfast'. Taking his leave, M'Coy asks Bloom to add his name to the list of mourners at the funeral. Bloom moves on, congratulating himself on having escaped the cadging gambit and indignant at the implied comparison between Molly and Fanny M'Coy ('Reedy freckled soprano').

Eventually Bloom is bold enough to take the letter from his pocket, fold it gently inside his newspaper, and then to read it furtively. It is a reply by someone called Martha to a letter of his, and there is a flower pinned to it. It later emerges that Bloom initiated the correspondence by inserting an advertisement in the *Irish Times*, 'Wanted smart lady typist to aid gentleman in literary work'. From among the applicants for this non-existent post Martha was selected. Something of the pathos of Bloom's emotional situation can be seen in his need, because of Molly's relationship with Boylan, to seek solace and vicarious female companionship in this underhand way. Martha's letter fondly takes him to task for sending her stamps. 'I am awfully angry with you', she writes. 'Are you not happy in your home you poor little naughty boy?' she asks, and 'O how I long to meet you'.

Bloom's memories reveal to us that Martha at first feigned indignation when she learned that the advertisement was a mere trick to establish a relationship; nevertheless she has suggested that they should meet one Sunday evening after rosary, but Bloom is unwilling to commit himself to what might produce a scandal and a serious domestic upheaval. Thus the relationship to Martha is a purely inert 'ideal' one. Bloom has no intention of bestirring himself to action.

Bloom's now rather purposeless wanderings take him into All Hallows' Church where mass is in progress. As a Jew and an outsider, Bloom harbours strange misunderstandings of both Catholicism and Protestantism. To him the mass, the togetherness it evokes, the miraculous healings and revelations, the practice of confession, and the hope of heaven all play their part in lulling people into a state of drugged contentment. After the service Bloom remembers that he has to call at the chemist's for some face lotion for Molly. Once more in an environment full of narcotics and perfumes, he orders the lotion to be made up, buys a bar of scented soap, and leaves the shop only to run into Bantam Lyons, who made a not very notable appearance in 'Ivy Day in the Committee Room' in *Dubliners*. Lyons borrows his newspaper. For today is the day of the Ascot Gold Cup race and Lyons is in search of tips. A casual remark by Bloom, that he was only going to throw away the newspaper anyway, is interpreted by Lyons as a coded tip to back an outsider called 'Throwaway'. This misunderstanding proves unfortunate for Bloom later in the day (in the 'Cyclops' episode). Very much a man of practical common sense in financial matters, he is the last person to have a flutter on a horse. As we take leave of him in this episode, he is walking towards the baths and already anticipating the pleasure of reclining luxuriously in a 'womb of warmth'.

Episode 6: Hades

Homer's Odysseus pays a visit to the Underworld, and Bloom today has to travel across Dublin in Paddy Dignam's funeral procession to the Glasnevin cemetery. The procession starts in Sandymount at the south-eastern end of the city and has to make its way to Glasnevin, north of the Liffey towards the west. Bloom finds himself sharing a cab with Simon Dedalus (Stephen's father), and with Jack Power and Martin Cunningham, the friendly, well-meaning couple who came to Tom Kernan's rescue in 'Grace' (*Dubliners*). They have not gone far when Bloom catches sight of Stephen in the street and tells his father so. Simon Dedalus wants to know whether 'that Mulligan cad' is with him. He guesses that Stephen is staying at his aunt Sally's, and he is full of contempt for the Goulding family, his wife's relations. As for Mulligan, 'His name stinks all over Dublin'. Bloom can sympathise with a father's concern for his son. As so often at this funeral his mind travels to the death of his own little son Rudy and to the growing little boy he might have been. Another loss recurs frequently to his mind too – that of his father, Rudolph. It is long before we hear the full story of this. However, Rudolph Virag (Hungarian for 'flower' – which explains Bloom's choice of 'Henry Flower' for his false name) settled in Dublin and changed his name to 'Bloom'. He was staying at the Queen's Hotel, Ennis, County Clare, on 22 June 1886 when he poisoned himself, leaving a pathetic note addressed to his son, lamenting his lost wife and his inability to put up with life longer. As the anniversary of the occasion approaches, the tragedy tends to be on Bloom's mind. A more immediate source of distress is revealed when they pass the Queen's Theatre and its advertisements bring the impresario 'Blazes' Boylan to mind. By a quirky coincidence Martin Cunningham catches sight of Boylan himself through the cab window. His appearance turns the subject of conversation to Molly Bloom's coming concert tour, and we learn that while she goes to Belfast with Boylan Bloom will be going to Clare for the sad anniversary of his father's death.

The sight of Reuben J. Dodd, a Jew and a well-known money-lender, introduces a piece of recent Dublin gossip. Dodd was to take his son to the Isle of Man to get him away from an unsuitable attachment when the boy jumped off the quay into the Liffey. The joke is that when a boatman pulled him out on the end of his pole, Reuben tipped the fellow two shillings for saving his son's life. Mr Dedalus, who values a son's life even less, thinks it was 'one and eightpence too much'. After this relapse into humour the company pull themselves together with thoughts of the solemn business they are about. While kindly Mr Power speaks of Paddy Dignam's 'breakdown' and attributes it to the 'heart', Bloom privately reflects that alcohol killed him. A passing funeral with a baby-sized coffin in the hearse evokes more solemnity about death and Mr Power innocently puts his foot in it by saying that suicide is 'the greatest disgrace to have in the family'. Martin Cunningham, who knows Bloom's story, cannot conceal his embarrassment and, later on when the opportunity arises at the cemetery, he explains to Mr Power what a *faux pas* he has made. But just now Bloom's thoughts revert to the scene in the hospital where his father died, to the letter he left, and to the proceedings at the coroner's inquest.

As the mourners journey across Dublin the reader is kept aware of what is about them along the route taken by the cortège – bridges over canals, schools, a theatre, churches, offices, a bridge under the railway, a hotel, a stonemason's yard – and all is exactly and methodically recorded as are all the walks taken by numerous characters around Dublin which Joyce so meticulously measured and timed. Thus Dublin's life passes before us. For instance, just after the procession has passed the end of Eccles Street where Bloom lives, they meet a drove of cattle being driven down to the docks and probably destined for Liverpool to become English roast beef. The sight stimulates reflection on a much disputed Dublin issue of the day which Bloom thinks should be solved by running a special tramline on which cattle-trucks could carry the animals down to the quays without crowding down busy city thoroughfares.

From this busy world the entry into the cemetery is indeed a visit to the world of the dead. The mourners leave their coaches. The coffin is shouldered by the bearers, and the mourners walk after it. From the quiet, sympathetic talk we learn that Dignam has left a widow and five children. The mourners file into the mortuary chapel and we follow the ceremony conducted by Father Coffey through the worldly eyes of Bloom whose mind is simply not attuned to Catholic practice.

> The priest took a stick with a knob at the end of it out of the boy's bucket and shook it over the coffin . . . Holy water that was, I expect. He must be fed up with that job, shaking that thing over all the corpses they trot up.

The ceremony over, the coffin is placed on a cart and pushed towards the grave, the mourners following. They pass the grave of Daniel O'Connell, 'the Liberator', who struggled arduously for the repeal of the Union, and Mr Dedalus points out his wife's grave to Jack Power and begins to weep. When they reach the Dignam grave, the mourners move to each side, the grave-diggers loop ropes round the coffin, and it is eased down into the depths. Then they fling clods of clay upon it and it disappears from sight.

Throughout this episode Bloom's thoughts continually revert to the mystery of life and death, but in a mode of reflection that contrasts sharply with Stephen's philosophical meditations on the origin and nature of being. Bloom's imagination takes him on less cerebral, less abstract, more concrete and down-to-earth mental journeys:

> Broken heart. A pump after all, pumping thousands of gallons of blood every day. One fine day it gets bunged up and there you are. Lots of them lying around here: lungs, hearts, livers. Old rusty pumps: damn the thing else.

The sheer magnitude of the world's daily toll of burials fascinates him. He readily reverts to imagery of decomposing bodies, of the gas they give off, of rats picking skeletons clean, and the like, but the flavour of such reflection is matter-of-fact rather than macabre or fearful. Such thoughts readily give place to cool-headed observations of the people around him, what they look like, what they are wearing, and what he knows of their personal lives.

At the end of the episode, however, a little incident brings home to the reader that element of social unsureness in Bloom which, along with his Jewishness and no doubt partly a product of it, makes him an outsider. As the mourners leave the cemetery the group around Bloom includes John Henry Menton, a solicitor and Dignam's former employer with whom, long ago, Bloom once had a slight altercation over a game of bowls and who (though Bloom does not know it) admired Molly and thought poorly of her choice of husband ('What did she marry a coon like that for?'). At this point Bloom, noticing a dinge in Menton's hat, tries to be helpful. 'Excuse me, sir . . . Your hat is a little crushed.' Menton deals with the matter and jerks out a terse 'Thank you' that makes Bloom feel he has been thoroughly snubbed.

Episode 7: Aeolus

In Homer Aeolus, the god of the winds, helps Ulysses on his way by giving him a leather bag in which winds unfavourable to his journey are sealed up. Unfortunately Ulysses's men think there is treasure in the bag, and they open it, with the result that they are blown off course. When Ulysses makes a second application to Aeolus for help, he is rebuffed.

Joyce seized on the idea of a god who could let winds loose on the world as an apt image for the daily press which fills a country with hot air, or gas, as we say. Since Bloom is by profession an advertising agent he has regular dealings with the press. (Joyce's own father did a little work of this kind for *Freeman's Journal* after he lost his official post.) Joyce's style in this episode is as restlessly busy as it was somnolently inert in 'The Lotus Eaters'. There is parody of journalistic idiom and methods throughout. In particular the text is punctuated by headlines which exude the flavour of turn-of-the-century newspapers.

It is against the background of the noise and bustle of the city centre that the episode opens – trams starting, time-keepers shouting their destinations, mail cars loading, draymen rolling barrels into vaults. Bloom enters the offices of the *Weekly Freeman and National Press* and the *Freeman's Journal and National Press*. He has a commission to handle today which was in his mind at the funeral. It involves a client, Alexander Keyes, a tea, wine, and spirit merchant who wants to renew his advertisement in the Dublin press and to use a novelty that he has tried out in a local Kilkenny paper. Punning on his name, he wants the advertisement to be headed 'House of Keys' (the name for the Manx parliament) and the symbol of two crossed keys encircled. The idea as Bloom explains, is to convey a suggestion of home rule (such as the Isle of Man enjoys). Against the background of incessant clatter from the printing machinery, of people rushing in and out, hither and thither, Bloom's little commercial mission seems to get all but submerged under sheer noise and bustle. What he is asking for, as tactfully as he can, is that if he places the new advertisement the press should insert a little paragraph somewhere among the news items boosting the Keyes firm as 'high-class licensed premises' answering a 'long-felt want'. The foreman is co-operative but stipulates that Keyes must give him a three-months' renewal of the advertisement. This condition presents Bloom with a further problem, since he is after all only conveying terms proposed by Keyes himself. Joyce skilfully relates the efforts of Bloom in this commercial task to his central personal dilemma in relation to Molly, for the key is the symbol of possession of the home (as we saw when Stephen handed his over to Mulligan), and the crossed keys suggest married harmony as does the talk of 'home rule' and the answering of 'long-felt want'. Moreover Bloom's reflections have already established tea as the symbol of homey warmth and refreshment.

Bloom moves on to the office of the *Evening Telegraph*. He hopes to telephone Keyes and persuade him to authorise a three-months' renewal. Inside the *Telegraph* office he finds a collection of Dubliners heartily enjoying a good jaw. There is Ned Lambert who was among the mourners at Dignam's funeral and who was greeted by Simon Dedalus as a fellow-Corkman, Simon Dedalus himself, and Professor MacHugh (a character based on Hugh MacNeill who taught for a time at Maynooth seminary). They are laughing uproariously at a speech made the day before by Dan Dawson which is printed in today's *Freeman*. Dawson is a politician known as 'Doughy Daw' because he used to be in the bakery business, and the nickname seems peculiarly appropriate to his form of oratory. While Ned Lambert is reciting its highfalutin rhetoric, the company is joined by J. J. O'Molloy, a down-at-heels solicitor with a dwindling practice who is heavily in debt through gambling, and who is on his way to see the editor in the hope of touching him for a loan. (Bloom is to meet O'Molloy again later in the day in Barney Kiernan's bar in the 'Cyclops' episode.) Then the editor himself comes in, Myles Crawford, Aeolus in person presumably. While Simon Dedalus and Ned Lambert go off for a drink, Bloom slips through to make his phone call to Keyes. Then Lenehan arrives, the seedy gadabout and punter who was Corley's confidant and hanger-on in 'Two Gallants' (*Dubliners*), and who is later to boast of having had intimate contact with Molly Bloom ('The Wandering Rocks' episode). Bloom fails to contact Keyes and goes rushing off in the hope of finding him in the Auction Rooms in Bachelor's Walk.

At this point a potentially more serious theme is introduced, if jocularly, when MacHugh begins to compare British civilisation to Roman imperialism as crude and materialistic, whereas the Irish, like the Greeks, have a culture of the spirit. Suddenly (for the episode is chockful of interruptions that chop all interchanges up into fragments as bittily inadequate as the reporting of the press) the company is joined by Mr O'Madden Burke and by Stephen Dedalus. O'Madden Burke is the elderly journalist who stood in for the official *Freeman* reporter to write up the concert ruined by Kathleen Kearney in 'A Mother' (*Dubliners*). (Joyce there described him as widely respected. 'His magniloquent western name was the moral umbrella upon which he balanced the fine problem of his finances.') Stephen Dedalus, of course, is intent on presenting Mr Deasy's letter for the press. Handing it over to Myles Crawford, the verse he wrote on the torn-off strip of it on the shore comes to mind, and the sample we get is not very distinguished given the creative excitement that seemed to be involved in its composition:

On swift sail flaming
From storm and south
He comes, pale vampire,
Mouth to my mouth.

Crawford appreciates Stephen's talent and suggests that he should write something for him. Then he launches into a recollection of the greatest scoop he has known. It was in 1882 (the text says 1881) when the members of the secret republican organisation known as the 'Invincibles' assassinated the British Chief Secretary and his Irish Under-Secretary in Phoenix Park. When *The New York World* cabled for details, the journalist Ignatius Gallaher wired back information about the assassins' movements by applying a code to an advertisement in a recent *Weekly Freeman*. While Crawford is getting excited about this long-past achievement, MacHugh announces that Bloom is on the phone, wanting to have a word with him, and Crawford says 'Tell him to go to hell'. MacHugh tempers this over the phone, telling Bloom, 'Come across yourself'. The irony is that these potentially influential Dubliners are engaged in sentimental glorification of Ireland's past, while the outsider Bloom cannot get a word in about a little matter of the practical present.

O'Molloy joins in to suggest that journalistic achievements are not to be compared with what is done by the great masters of oratory. He cites a speech by Seymour Bushe, a barrister, made at a murder trial. MacHugh caps this by quoting a magnificent piece of oratory in a speech made by John F. Taylor, another barrister, at a college society debate about the revival of the Irish language. Taylor argued that the attempt to stifle the revival of Irish was as futile as would have been any Egyptian attempt to try to persuade Moses that the Israelites should submit and accept the mature religion and language of Egypt. Thus a tyrannical overbearing Egypt, like imperial Rome, is compared to the British empire and the Irish are the people with the culture and spirituality of the Jews and the Greeks – though the living Jew is not getting much attention at present. The sonorous rhetoric of Taylor, quoted by MacHugh, stirs Stephen, and we sense that, while Crawford's appeal to him to write something for him might lead him to profitable journalistic work (like Gabriel Conroy in 'The Dead'), Taylor's emotional cadences might lure him into cosy accommodation with the Irish nationalist movement. Moses, of course, is another leader who, like Pyrrhus, like Parnell, died without reaching his promised land. Poor Bloom, too, seems unlikely to reach his objective, for as the company adjourn to a bar, he comes running after Crawford. He has spoken on the telephone to Keyes, who will order a two-months' (not a three-months') renewal of his advertisement, provided he gets a paragraph boosting the firm in the *Telegraph* as well. 'What will I tell him, Mr Crawford?' 'He can kiss my arse,' says Crawford, and that seems to be as near as Bloom will get to commercial success today. That bottom-kissing is also as near as he will get to another more personal kind of success becomes evident in the 'Ithaca' episode when he retires to bed at his wife's side. The theme is underlined by a parable which Stephen tells about two old ladies who climb to the top of the Nelson Pillar one day to get a view of Dublin, and which he calls 'A Pisgah Sight of Palestine'.

The general impression the episode leaves is of a Bloom whose tentative unassertiveness can scarcely impinge on an Irish community loud in sentimental obsession with its own imaginatively falsified history. New meaning seems to be added to Mr Deasy's statement about Ireland and the Jews. 'She never let them in.'

Episode 8: The Lestrygonians

In Homer the Lestrygonians were a race of cannibalistic giants who devoured many of Odysseus's followers. In Bloom's day it is now lunch-time and thoughts of food impinge frequently on his musings as he treads the streets of Dublin. We find him walking south over O'Connell Bridge, purchasing Banbury cakes and throwing crumbs to the gulls. His ultimate destination is the National Library in Kildare Street, where he is to look up the files of *The Kilkenny People* for a copy of the Keyes advertisement. He intends to eat lunch en route and eventually turns into the Burton Restaurant in Duke Street. But the sight of the swilling and guzzling going on there repels him like a Lestrygonian horror, and instead he moves on down the street to Davy Byrne's, where he orders a sandwich and a glass of beer.

The external action of the episode is minimal, but Bloom's thoughts, occasioned by what he sees about him and the people he meets, fill out our picture of the epic hero's background and character. In particular his thoughts continually revert to Molly with love and, indeed, with sexual hunger. It is here that we learn that it is ten years since little Rudy died and that since that traumatic experience he and Molly have not had a full sexual relationship. The years of married life before the loss of Rudy are looked back upon now as idyllic years of happiness. As for Boylan, the adulterer, he is not so much reflected upon as *not* reflected upon. On this matter Bloom clearly cannot bear to face reality. The man's name does not form itself even in his mind. Boylan is just 'he' and 'him'. For instance, an advertisement for treatment of venereal disease produces in Bloom the agonisingly expressive but inarticulate reaction: 'If he . . . O! Eh? No . . . No. No, no. I don't believe it. He wouldn't surely? No, no.' That is how the intolerable question is pushed aside, the question: Might Boylan infect Molly with venereal disease? Bloom's professional interests as an advertising agent naturally surface repeatedly as he studies passing examples of effective and ineffective advertising. Sandwich-boardmen employed by the stationer, Wisdom Hely, remind him that he was working for Hely himself at the time of his marriage, and how frustrated he was by Hely's ham-fisted advertising techniques ('You can't lick 'em. What? Our envelopes').

Bloom's inclination to brood nostalgically on earlier days is encouraged by a chance meeting with an old flame, Josie Breen, formerly Josie Powell. She married Denis Breen who has since become feeble-minded. Last night, she tells Bloom, he had a nightmare. 'Said the ace of spades was walking upstairs.' So one more image of a dark intruding wanderer joins Haines's black panther and Stephen's oriental stranger. Bloom finds Mrs Breen's dowdiness and shabbiness a strong contrast with the qualities of the girl with whom he played charades at a party long ago. She gives him news of Mina Purefoy, who has been three days in labour in the Maternity Hospital to which Stephen and his medico friends are to repair later in the day ('Oxen of the Sun' episode). Bloom, ever sensitive to suffering, reacts negatively now against childbirth for the crudity and pain it involves. This reaction is in keeping with that over-sensitivity in his physical and emotional relationship with Molly that is holding him in sexual exile from his own home. He dislikes large families and recalls the repetitive routine of breast-feeding with distaste. Yet in contrast to this reaction against the processes of natural fertility (and no doubt *because* of this reaction) the displays of fine silks and women's underwear in the shop windows in Grafton Street mingle with imagery of voluptuous bodies, perfume, and the fruits and spices of the east to stimulate moods of cerebral sensuality that are to culminate later in the day (in the 'Nausicaa' episode) in masturbation. Certainly this episode powerfully realises the epic aspect of the hero's long wandering exile from home and from his loved wife.

The obsessive longing for Molly rises again when Bloom goes into Davy Byrne's and enters into conversation with one of the regulars, Nosey Flynn. Flynn turns the talk to Molly's coming tour and names Bloom's unnamable name. 'Isn't Blazes Boylan mixed up in it?' Smothering the surge of wounded yearning within, Bloom agrees. 'He's the organiser in point of fact.' And his eyes catch sight of the clock hands now at two. Two hours to go before Boylan is due at his home. His thoughts turn again to the orange-groves of the Agendath Netaim advertisement and soon after to the fond recall of how he and Molly lay long ago making love on Howth Hill. What makes the particular memory especially touching for the reader is that it is the climactic recollection in Molly's mind on the very last page of the book.

As Bloom is leaving Davy Byrne's, Paddy Leonard, Bantam Lyons, and Tom Rochford come in. In talk about the Ascot Gold Cup race Lyons tells the others that Bloom gave him a tip for the winner, an error which is to bring trouble upon Bloom later. Meanwhile Bloom moves on, ever musing, towards the library and, just before getting there, catches sight of the unnamed adulterer himself. The shock, the shame, and the embarrassment of this climactic experience are registered in terse, fearful gasps of realisation that underline the pathos of the hungry longing for Molly that has never been long absent from his mind in this episode.

Episode 9: Scylla and Charybdis

After an episode that kept the reader moving largely in the mind of Bloom we find ourselves with Stephen Dedalus again. The 'action' in the episode is minimal, as it was in the 'Proteus' episode in which Stephen was last the centre of interest. Moreover the lines of thought shift from the predominantly earthy – or at best rather half-baked intellectual – level of reflection associated with Bloom to a level of academic cerebralism characteristic of Stephen. Stephen is in the National Library at about 2 o'clock. He has not kept his promise to meet Mulligan at the Ship Inn at 12.30. Instead he has sent him an enigmatic telegram with an aphorism quoted (though not exactly) from Meredith: 'The sentimentalist is he who would enjoy without incurring the immense debtorship for a thing done.' But later in the episode Mulligan, now 'mine enemy' in Stephen's eyes, tracks him down to the library where Stephen is deep in serious scholarly conversation with T. W. Lyster, the librarian and a Quaker, with R. L. Best, a younger librarian, with a third member of the library staff – W. K. Magee, an essayist who used the pseudonym 'John Eglinton' – , and with George Russell, the eminent poet and man of letters who used the pseudonym 'AE'.

This is the one episode in *Ulysses* which touches closely on the life of literary Dublin at a time when Ireland's culture was dominated by a number of very great writers, W. B. Yeats, George Moore, Edward Martyn, Lady Gregory, J. M. Synge, James Stephens, and AE himself. The Irish Literary Theatre had been founded in 1899 and its successor, the Irish National Theatre, moved to the Abbey Theatre in 1904. Joyce was struggling to make his way as a young writer with little to show publicly for the talent he laid claim to. He was proud, overly sensitive to slight or rebuff, and some of his personal habits did little to recommend him. In this episode there is gossip about the known literary figures which makes Stephen Dedalus feel like an outsider. In the company of AE and the librarians he assumes the role of the young man ready to shock by seemingly outrageous challenges to received opinion. In particular he expounds his theory of *Hamlet* to which Mulligan and Haines referred in the opening episode, 'Telemachus'.

Stephen identifies Shakespeare not only with Hamlet but also with Hamlet's murdered father, and therefore with the Ghost. (The fact that Shakespeare is known himself to have performed the part of the Ghost on stage corroborates the identification.) Moreover Shakespeare had a son, Hamnet, who died at the age of eleven, the age little Rudy would now have reached, and to this extent there is a certain parallelism between Shakespeare and Bloom. In the play Shakespeare, as the Ghost, comes on stage to tell his son, 'You are the dispossessed son: I am the murdered father: your mother is the guilty queen'. Thus Ann Hathaway is under judgement. Shakespeare was eighteen and Ann Hathaway twenty-six when she became pregnant and married him. A boy of eighteen does not masterfully seduce a woman of twenty-six. It is the other way round. Shakespeare was sexually destroyed when Ann Hathaway seduced him. He was wounded as Adonis was wounded by the boar and beaten by the huntress, Venus, in Shakespeare's poem, *Venus and Adonis*. Shakespeare was wounded sexually in such a way that he was obsessed as a writer with the compensatory dream of masterful ravishing achieved by Tarquin in the poem, *The Rape of Lucrece*, and laid claim to by Iachimo in the play, *Cymbeline*. After being sexually destroyed Shakespeare is the ghost of his former living self.

In half-serious vein Stephen suggests that in putting himself into his play as both ghost-father and son who pays the price of evil, Shakespeare was only doing what God does in entering his created world as Holy Ghost and as suffering Son. Moreover the theory implies that Joyce enters his own created world in the person of Bloom as well as in the person of Stephen. (Bloom is the ghost-father of the lost son, Rudy.) Other parallels are drawn too, some explicitly, some implicitly. As Eve, the great mother of all, was soiled by sin, so Hamlet finds his mother Gertrude, and by transference all women, soiled by sin. Shakespeare's obsession with wifely infidelity and his emphasis on broken vows indicates that Ann Hathaway was unfaithful. Small wonder that from the day of her marriage to the day of her death there is no news of her except that she had to borrow money from her father's shepherd and that Shakespeare bequeathed her his second-best bed. Meanwhile for twenty years Shakespeare lived a rich, successful life in London.

In *Hamlet* two deeds rankle in the Ghost's mind – his wife's breaking of her vow and his coarse brother's replacement of him. Shakespeare himself had three brothers, Gilbert, Richard, and Edmund. Gilbert was seemingly of little account to the poet-dramatist, but he made of 'Richard' and 'Edmund' two of the three blackest villains in all his works, Richard Crookback (*Richard III*) and Edmund in *King Lear*. And *King Lear* was actually written while brother Edmund lay dying in Southwark. Shakespeare's Richard III, the only totally depraved king in Shakespeare, 'a whoreson crookback, misbegotten, makes love to a widowed Ann . . . woos and wins her'. The sub-plot of *King Lear*, in which Edmund figures, is 'lifted out of Sidney's *Arcadia* and spatchcocked on to a Celtic legend'. Shakespeare was plainly obsessed with the theme of the false, adulterous, usurping brother, and with the theme of banishment from home.

When John Eglinton asks Stephen whether he believes his own theory Stephen promptly replies 'No'. For the reader perhaps the most interesting ideas thrown up in the theorising are those comments on the artist's relationship to his created work which can be applied to Joyce and to *Ulysses* itself. These comments draw a parallel between the human creator's role and the divine Creator's role. As God created his world and put his own Son in it to be sacrificed and to rise again, and entered that world too as the Holy Ghost, so Joyce puts himself into *Ulysses* as Stephen Dedalus whose 'suffering' in the climactic Nighttown episode is paralleled with Christ's, and who like Christ cries out 'I thirst'. Joyce puts himself into *Ulysses* too as the ghost-father

Bloom. The universal dimensions of the pattern laid down in *Ulysses* are further defined in the character of Molly Bloom, who as the faithless wife embodies again the weaknesses of Eve who betrayed mankind.

It is just after Stephen's mocking comparison between the way God and Shakespeare enter their respective worlds as Ghost-father and suffering Son, that Mr Lyster announces to the librarian: 'There's a gentleman here, sir . . . From the *Freeman*. He wants to see the files of the *Kilkenny People* for last year.' So the 'dark figure' of Bloom is briefly seen and mocked by Mulligan as 'Ikey Moses' and 'Jehovah'. Indeed Mulligan's reference to Bloom's 'pale Galilean eyes' echoes a Swinburnian mockery of Christ. And the figure intrudes again at the end of the episode as Stephen and Mulligan are leaving the library. 'A man passed between them, bowing, greeting', and Mulligan whispers 'The wandering jew'. Moreover his 'dark back' is seen as he goes down with the 'step of a pard'. (Leo-pold, not -pard, is the black panther of Haines's nightmare.)

The reader who comes to *Ulysses* fresh from the *Portrait* may be disappointed that the figure of Emma Clery seems to have disappeared from Stephen's world. But buried near the end of this episode there is an unexplained momentary glimpse by Stephen of a young lady working in the library. It perhaps represents the reader's last glimpse of Emma in Joyce's work: 'Is that? . . . Blueribboned hat . . . Idly writing . . . What? Looked? . . .'

In Homer Ulysses has to steer a perilous course between the deadly whirlpool Charybdis and the rock where the many-headed monster Scylla lurks. Stretching out her six necks, she seizes men from passing ships. Joyce's use of this idea from the *Odyssey* is a very intellectualised one. Certainly Bloom's progress from the library between Stephen and Mulligan might be seen as an Odyssean escape, but Stephen's sharp dialectical aggressiveness against the misty abstract talk of Russell and the librarian suggests the contrast between the monster and the whirlpool.

Episode 10: The Wandering Rocks

In Homer Ulysses is warned to steer clear of the dangerous wandering rocks, and on the basis of this warning Joyce constructed the central episode of his epic. In a sense it breaks into the action, for it gives a bird's eye view of people moving about Dublin's various streets at the same hour of day. In many sections of the episode Joyce takes quick glances at the movements of various minor figures in the epic, often returning more than once to note their progress, so that an elaborate choreography emerges, as flashbacks link one section with another and the episode as a whole with earlier episodes in the book. Here there is space to describe only the more outstanding vignettes. Joyce was always methodical in the patterning of his work. As there are seventeen episodes besides this one in the whole book, so 'The Wandering Rocks' contains seventeen episodes sandwiched between an introductory one and a closing one. The introductory one traces the progress across Dublin of Father Conmee, the representative of ecclesiastical authority. The closing one traces the progress of the Earl of Dudley, the Lord Lieutenant and therefore the representative of civil authority. Enclosed within this outer framework the seventeen sections present a cross-section of Dublin life between 3 and 4 o'clock in the afternoon. This is therefore Dublin's episode rather than that of any one or more of the main characters in the book, though of course we catch glimpses of them here and there, as well as of so many others whom we have met or heard of in earlier episodes. Their movements are very exactly worked out. Joyce toiled at this episode with a map before him, a ruler, and a stop-watch in his hand.

(i) Father Conmee is the former rector of Clongowes College to whom Stephen appealed after the unjust pandy-batting in the *Portrait*. In real life he helped the Joyces by getting James a place at Belvedere College, and Joyce spoke well of him. Here Father Conmee is pictured journeying northwards from Mountjoy Square to Artane on an errand of mercy. Kind-hearted Martin Cunningham has written to him about the bereaved Dignam family and Father Conmee is going to see whether he can place one of the Dignam boys in the Artane orphanage, as Tom Kernan told Bloom in 'Hades'. Father Conmee starts his journey on foot, continues it by tram, and completes it on foot. His reflections are those of a kindly, humane priest, interested in Dublin and its people, and knowledgeable about its past. He reads his office on the last stage of his journey. And he catches sight of Lynch and his girl friend coming from a field.

(ii) Here are further glimpses of the people Father Conmee glimpsed on his walk, including Corny Kelleher, the undertaker who was present at Glasnevin for the Dignam funeral, and a one-legged sailor who was begging in the street when Father Conmee left the presbytery and received the Father's blessing. He is just now passing Bloom's house in Eccles Street and Molly's white arm throws a coin through the window.

(iii) As the one-legged sailor turns into Eccles Street singing 'The Death of Nelson', he passes Katey and Boody Dedalus. We again see Molly's arm throwing the coin.

(iv) Katey and Boody Dedalus reach home and join Maggy there. The

Dedalus children are plainly suffering privation. There is talk of failing to get anything for some books at the pawnshop, and of a forthcoming meal of bread and pea-soup begged from the nuns.

(v) Blazes Boylan is having a basket of fruit made up for Molly at Thornton's, the fruiterer and florist. He wants it delivered by tram. He flirts with the shop-assistant. He asks to use the phone. Meanwhile we glimpse again the HELYS sandwichboardmen whom Bloom saw in 'The Lestrygonians' episode and see Bloom himself looking at books for sale on a street-hawker's cart.

(vi) Stephen Dedalus is talking in the street outside Trinity College to Almidano Artifoni, the music teacher, who urges him to pursue his musical career as a tenor.

(vii) In Blazes Boylan's office his secretary Miss Dunne hides a library copy of Wilkie Collins's thriller, *The Woman in White*, in her drawer and goes back to her typing. The phone rings, bringing Boylan's voice from the fruit shop. She tells him that Lenehan has called in and will be in the Ormond Hotel at 4 o'clock. (But this is the hour of Boylan's meeting with Molly.)

(viii) We see again two of the characters present in the *Freeman* office in the 'Aeolus' episode, Ned Lambert and Jack O'Molloy. They are in the ancient council chamber of St Mary's Abbey which Ned is showing to a clergyman, the Reverend Hugh C. Love. Love is writing a book on the Fitzgeralds, and this is the very place where 'Silken Thomas' (Lord Offaly) declared himself in rebellion against Henry VIII in 1534.

(ix) Among a number of brief snapshots we see the gates of the Phoenix Park drive opened wide to let the vice-regal cavalcade through for its progress through the city. We also see Lenehan and M'Coy walking past Bloom as he looks at second-hand books on the hawker's cart. Lenehan boasts about an annual dinner at Glencree Reformatory at which Bloom and Molly were present. They were driven back by night over the Featherbed Mountain and Lenehan, squashed against Molly in the cab, made the most of the rocking and jolting to paw her breasts.

(x) Bloom is now looking in a bookshop for a book for Molly. He picks up one called *Sweets of Sin*, an erotic novel. Riffling through it he comes across lurid sentences that are to linger in his mind. ('Her mouth glued on his in a luscious voluptuous kiss while his hands felt for the opulent curves inside her déshabillé.') He decides to take it.

(xi) Dilly Dedalus has found her father in the street and tells him that it is time he went home. In search of money, she manages to squeeze one shilling and twopence out of him. We catch sight of Tom Kernan walking down James's Street and of the vice-regal cavalcade on its progress.

(xii) Tom Kernan, the tea-merchant of 'Grace' (*Dubliners)*, walking along James's Street, is pleased with himself for having just booked an order. Denis Breen and his wife cross O'Connell Bridge. Breen, mentally sick, is seeking legal advice about imaginary persecution. The vice-regal cavalcade is sighted again.

(xiii) Stephen Dedalus is looking in a lapidary's window, studying the stones and jewels. The two old widows seen on the shore in the 'Proteus' episode are now sighted trudging through Irishtown. Stephen moves on and stops to look at books on a book-cart in Bedford Row. His sister Dilly appears. She has bought a French primer for a penny, and Stephen is touched by the pathos of the child's situation in a family that is being dragged down to utter poverty.

(xiv) In powerful irony we catch sight immediately afterwards of Simon Dedalus, the cause of all the misery, as he meets one of his boon companions, Father Cowley, a spoiled priest whose house is now besieged by bailiffs. It appears that Reuben Dodd, the money-lender, is pressing for payment of debts. Another crony turns up, Ben Dollard, the amateur bass soloist. He has seen John Henry Menton, the solicitor, and sorted out Father Cowley's immediate legal problem. The landlord has already distrained for unpaid rent and has prior claim, so the money-lender's writ for possession is worthless.

(xv) Glimpses are given of Martin Cunningham and Jack Power in conversation about helping the Dignam children, of councillors outside the city hall, of John Henry Menton, of Blazes Boylan, and of the Lord Lieutenant's vice-regal cavalcade.

(xvi) Buck Mulligan and Haines are in a restaurant where they see John Howard Parnell, the great man's brother and city marshal. Mulligan tells Haines that the Jesuits drove Stephen half-mad with fear of hell. As for Stephen's literary future: 'Ten years, he said, chewing and laughing. He is going to write something in ten years.' But the Englishman does not laugh it off. 'Still, I shouldn't wonder if he did after all.'

(xvii) There are further glimpses of Almidano Artifoni and others.

(xviii) Young Patrick Aloysius Dignam is dawdling along a street, reluctant to go home to a house of mourning. It would appear that he is the youngster whom Martin Cunningham has asked Father Conmee to place at Artane. He and we catch sight of Blazes Boylan with a flower between his lips which he picked up in the florist's. Boylan is grinning as he listens to the talk of a drunk who, we learn later, is none other than Bob Doran, on his annual spree, the clerk who was trapped into matrimony in 'The Boarding House' (*Dubliners*). Young Dignam's boyish musings about death end the section.

(xix) The Lord Lieutenant and his Lady, the Earl of Dudley and Lady Dudley, are driven with their cavalcade through the streets of Dublin. They too are on a mercy mission of a kind; for they are to open the Mirus Bazaar in aid of Mercer's Hospital. Their progress takes them in succession past many of the characters whose movements have been traced in this episode.

Episode 11: The Sirens

The Sirens were sea nymphs whose melodious voices enchanted all those who heard them and lured them to their deaths. In Homer Ulysses is warned in advance of this peril and he has the ears of his followers stopped up with wax so that they shall not hear the voices of the sirens as they sail past them. He orders his men to tie him firmly to the ship's mast so that he cannot get free when he hears the irresistible voices.

The scene is the Ormond Hotel. Two barmaids, bronze-haired Lydia Douce and gold-haired Mina Kennedy, stare out through the window as the vice-regal cavalcade goes by, then settle down to gossip. They are in a skittish, giggly mood when Simon Dedalus comes in and orders whisky, playing up to Lydia's flirtatiousness. Then Lenehan arrives, for he made an appointment with Boylan, through his secretary, to meet him here in the Ormond at 4 o'clock. Lenehan, who drank with Stephen in Mooney's earlier in the day, brings 'greetings from the famous son of a famous father' to Mr Dedalus and evokes some very dry sarcasm in reply. Lenehan has turned his attention to chatting up Mina Kennedy when Boylan arrives and both the barmaids play up to the newcomer.

Throughout these early pages of the episode we have had intermittent glimpses of Bloom, first walking along Wellington Quay on the opposite side of the river Liffey, then crossing over by Essex Bridge, buying paper and envelopes to write to Martha, and then by an odd coincidence catching sight of Boylan's jaunting car in the distance. Boylan is very much on his mind because he is due to call on Molly at 4 o'clock. Now, seeing Boylan's car outside the Ormond, Bloom realises that Boylan himself must be inside the hotel and he is curious why he has not yet gone to Eccles Street. At that moment he bumps into Richie Goulding, Mrs Dedalus's brother, who works for Collis and Ward, the solicitors, and the two of them join up for a snack and go into the Ormond together. When the clock strikes four Bloom wonders whether Boylan may have forgotten his appointment. 'Perhaps a trick. Not come: whet appetite. I couldn't do', he muses pathetically. But a few minutes later Boylan dashes off, Lenehan following him, and for the rest of the episode we keep being reminded of the jingling and trotting of his progress by jaunting car across Dublin to Bloom's home.

Ben Dollard and Father Cowley come in, Ben still trying to comfort the beleaguered debtor. Dollard goes to sit on the piano stool and calls on Simon Dedalus for a song. The three friends around the piano reminisce about an occasion when Ben was due to sing in public and did not have an appropriate suit for the occasion. They were rescued by none other than Molly Bloom who ran a little business on the side in hiring out smart clothes. The trousers of the borrowed suit turned out to be indecently tight, as Bloom and Molly well remember at other points in the book. Meanwhile Bloom has got his liver and bacon, Richie his steak and kidney, and at first they eat in silence. Then Father Cowley sits down at the piano and Richie Goulding reminisces about a performance of Bellini's opera *La Sonnambula* at which the tenor Joe Maas sang the aria 'All is lost now'. He drones on about the beauty of this song and Bloom reflects that all seems to be lost with the once rollicking Richie himself, a now seedy, decaying figure.

Simon Dedalus starts to sing 'M'appari' from Flotow's *Martha*, Father Cowley accompanying. Bloom's musings are given new and potent emotional dimensions by the words and music of the aria, which in the opera is sung by the hero Lionel in lament and longing for his lost beloved, Martha. The coincidence involved in the two names, Lionel and Martha, is touching. (The 'Leo' of Leopold is Latin for lion.) But it is of Molly, not the unseen Martha, that Bloom day-dreams, tenderly recalling how they first met. The climax of the song, dramatically and lyrically rendered by Simon Dedalus, evokes in Bloom a powerful emotional experience of release and temporary sense of community with others. As so often, Bloom's emotional life moves in physical isolation from the one he really loves. It is ironic that he sits immobile, indulging in the sentimental climax of an erotic song, while Blazes Boylan is driving his mare jog-trot up towards Eccles Street, intent on a real sexual adventure with Bloom's own wife. And it is equally ironic that Bloom now asks the waiter for pen, ink, and blotting-pad, to carry on his paper-relationship with Martha. Taking out his notepaper, he conceals it within his newspaper and writes a letter to Martha, pretending to Richie that he is answering an advertisement. He ends the letter with a PPS, 'I feel so sad today, so lonely', addresses the envelope and blots the blotting-pad so that the address cannot be deciphered. He plans to buy a postal order and enclose it in the envelope.

More music is called for, and Ben Dollard is prevailed upon to sing

'The Croppy Boy'. This touching ballad was one which Joyce sang in public in Dublin. (Its text is given in full in the section on 'Historical background' in Part 1 above.) The ballad carries significant overtones. It is a story of betrayal, and even as it is sung, Boylan is knocking on Bloom's door. Moreover the croppy boy's confession tells how once he hurried through the graveyard and forgot to say a prayer for the repose of his mother's soul. He is not the only son in our story to have failed to pray for his mother's rest.

As the song nears its end Bloom rises to go. Outside in the street he sees another chance acquaintance coming his way whom he regards as dangerous. It is a whore in a sailor hat who once revealed that she knew Molly. (She turns up again in the 'Eumaeus' episode.) To avoid her he stares in a shop window. Among other antiques he sees a portrait of Robert Emmet, the patriot and martyr. He reads the hero's noble last words at his trial: 'When my country takes her place among the nations of the earth, then and not till then let my epitaph be written. I have done.' But the food and drink have made Bloom gassy, and he accompanies his recitation of the words with an unseemly burst of wind.

Joyce's stylistic experimentation in this episode effects one of his most skilful and brilliant achievements. The use of words is such that every possible approximation to music is explored. In terms of structure figures, phrases, and themes are stated, repeated, developed as they would be in symphonic form. There are elaborate manipulations of words and syllables in onomatopoeic imitation of musical devices, instrumental and vocal. Rhythmic patterns are tapped out or hammered out in musical configurations. Vowel and consonant, phrase and cadence are disposed with such attention to aural effect that pitch and tone colour appropriate to woodwind, brass, strings, or percussion are brought to the listening reader's ear and mind. Moreover a 'fugal' manipulation of central themes (like Boylan's ride across Dublin and Bloom's thoughts of Martha) weaves the narrative strands of the 'action' together in a carefully contrived counterpoint.

Lines and phrases from well-known songs from opera, the concert hall, and the drawing-room are frequently quoted or worked into the text. To those who recognise them they bring their melodic shape with them to enrich the texture further.

Episode 12: The Cyclops

'The Cyclops' is at once the most savagely satirical and the funniest episode in the book so far. The Cyclopes were giants who had one eye in the middle of their foreheads. They lived on the west coast of Sicily. Ulysses and a dozen of his followers were captured by the Cyclops Polyphemus and imprisoned in his cave. He blocked the entrance with a huge rock and began to eat two of Ulysses's men a day. Ulysses tempted Polyphemus with some fine wine he had and then, while Polyphemus lay in a drunken sleep, plunged into his one eye the sharpened tip of a stake red-hot from the fire. Even so the sightless giant determined that his victims should not escape, but he had to let his sheep out of the cave to graze and Ulysses and his men clung to the underbellies of the sheep and slipped out through Polyphemus's grasp.

This episode is set largely in Barney Kiernan's bar in Little Britain Street. The bar is the Cyclopean cave, and for Polyphemus we have an unnamed 'Citizen', a specimen of one-eyed revolutionary nationalism, intolerant of all moderation, ferocious in savage denunciation of all and sundry, blind to everything except the Irish cause. He sits there with his dog Garryowen, sponging on others for drinks. Joyce based him on Michael Cusack, a tough, broad-shouldered nationalist who founded the Gaelic Athletic Association and who (we learn from Richard Ellmann's *James Joyce*) would enter a pub and shout at the waiter 'I'm Citizen Cusack from the parish of Carron in the Barony of Burren in the County of Clare, you protestant dog!'

Much of what happens here is described by a nameless narrator, fluent in the crudest idiom of the Dublin bar-haunter. The pub's habitués are garrulous gossipers with scarcely a good word for anyone. In this respect the episode complements the scathing picture of city bar-life in 'Counterparts' in *Dubliners*. Here, however, a note of sinister menace is added. The prevailing atmosphere of hostility and violence is created partly by the malicious and sarcastic gossip. In this atmosphere of political fanaticism and bigotry, of personal spite and venom, gentle, tolerant Ulysses–Bloom finds himself trapped in a menacingly alien environment.

Joyce took the hint provided by the gigantic stature of the Cyclops to vary the texture of the style in a striking way. The method has been labelled 'Gigantism'. For the flow of crude bar-room gossip is periodically interrupted by voices which seize upon the events described or the features of characters discussed and expand the matter in grossly exalted rhetoric, hilariously parodic. Thus discussion of a meeting about the foot-and-mouth disease and the Irish cattle trade is interrupted by an idealised picture of the natural produce of Ireland and its marketing in the style of Celtic saga. Similarly the account of the Citizen sitting with his dog is interrupted by a heroic description of this mighty figure in epic proportions which are farcically hyperbolic:

> The widewinged nostrils, from which bristles of the same tawny hue projected, were of such capaciousness that within their cavernous obscurity the fieldlark might easily have lodged her nest.

This kind of inflation in sheer magnitude is matched by inflation by aggregation. For a 'row of seastones' dangles from his girdle, on which are 'graven with rude yet striking art the tribal images of many Irish heroes and heroines of antiquity, Cuchulin, Conn of hundred battles, Niall of nine hostages . . .'. But the list of Irish heroes and heroines thus embarked upon runs out of control, and eventually takes in such notables as 'The Man that Broke the Bank at Monte Carlo', 'Thomas Cook and son', and 'Lady Godiva', as well as 'William Tell', 'Napoleon', and 'the Colleen Bawn'.

Thus Joyce exaggerates the romantic and idealistic element in Irish nationalism to a point of absurdity. The moral implication is that characters like 'the Citizen' attribute a grossly disproportionate stature and magnitude to themselves and their cause. The artistic effect of the inflationary technique is to swamp the quiet voice of reason represented by Bloom under a deluge of wild overstatement. Bloom drifts in here in search of Martin Cunningham. This too is an errand of mercy, for Bloom has been to the Dignams' about the widow's problems in connection with an insurance policy and he is to report to Martin Cunningham on his findings. So he drops in here in the middle of a drinking session involving the narrator, the Citizen, Joe Hynes, and Alf Bergan, not to mention Bob Doran who is sitting drunk in a corner. (He is the man who was tricked into marriage by Mrs Mooney in 'The Boarding House' in *Dubliners*. Bloom caught sight of him on his annual spree in 'The Lestrygonians' episode. Boylan was seen talking to him in the street in 'The Wandering Rocks'.)

As Bloom comes in the talk is of an execution due at Mountjoy Gaol. Alf Bergan has a collection of hangmen's letters and Joe Hynes reads one out. It is an application from a Liverpool hangman called 'H. Rumbold' to officiate in Dublin. Bloom gets involved in a discussion about capital punishment, but when the Citizen demands a toast to the memory of the dead, calling 'Sinn Fein', immediate dialogue is buried under a vast interpolation. It is a hilariously parodic description of the public execution of a revolutionary carried out with all the panoply of state before a vast concourse of people ('Every lady in the audience was presented with a tasteful souvenir of the occasion in the shape of a skull and crossbones brooch . . .'). Bloom then blunders by defending St Patrick's Anti-Treating League formed in 1902 to combat drunkenness by discouraging the practice of treating others to a round of drinks. He refuses to drink and it is assumed that he is trying to avoid having to stand a round. Thus Bloom's temperance and moderation in another respect put him at loggerheads with the present company. The Citizen, of course, it is pointed out, does well for himself out of free drinks extorted from others by the moral blackmail of his revolutionary zeal and the menace of his fearsome dog. Bloom unwittingly gives further annoyance by gently airing his modest knowledge of issues such as foot-and-mouth disease, athletics, and even the effect on the genitals of death by hanging.

Bob Doran has staggered out. Ned Lambert and J. J. O'Molloy have joined the company. The Citizen tries to provoke Bloom by talking of the damage done to the country by immigrants. Meanwhile with a few quiet words, with a little bit of cunning and generosity, Bloom seems to bring off his one positive achievement to date. He tells Joe Hynes that 'he needn't trouble about that little matter' until next month, clearly referring to the money he owes, and in return suggests that Hynes should put in a word to Myles Crawford about renewing the Keyes advertisement. 'Consider that done', Joe replies. But such little arrangements are swamped under the prevailing talk of pornography and brutality.

John Wyse Nolan and Lenehan come in, Nolan talking about a City Council meeting on the Irish language question, which sparks off a virulent anti-English outburst by the Citizen. Lenehan brings too the news that the Ascot Gold Cup has been won by an outsider, Throwaway, and that those who backed the favourite, Sceptre, have all lost heavily. The Citizen develops his tirade against England and the ruin she has brought upon Irish trade and Irish forestry, eventually prophesying a resurgence of Irish merchant-shipping and the birth of an Irish navy. There is mockery of English brutality and oppressiveness, of the British monarchy and British hypocrisy, and amid the excessive rhetoric of hatred and contempt Bloom interposes here and there a moderating word of reason and tolerance to which no one is prepared to listen. His advocacy of universal love instead of hatred earns him ridicule as 'a new apostle to the gentiles'. When he goes off to look for Martin Cunningham it is immediately assumed by Lenehan that he has gone to collect his winnings on the Gold Cup race, for Bantam Lyons's mistaken notion that Bloom gave him Throwaway as a betting tip has gone the rounds. The company join in denigrating Bloom and his family. The abuse continues when Martin Cunningham, Jack Power, and Crofton come in, and Cunningham calls for charity, 'God bless us all here, is my prayer'. Even the Citizen says 'Amen' to that. The moment of harmonious piety is expanded in one of Joyce's most extravagant interpolations into a massive religious ceremony attended by a great concourse of the faithful.

When Bloom returns, explaining that he has just been round to the court-house looking for Martin Cunningham, the narrator and the Citizen assume that he is lying; that he has been to collect his winnings and is too mean to stand drinks all round. The air of menace and hostility intensifies. Martin Cunningham, Jack Power, and Crofton go out with Bloom and get into a waiting jaunting-car. The Citizen gets up and staggers heavily to the door shouting 'Three cheers for Israel'. Martin is urging the driver to make off while Jack Power tries to get Bloom to sit down in the car instead of responding to the Citizen's provocation. But Bloom makes a spirited defence: 'Your God was a jew. Christ was a jew like me!' The Citizen is furious. 'By Jesus . . . I'll brain that bloody jewman for using the name'. He flings a biscuit tin at Bloom. Mercifully the sun is in his eyes and his aim is bad. But the horse takes fright, and the car speeds away with the Citizen's dog chasing behind it. A last interpolation presents Bloom in the jaunting-car as Elijah in the chariot which ascended to heaven amid clouds of angels.

Episode 13: Nausicaa

In Homer's *Odyssey* Poseidon, god of the sea, is angry with Odysseus for blinding his son Polyphemus the Cyclops, and when Odysseus escapes from Calypso on a raft, Poseidon stirs up a storm that throws Odysseus on the coast of Scheria. Here he is discovered, naked and exhausted, by Nausicaa, daughter of King Alcinous, when she comes down to the beach with her maids to wash her linen. She cleans Odysseus, clothes him, and takes him to her father's palace where he is hospitably welcomed and entertained.

The scene is the Sandymount shore at 8 o'clock in the evening. Gerty MacDowell (our Nausicaa) is sitting on the rocks with her friends, Cissy Caffrey and Edy Boardman. The three girls are looking after Cissy's twin brothers who are four years old and also Baby Boardman in his push-car. Bloom is sitting at a distance watching them. Like Odysseus he is 'storm-tossed' if only in the sense that he has suffered a series of emotional frustrations today that have left him isolated and defenceless if not naked and prostrate. There is the consciousness of being turned into an outsider in his own home by his wife Molly and her adultery with Boylan. His commercial efforts in the newspaper office brought him a sharp rebuff. His mild attempts to speak with the voice of reason in Barney Kiernan's brought the vulgar wrath of the nationalist on his head, and he has had a narrow escape from physical violence. Moreover, though he is unaware of the fact, his friendliness in offering his newspaper to Bantam Lyons as something he was going to 'throw away' has backfired against him. Above all, sexually repressed and sexually excited by what he has seen in the streets and shop windows of the city, he is in the mood to be 'rescued' from deflation by surrendering himself to visual self-indulgence in femininity.

This is what Gerty MacDowell has to offer. It has to be remembered that Bloom is still captive emotionally to his Penelope at home. The lack of sexual fulfilment with Molly is an aspect of his fastidious shrinking from the messy crudities of childbirth and, by correspondence, from the natural processes that produce fertility. Bloom is an advertising agent, existing professionally in a 'paper' world, in talk about commodities rather than commodities themselves. His love-affair with Martha is a purely verbal one conducted on paper. And this brief love-affair with Gerty which solaces him in the present episode is a purely visual one. There is no real contact.

Gerty is the perfect partner for such an encounter. Though her thoughts present her as twenty-one, she seems like a retarded adolescent whose head is stuffed with cheap girlish romanticism bred of sentimental novelettes and women's magazines and nourished by the more sentimental pieties of popular Catholic teaching. Throughout the episode most of what takes place is what passes through the minds of Gerty and Bloom. Joyce chose to present Gerty's thoughts and feelings in what he called 'a namby pamby jammy marmalady drawersy style'. It is both highly comic and strangely pathetic to have a foolish girl's thoughts and dreams articulated in an idiom that blends what is natural and homely to her with the terminology of the advertisements, novelettes, and pious exhortations that have encouraged her to image herself as the feminine ideal.

> The waxen pallor of her face was almost spiritual in its ivorylike purity though her rosebud mouth was a genuine Cupid's bow, Greekly perfect. Her hands were of finely veined alabaster and as white as lemon juice and queen of ointments could make them . . .

Very little happens in the episode. The twins play ball and run about. Cissy looks after them. Gerty becomes conscious that Bloom is staring at her 'and there was meaning in his look'. The dark eyes and the 'pale intellectual face' appeal to her. 'He was in deep mourning, she could see that, and the story of a haunting sorrow was written on his face.' Thus he is mentally transfigured into the 'dreamhusband' who might take her crushingly into his arms. Such aspirations are mixed up in her mind with remembered pieties from the confessional and with liturgical phrases about the Virgin Mary ('Refuge of sinners. Comfortress of the afflicted') that confer a pseudo-religious status on Gerty's sexual self-projection. A fireworks display from the Mirus Bazaar and, in particular, rockets shooting up into the sky give Gerty the opportunity to lean back so far in looking up that her legs, thighs and knickers are on display as a reward for Bloom's patiently adoring gaze. The exhibitionism brings Bloom's voyeuristic self-indulgence to the climax of an emission. A moment later, when Gerty stands up and walks away, Bloom is shocked to see that she is lame.

Joyce enriches the texture of this encounter between Bloom and

Gerty by giving us intermittent reminders of a service that is taking place in the parish church nearby dedicated to the virgin Mary as Star of the Sea. Father John Hughes is conducting a men's temperance retreat and the service of Benediction is in progress. The retreatants, abstainers from alcohol as Bloom is an abstainer from real conjugal sex, are thus involved in adoring the Blessed Sacrament as Bloom is involved in adoring Gerty. Like Bloom's, their adoration stops short of real communion.

When the girls have gone Bloom lapses into musing that gets ever dreamier and more incoherent until he finally dozes off to sleep. The recurring themes of his fragmentary musings are characteristic – the recent seductive self-display by the lame girl, a brief past encounter with a harlot, early memories of Molly, Milly's childhood, Martha's letter, the incongruous physical partnerships of some marriages, feminine perfumes and smells, and especially happy memories of Molly at parties and on Howth Hill where they made love. In the mood of drained inertia and somnolence even the brawler and ranter in Barney Kiernan's comes in for a forgiving thought ('Perhaps not to hurt he meant'). But what is perhaps especially notable about this episode is the way it contrasts with and yet complements the trains of thought pursued by Stephen on this very shore that same morning ('Proteus' episode). For Bloom's thoughts have been essentially rooted in experience of the senses, in sight and smell and touch, while Stephen's thoughts were highly intellectualised, abstract, and metaphysical. Moreover Bloom's evening reflections have drifted lazily and dreamily into vagueness and incoherence, whereas Stephen's morning meditations were sharp, condensed, and alertly marshalled.

Episode 14: Oxen of the Sun

Helios, the sun god, has sacred cattle on the island of Thrinacia. When Ulysses and his men arrive there, he urges them not to kill the cattle for food and they ignore his command. As a result of this sacrilege their ship is wrecked by a thunderbolt and only Ulysses is saved.

In so far as a sacrilegious offence is committed in this episode it is through the improper behaviour of a group of ribald students in the Holles Street Maternity Hospital. The patients, like the sacred oxen, are living representatives of fertility. Bloom, who is with the students, alone disapproves of their behaviour. He is visiting the hospital to enquire after the progress of Mina Purefoy, of whose long labour he learned this morning from Josie Breen in 'The Lestrygonians' episode. He is pressed to join the students, who are waiting for Buck Mulligan, and somewhat reluctantly agrees.

The stylistic experimentation reaches a new complexity in this episode. Joyce took great pains to construct it on the basis of the month-by-month growth of the foetus in the womb. A great deal of attention was paid to physiological technicalities in dividing the episode into nine sections. But what the general reader will find more digestible is that Joyce devised a parallel series of parodies of English prose style in rough chronological sequence.

Thus the early paragraphs are written in a pre-English style that is undisciplined and confused, though the flavour of Latin syntax is detected through the chaos. Next a firm Anglo-Saxon idiom is employed in description of the midwives, with imitation of alliterative verse ('Before born babe bliss had'). In the same idiom is recounted the arrival of Bloom, who is admitted by Nurse Callan. He asks after Mrs Purefoy and is told that, after three full days of labour, the birth is now near. The student doctor Dixon comes in and presses Bloom to join himself and others at a gathering. The group consists of three medical students, Dixon, Lynch, and Madden, together with Lenehan, Crotthers, Punch Costello, and Stephen. They are waiting for Mulligan too, drinking beer and eating tinned sardines. By this time a Middle English flavour has become firmly established in the idiom.

Bloom joins the students, chiefly out of concern for Stephen. He was with Simon Dedalus at the funeral this morning and from what was said then he cannot but be aware of the strained relationship between father and son. The young men are arguing over the old question whether the life of mother or baby should be of first concern in childbirth. They are already merry and have to be admonished by a sister for their noisy roistering at a time when a cry from the labour ward suggests to Bloom that Mrs Purefoy's time must be very near. Stephen preaches a mock-sermon whose blasphemies, it appears, spark off a fearsome thunderclap. In general the blasphemy, the bawdy, the mockery, and the flippancy in which the riotous company indulge clearly represent an offence against the proprieties of a Maternity Hospital, and the talk of contraception and abortion offends against the code of fertility.

By the time Mulligan and Bannon arrive, Joyce has reached the eighteenth century, and Addison and Steele, in his progress through English prose styles, having parodied many writers including Mandeville, Malory, the Bible, Sir Thomas Browne, John Bunyan, and Pepys, on the way. Mulligan contributes to the ribaldry with a claim that he is planning to set himself up on Lambay island as a Fertiliser and Incubator. His national farm will counter the ill-effects of nuptial sterility, and he will personally service all female applicants, irrespective of class. There is more ribaldry and more praise of contraception until the roisterers are interrupted by Nurse Callan. She comes with a message for Dr Dixon, who thereupon departs. Throughout the outpouring of jocular obscenities and crude wit Bloom is the only one to turn his mind in sympathy to poor Mrs Purefoy in her long ordeal, and he is genuinely glad when the news comes through that her child has been born.

Among the rest of the company, however, the news merely evokes an outburst of obstetrical discussion which explores various kinds of abnormalities, such as the birth of freaks, conception by rape, and unnatural intercourse between women and animals, and the legal and theological questions raised when one Siamese twin dies before the other. Then mood and tone are transformed as Joyce parodies the style of the eighteenth-century Gothic novel in order to present the brief appearance of Haines the Englishman, as an apparition from behind a secret panel, burdened with remorse and guilt, trying his tongue at a Synge-like brogue, claiming that only laudanum can obliterate his crime from his memory, and asking to be met at Westland Row station at 11.30.

Meanwhile Bloom is lost in reverie, recalling his childhood, his first entry into commercial life, selling trinkets, and his first encounter with a whore, then indulging in idealised pictures of Martha and Molly. At the same time, in an odd conjunction of interests, Stephen's thoughts have been led back to his childhood by Costello who was with him at Clongowes. Lenehan gives an account of the Gold Cup race in which the dark horse, Throwaway, overtook the favourite, Sceptre, in the straight. By this time the reader has learned to associate Bloom with the 'outsider', the 'dark horse', and the throwaway, and the cocksure, flamboyant Blazes Boylan with the favourite, Sceptre, so that in the result of the race for the treasured prize we seem to have a forecast of what ultimately is to be the final outcome of the rivalry between Bloom and Boylan for Molly.

Joyce has by this time parodied the style of a number of nineteenth-century prose writers, but increasingly the style becomes a hotch-potch marked by verbosity and circumlocution, and the debate among the students gets correspondingly more jumbled, irrational, and chaotic. This development is appropriate to the increasing drunken excitement of the speakers: but it also seems to suggest an erosion of cultural standards and disciplines. Modes of discourse appropriate to medical, sociological, or even sentimental purposes are picked up, burlesqued, and jumbled together so that the final effect is of hysterical artificiality running riot. But when we return to take a glance at Mina Purefoy and her baby, mother and child are presented in a sentimental Dickensian style. Husband and family are sentimentally grouped in imagination around her, and upon this nativity scene another impinges. This scene takes place in the mind of Bloom, who is stirred by Stephen's unhealthy talk, obsessed with physical crudities. He calls to mind by contrast a scene long ago when he was at a May-time evening party at

Roundtown and Stephen, then a little boy of 'four or five in linsey woolsey', frowned as he was encircled by the hands of Molly and other young ladies, indeed looked reproachfully towards his mother. A third nativity scene is briefly touched upon, for a sudden quietness descends like the quiet of 'the vigilant watch of shepherds and angels about a crib in Bethlehem of Juda long ago'.

Quietude is rudely broken by the utterance of 'the Word' – and the word is 'Burke's', the name of a pub, to which the company forthwith repair. Leaving the hospital, they caper through the streets, having plainly been granted by intoxication a gift of tongues that reveals itself in an outburst of talk so compounded of mixed idioms, slang, quotations, and abbreviations that it reads like gibberish which it would tax even the most fervent Joycean to interpret in exact detail. What is clear, however, is that the company drink whiskies and beers in the pub and then move on to absinthe, and when the landlord calls Time and turns them out, Stephen and Lynch go for the train to take them to Amiens Street station and the red-light district.

Episode 15: Circe

Circe was an enchantress expert in the use of potent magic herbs, and when Ulysses visited her island she drugged his companions and turned them into swine. Ulysses, however, was protected from the same fate by a herb, moly, given him by Hermes. He was thus able to threaten Circe with the sword and to order his followers to be restored. Subsequently Ulysses was taken to Circe's bed and remained a year with her. For Ulysses's visit to the island where the enchantress turns men into animals we have the visit of Stephen and Bloom to 'Nighttown', the red-light area of Dublin where men are bestialised by prostitution. At the turn of the century the area around Talbot Street, Montgomery Street, and Mecklenburg Street was estimated to be inhabited by some two thousand prostitutes.

This episode represents the climax of the story and the Homeric parallel does not fully account for the importance Joyce gives to it, for it is the longest episode in the book and is contrived with a degree of artistry that makes it both the most compelling thing that Joyce wrote and one of the most outstanding tours de force in world literature. To appreciate the significance of the episode, one must realise that the Homeric parallel was not the only model Joyce took in constructing *Ulysses*. For instance, the work is divided into three books like Dante's *Divine Comedy*, and the three books have aspects of a *Purgatorio*, an *Inferno*, and a *Paradiso*. It is clear that, as Dante is led down into the *Inferno* through circle after circle till he reaches the depths of Hell and the place of ultimate betrayal, so Bloom is conducted through various spheres of twentieth-century unreality and artificiality till he reaches the depth of the Dublin inferno where Irish womanhood is for sale and where men are turned into animals.

Joyce cast this episode in dramatic form with very full 'stage' directions. Stephen and Lynch have had a potent mixture of drinks and in their intoxicated condition the borderline between reality and dream, or reality and nightmare, is a faint one. Bloom too has perhaps drunk a little more than he should. In any case his day has been packed with musings and memories that have given as much substance to what passes in the mind as to what happens in the outer world around him. Thus Joyce intensifies the mingling of mental life and external life by giving the substance of both comparable status. In this episode what passes in the mind, and indeed what rises up from the unconscious, is articulated in the same dramatic form as what is said and done in reality. Thus the reader follows Bloom and Stephen through the external activities of the night and at the same time sees this layer of 'normal' behaviour interwoven with the stuff of reflection, musing, and dreaming, and often breached by the incursion of stuff from the hidden unconscious.

At the beginning a sordid scene in Mabbot Street is presented in vivid imagery: a deaf-mute idiot, a pigmy woman, a 'gnome' ransacking a rubbish tip, a bandy child, a drunken navvy, and behind them the noise of crashing plate, screaming woman, and swearing man. A couple of English soldiers, Privates Carr and Compton, pass by, looking mockingly at Stephen and Lynch who enter as though pantomiming the mass. Soon Bloom arrives, out of breath with trying to keep up with them, and slips into a butcher's shop to get a pig's crubeen and a sheep's trotter. There are a cluster of minor near-misses as two cyclists almost run him down, a tram almost hits him, and the Caffrey children collide with him. These near-misses spark off a series of imaginary encounters in which earlier frustrations and guilts are materialised: his father and mother rebuke him as a boy, Molly appears in splendid Turkish costume to call him a stick-in-the-mud and he apologises for having forgotten to collect the skin lotion from Sweny's. Gerty MacDowell also reappears to remonstrate with Bloom, then Mrs Breen, with whom he re-enacts a memorable personal success he had with her as lion of a party long ago. (He mentally compared her present dowdy appearance with what she had been like in the old days when he met her in the street in 'The Lestrygonians'.)

In the outward world meanwhile whores call out indecent invitations from lanes, doors, and corners. Bloom begins to wonder if his pursuit of Stephen is a wild-goose chase. In this apprehensive mood two policemen are transfigured for him into symbols of repressive authority. They challenge and question, reprove and threaten him. So begins a lengthy trial of Bloom in which numerous long-standing guilty memories surface, those he has injured or offended confront him, and he marshals the skills of the advertising agent as well as the belief in his own comparative 'innocence' in his defence. Thus Martha appears, sobbing about a 'breach of promise' and calling upon him to clear her name. Philip Beaufoy (the author of the winning story in *Titbits* which Bloom read with some envy and admiration in the privy in the 'Calypso' episode) emerges to discredit Bloom's claim to follow a literary career by calling him an ignorant 'pressman johnny'. Then graver hidden guilts surface. Mary Driscoll, a servant girl who worked for Molly, accuses him of sexual assault. Bloom replies with what is meant to be a tear-jerking appeal to sympathy, and J. J. O'Molloy, the failed barrister, rises to his defence. O'Molloy's submission is that Bloom is 'of Mongolian extraction and irresponsible for his actions. Not all there, in fact'. Bloom is howled down by the hostile court and tries to mollify his accusers by giving references of some importance in the city. But his claim to have moved in society circles is immediately countered by the appearance in court of society women whom he has apparently admired at a distance and sometimes tried to approach. They are well-built, masterful women, Mrs Yelverton Barry, Mrs Bellingham, and the Hon Mrs Mervyn Talboys. They claim that Bloom desired to be ridden and whipped by them, and are all agog to remove his trousers and set to work. Jurors and police are disgusted; and the recorder puts on his black cap and condemns Bloom to death. The call goes out, 'Who'll hang Judas Iscariot?' Whereupon H. Rumbold, whose letter of application for work as an executioner was read in the 'Cyclops' episode, puts in an appearance with the tools of his trade at the ready.

The dream world fades into reality. Bloom is plodding his way through Nighttown. Zoe Higgins, a whore, comes tripping down the steps of a house and accosts him. She takes his arm and snuggles up to him. The warmth and admiration she brings destroy all trace of Bloom's despair. Frustration is replaced by self-assurance, and he embarks on a new self-projection as exaggeratedly confident and victorious as his former one was tentative, apologetic, and defeated. Refusing Zoe's request for a cigarette, he expresses his opposition to smoking in the rhetoric of a radical agitator. He is transformed into a Dublin alderman proposing as his election manifesto the immediate construction of the tramline he suggested in the 'Hades' episode for transporting cattle from the cattle-market to the docks. In a flash he becomes a celebrated public figure acclaimed by the city authorities. The long-felt inner need for acceptance and approval is satisfied in a public ceremony in which triumphant Bloom is born on a white horse in magnificent procession, then, mantled in gold, ascends the Stone of

Destiny to receive the homage of archbishops, bishops, peers, and nobles, and the acclamation of the common people. Bloom's wish-fulfilment dream gives him popularity alike with the British establishment and the Irish nationalist circles. He orders the building of the 'new Bloomusalem'. When a dissenting voice is raised, he has only to raise a finger and the objector is shot.

Bloom's picture of himself, familiar to the reader from long following the workings of his mind, is exaggerated in all its aspects, so that his good-nature, his compassion, and his sense of fair play are projected on a massive scale as he dispenses bounty, embraces the afflicted, and as judge answers the queries of all comers on all subjects with encyclopaedic comprehensiveness. Again his progressive, liberal humanism is expressed in proclamations of universal tolerance, religious reunion, and the free distribution of electric washers.

Bloom's moods of confidence today have, however, been frequently ruined by rejection, and this glorious self-fulfilment is rudely interrupted. He is accused of hypocrisy and faces a howling mob. On the defence once more, he calls medical evidence. Mulligan and other young medicos testify that he is a specimen of 'the new womanly man' and about to have a baby. Thus there is sympathy for him again. Encouraged, he brings forth eight children, handsome and intelligent. He is proclaimed Messiah; in response to popular request he performs instant miracles, and a papal nuncio traces his descent from Moses. The glory does not last. The guilt of his masturbation arises to incriminate him, persecution begins, and a pantomimic 'crucifixion' ensues in which the Fire Brigade set fire to him in a seamless garment. 'Weep not for me, O daughters of Erin' he cries from amid the flames, and massed choirs sing the Hallelujah chorus.

In the external world, meanwhile, Zoe tries to clinch a deal for ten shillings and she takes him into the house. In the 'stage' directions animal imagery (for instance a client with 'an ape's gait', 'goatee beard', and 'two-tailed black braces dangling at heels') suggests entry into the inner haunts of the Circe who bestialises men. In the music room Bloom and Zoe find Stephen fiddling with the pianola, Lynch sitting on the floor, Kitty Ricketts sitting on the edge of the table, and Florry Talbot lolling on a sofa. Stephen is talking pompous intellectual nonsense which nevertheless, if the meaning is teased out, adds to some of the themes in his thinking earlier in the day. Florry Talbot remarks 'They say the last day is coming this summer', and the apocalyptic theme of the end of the world is expanded in hallucinatory events. Even the whores are touched to confess how first they fell into sin. Stephen's companions of the drinking bout and his fellow-conversationalists from the National Library ('Scylla and Charybdis') put in appearances to play their part.

Bloom is concerned with earthier matters, stirred by the sight of Zoe's bare flesh when Lynch lifts the side of her slip. He ponders an injection mark on her thigh, notes Kitty's skinniness and Florry's more cushioned build. An elaborate consideration of women in crude anatomical and sexual terms is made through a hallucinatory inner dialogue between Bloom and his grandfather, Lipoti Virag, from whom he seems to have derived his more technical physiological interests. By contrast another side of Bloom's personality asserts itself when 'Henry Flower' (his pseudonym in the correspondence with Martha) appears, darkly mantled, equipped with a dulcimer, to give a stagey operatic rendering of 'There is a flower that bloometh'.

As Bloom's character is projected in different personae such as those of Virag and Henry Flower, so Stephen's is projected in two competing personae, Philip Sober, who advises him (like Mr Deasy in the 'Nestor' episode) to watch what he is spending, and Philip Drunk, who gives way to wild fancies. Florry suspects that Stephen is a product of the Roman Catholic seminary at Maynooth (his pseudo-theological chatter would encourage this inference) and there is consequent talk of priests who visit the brothel. There is profane talk too about Christ's paternity, reflecting again the pervasive theme of the nature of fatherhood which is to reach its end in Stephen's 'discovery' of Bloom. When Florry says to Stephen 'I'm sure you are a spoiled priest', Stephen is mentally metamorphosed into a Cardinal, Primate of All Ireland, equipped with a rosary of corks and a pectoral 'corkscrew cross'.

Bella Cohen comes in. She was in real life a notorious brothel-keeper. She is pictured as huge in build and masterful in temperament. This combination of qualities appeals to that element in Bloom's character which makes him admire large, imperious women. Here her entry sparks off an extravagant hallucinatory passage in which Bloom seeks to be dominated by her and to play the yielding woman to her masterfulness. Mentally he ties her bootlaces. She orders him down on hands and knees and then (temporarily masculinised by Joyce as 'Bello') pins him to the floor. He creeps under the sofa to escape her 'heel discipline' (thus 'bestialised' into a dog), but she coaxes him out, then turns her wrath on him, slaps him, gets the girls to hold him down, mounts him, and orders him to change his male clothes for female dress. Thus Bloom is feminised. 'The Sins of the Past' proclaim his secret perversions: exhibitionism, voyeurism, and coprophilia. Bella imposes appropriate punishments on him such as swabbing out ladies' lavatories and acting the whore, and then offers him for sale. The auctioneer knocks him down to a bidder stocking up a Caliph's harem.

Bella taunts Bloom for his lack of virility in allowing a 'man of brawn' to supplant him with Molly. ('Brawn' for Boylan fills out the sequence of correspondence: Bread for Bloom, Brains for Stephen, Blood for Molly.) The unmasking of Bloom's fastidious revulsion against his marital duties is effected in crude burlesque. He has pursued other women while his home has been desecrated. The fit sequel to this self-imposed domestic rejection is that he should be buried in the shrubbery privy. As the nightmare continues, Jews wail Bloom's passing and, after death, he wakes to the vision of a Nymph. She is the very Nymph whose naked picture, given away in an issue of *Photo Bits*, hangs over his bed. (It is described in the 'Calypso' episode.) From that advantageous position she has learned a lot about Bloom's private habits. She also seems to be informed about his less respectable private indulgences in the open air. But finally, in response to repeated recriminations from this supposed specimen of stone-cold chastity, Bloom calls her bluff, asserts his virility, and she flees.

In the real world Bella Cohen gets down to brass tacks. 'Who's paying here?' The charge is ten shillings each. Stephen puts down thirty shillings (almost half this morning's pay from Mr Deasy in the 'Nestor' episode), but Bloom pays for himself and gives ten shillings back to Stephen. Stephen is in fact so drunk that Bloom suggests he take over his cash to keep it safe, and Stephen acquiesces.

By a deft psychological move Joyce floats Bloom off into another fantasy. Zoe and Florry begin to whisper and giggle together so that Bloom feels excluded, and immediately the drama of his domestic exclusion is enacted. Boylan is telling Lenehan of his sexual achievements, and we see Boylan jump into a car and enter Bloom's home, treating Bloom as the footman. 'Show me in. I have a little private business with your wife . . .' Bloom is told how he may watch through the keyhole, and the two barmaids from the Ormond Hotel (also watchers through a window and giggling girls from whose confidences Bloom was excluded in the 'Sirens' episode) give a running commentary on Boylan's hearty sexual antics with Molly.

Stephen meanwhile is rambling drunkenly and when his talk touches on perversions he is rebuked by Bella, but it is explained that he is fresh from Paris. Zoe wants to hear all about it and Stephen burlesques the chatter of a Paris brothel, advertising absurd perversions. But suddenly the memory of last night's dream (first recalled in the 'Proteus' episode) recurs to him, in which the oriental stranger greets him over the red carpet, and Bloom moves towards him as if to bring it to fulfilment. However, Stephen turns from proferred acceptance, giving in to his obsessive urge to flee. So the image of flight is concretised in a wild horse-race.

Privates Carr and Compton, accompanied by Cissy Caffrey, pass by in the street outside, and the scene within grows ever more delirious.

Zoe puts pennies in the pianola. The music starts and a mad dance ensues. Stephen dances with Zoe till she is giddy, then seizes Florry and Kitty in turn. Soon all are wheeling and whirling. At the climax Stephen totters to a standstill, his head a mass of circling stars, only to see the ghost of his mother rising through the floor, and the guilt of his disobedience at her death-bed surfaces. 'They said I killed you, mother', he cries. To the others he is white and deathly as he refutes his mother's pious warning, 'Beware! God's hand!'. He summons up all his powers of resistance and shouts '*Non serviam*'. (This repetition of the slogan 'I will not serve that in which I no longer believe . . .' from the *Portrait* turns to positive account the rebellious *Non serviam* of Lucifer which the retreat sermons presented as the origin of all evil.) And while his mother calls upon the 'sacred Heart of Jesus' to have mercy upon him, he shrieks 'No! No! No!', lifts his ashplant, smashes the chandelier, and dashes madly from the room. There is a stampede after him. Bella detains Bloom. She wants to be paid for the broken lamp. He throws a shilling down angrily, then makes his furtive way along the street, in imagination pursued and recognised by various acquaintances.

Soon Bloom comes upon a menacing little scene. A crowd is gathering. Cissy Caffrey is complaining that Stephen ran after her when Privates Carr and Compton left her for a moment to relieve themselves. 'Was he insulting you while me and him was having a piss?' Private Carr asks her. Stephen is talking drunkenly in his pompous way. Bloom, ever resourceful, comes up, calls Stephen 'Professor', and says the 'carman is waiting'. But Stephen is in no mood to be pushed around and in his intoxicated state taps his own head and says, seemingly adapting a sentence of William Blake's, 'But in here it is I must kill the priest and the king'. Private Carr is roused. 'What's that you're saying about my king?' he demands. Cissy Caffrey is elated. 'They're going to fight. For me!' And while the hallucinatory images of Edward VII, the Croppy Boy, and various other historic characters give the wider dimensions of the British-Irish struggle to the encounter, Private Carr punches Stephen in the face and he collapses, stunned.

Two policemen arrive and the soldiers clear off. Bloom deals tactfully with the police, then turns his attention to Stephen. He tries to waken him, and Stephen responds with groans and incoherent mutterings. Among the mutterings are phrases from the song which Stephen sang for his mother on her death-bed (Yeats's 'Who goes with Fergus?' from his play *The Countess Cathleen*), an occasion recollected right at the beginning of the book in the 'Telemachus' episode. Bloom misunderstands the fragmentary phrases and concludes from reference to a 'white breast' that Stephen must be in love with a Miss Ferguson.

('Best thing could happen to him . . .') At this climax of the whole book Bloom is so tenderly and solicitiously attentive to Stephen that the long-felt paternal hunger for the lost son wells up in him and he sees a sudden vision of little Rudy, aged eleven, as he would now have been had he lived. The father has found a son.

Book III (The Homecoming)

Episode 16: Eumaeus

Homer's Eumaeus is an Ithacan swineherd. Odysseus, having reached Ithaca, his homeland, comes to Eumaeus's hut disguised as a beggar. Here he learns from this faithful swineherd how Penelope is tormented by the insolent, riotous suitors. Telemachus comes back from Sparta and Odysseus reveals himself. Then they concoct a scheme for dealing with the suitors.

This episode has the atmosphere of calm after storm. It is a weary exhausted calm, and Joyce represents it so in a weary, rambling prose style. Syntax is unsure. Logic is vague. Sentences wander off into factual and grammatical inconclusiveness.

Bloom brushes down Stephen's clothes, gives him his hat and his ashplant and tries to restore him generally. Stephen wants a drink but it is after midnight and Bloom thinks the best place near at hand would be the cabmen's shelter near Butt Bridge. They make their way into Amiens Street but do not manage to find a cab they can hire, and so are compelled to continue on foot. Bloom gives some sound fatherly advice to Stephen about the dangers of drinking and whoring. As they pass a watchman's brazier and sentry box, Stephen sees that the watchman is Gumley, a former friend of his father's who inherited a decent estate and proceeded to squander it with even more thoroughness than Simon Dedalus, and is now reduced to the level of corporation night watchman. They also meet John Corley (Lenehan's friend in 'Two Gallants', *Dubliners*) who borrows half-a-crown from Stephen. Bloom continues to be solicitous for Stephen's welfare, mentioning that he met his father this morning and suggesting that he might go home, for he has a poor opinion of Mulligan and his influence on Stephen.

Reaching the cabmen's shelter they sit down among an odd assortment of customers and order a coffee and a bun. A red-bearded sailor accosts Stephen, asks his name, and then claims to know Simon Dedalus, a marksman he saw performing brilliantly in Stockholm with a touring circus. The sailor, who claims to be W. B. Murphy of Carrigaloe, launches into highly coloured traveller's tales. The travel talk sets Bloom the businessman musing on the commercial possibilities of the developing tourist trade. The immediate environment is sordid enough; the sailor displays a trick tattoo on his chest whose grim face is wreathed in smiles when he pulls the skin in a certain way, and a seedy looking street-walker peers round the door and catches Bloom's attention because she is the same one he saw this afternoon on Ormond Quay (in the 'Sirens' episode) and avoided looking at because she knows Molly. She sets Bloom moralising on prostitution. He thinks brothels ought to be licensed and medically inspected. While Bloom talks thus on his level of hygienic politico-social comment, Stephen sticks to his intellectual and metaphysical vein. 'In this country people sell much more than she ever had and do a roaring trade. Fear not them that sell the body but have not power to buy the soul.' The aphorism leads to a discussion of the 'soul' in which wide divergences between the two minds are evident.

By degrees Bloom manoeuvres the conversation from talk of the sailor's dubious yarns of travel to the temperament of Spaniards and praise of Mediterranean female contours. But there is also talk of different kind going forward. It so happens that the keeper of the shelter is James Fitzharris, nicknamed 'Skin-the-goat', who played a crucial part as one of the 'Invincibles' in the Phoenix Park assassinations of 1882. When the matter was discussed in the newspaper office in the 'Aeolus' episode we learned how, immediately after the murders, 'Skin-the-goat' drove a decoy car back to Dublin while the assassins got away by detour. Here the shelter-keeper launches into regret for the falling off of Irish shipping, putting the blame on the British. Ireland would be a land of wealth and plenty but for England's exploitation of the country and its penal taxation. But he can foresee the day when Germany and Japan will bring England down. The sailor's comment that the Irish Catholic peasant is 'the backbone of our empire' stirs 'Skin-the-goat's' anger further. No Irishman worthy of his salt would serve the empire.

Bloom regrets the altercation. He recognises that 'Irish soldiers had as often fought for England as against her, more so, in fact' and the wise course is to make the best of both countries. He tells Stephen of his encounter with the Citizen in Barney Kiernan's ('Cyclops' episode) and how he insisted that Christ was a Jew. He presses his philosophy of good-will and mutual tolerance. So-called nationalistic causes are often financial struggles at bottom. Jews increase a country's prosperity. Being a good Irishman is nothing to do with class or creed. Bloom would like to see everyone with a nice tidy income in an Ireland where all can live well if they work. 'Count me out', says Stephen on the mention of 'work', beginning to resist Bloom's clichés more sharply. He refuses to regard himself as having a duty to Ireland. Indeed he suggests that they change the subject. The note of ill-temper sets Bloom wondering whether Stephen is still intoxicated or whether the deficiencies of his home life have soured him. He broods on the way some promising young men go to seed while on the other hand some youngsters from the lowest social level struggle to the top by sheer force of natural ability. At this point Bloom's commercial instincts come to the aid of his natural compassion in recommending a continuance of the outlay of money on Stephen's behalf. For Stephen is a person of such uncommon calibre that he can provide intellectual stimulation that would amply repay him. Moreover, making contacts of this unique kind is the very stuff of interesting living.

Bloom picks up the pink sporting edition of the *Evening Telegraph* and sees that C. P. M'Coy and Stephen have had their names added to the list of mourners at the Dignam funeral. At Stephen's request he also locates Mr Deasy's letter, and he reads the Ascot Gold Cup race results too. Meanwhile a cabman in the shelter has raised the inevitable public topic – the theory that Parnell is not dead but will return. This fanciful notion takes its place among other instances that have occurred to Bloom's mind in this episode of a fabulous wandering hero's return. The figures include Rip van Winkle, Enoch Arden, and the Flying Dutchman, all of whom return, like Odysseus himself. There is talk of Kitty O'Shea and Bloom broods, somewhat ironically, on the kind of triangle where a commonplace husband is displaced when a 'real man' arrives on the scene. The theme of passionate women sets Bloom pondering again on the warm-blooded Spaniards. He takes a photograph of Molly from his pocketbook and lays it before Stephen for his comments. Stephen observes a large woman with a low-cut evening dress, ostentatiously displaying an ample bosom as she stands by a piano. The photograph gives a speaking likeness of his wife's face, Bloom observes, but scarcely does full justice to her figure. On this subject, Molly's generous contours, he dwells with enthusiasm. Stephen thinks her handsome. Bloom appreciates this approval of Molly and, by an odd sequence of logic, allows his thoughts to wander on the subject of matrimonial triangles and divorces, by which route he is led back to the topic of Parnell, whose hat he once rescued during a fracas around the great leader.

Then Bloom takes up again his paternal reflections on Stephen's well-being, regretting the way he wastes his time in brothels and runs the risk of getting venereal disease. He cannot bear to think of Stephen being houseless and homeless, the victim of mean landladies. He finds himself fascinated by Stephen's peculiar conversation, being several years his senior 'or like his father', and he is horrified to discover by questioning him that he last ate a meal 'the day before yesterday'. Ironically, perhaps, Bloom's sense of fellowship with Stephen is encouraged by a feeling that their respective minds, though not in agreement about everything, tend to move 'in the one train of thought'. It is time to go to bed, and Stephen cannot go back to Sandycove. Bloom would like to take him back to Eccles Street, but is unsure how Stephen would react to the suggestion. He takes the plunge, however, and invites Stephen to come home with him. Privately he indulges wild notions that Stephen might even sing duets with Molly on a tour of English holiday resorts. He pays the bill and takes Stephen, still rather weak in the knees, out into the open. The air will do him good, he assures Stephen, and puts his arm through his companion's to support him as they walk.

They talk together about music, Bloom revealing a lively but not very discriminating taste for tuneful nineteenth-century composers, and incidentally dropping a few amusing inaccuracies into the discussion. Stephen's more austere taste is for the English Elizabethan and Jacobean contrapuntalists. Bloom insists that his wife would be delighted to make Stephen's acquaintance. Stephen sings an old German song as he walks. Bloom is enthusiastic about his fine voice, and at once foresees that, properly trained, Stephen could soon have Dublin's musical world at his feet. He could at one and the same time make money and raise the cultural level of Dublin's musical taste. But he has one caveat for Stephen, and that is that he should break off his connection with Mulligan who is only too ready to disparage him in his absence.

Stephen does not himself reply to the new temptation to make profit from his art, but a nearby horse adds its comment by dropping three turds.

Episode 17: Ithaca

Homer's Penelope declared that she would marry the man among the suitors who could string her lost husband's bow and shoot an arrow through twelve axe-heads. Odysseus alone, in disguise, was able to bend the bow and shoot the arrow as required. Having done so, he shot down the suitors with the pre-arranged help of Telemachus and Eumaeus. Odysseus's knowledge of the peculiar construction of her bed convinced Penelope that he was indeed her lost husband.

A catechetical mode of presentation is adopted. That is to say, the whole episode is presented in questions and answers. The answers are not just exact and specific, but they tend also to amplify the information given to an encyclopaedic degree, often putting events and trains of thought into the context of the universal. Thus this is the most satisfying episode in the book, satisfying in that it clears up unanswered questions in the reader's mind and fills out much that has been half-hinted at or inadequately explained, and does so in a style that delights by its sheer lucidity, poise, and intellectual thoroughness.

Bloom returns home bringing Stephen with him. To what extent the developments in this episode may be interpreted as forecasting the finishing off of the rival Boylan and the reinstatement of husband with wife is a matter which Joyce does not make clear beyond dispute. This may be thought odd in view of the fact that the episode is packed full of clarifications. If the rather meandering, inexact, and inchoate style of the 'Eumaeus' episode may be said to represent the mentality of Bloom (and the forthcoming 'Penelope' episode of course the mentality of Molly), the precise, comprehensive, and conclusive style of 'Ithaca' must be, if not solely representative of Stephen's mentality, at least predominantly so. Indeed there is much to suggest that it is representative of the Bloom mind when infused with the intellectual vigour of Stephen's. The text suggests a coming together of personalities, a communion of two beings perhaps necessary to each other for full living. Moreover, Stephen's sufferings at the hands of the British soldiers in the 'Circe' episode was presented in imagery of the Crucifixion, and Joyce sustains aspects of this parallelism between Stephen and Christ in the present episode. Thus, in taking Stephen–Christ into his home, Bloom, the epitome of common humanity, creates a relationship in which the light of sheer intellectual lucidity and comprehensiveness is shed on the homely scene.

The two walk back to Eccles Street. Bloom, who forgot this morning to transfer his latchkey into the trousers of his mourning suit, has to lower himself into the basement and get in through the scullery door. There he takes off his boots, lights a candle, and then comes to the front door to admit Stephen. They get into the kitchen, where Bloom kneels down to light the fire, reminding Stephen of Brother Michael lighting the fire in the sick-room at Clongowes and of the Dean of Studies performing the same task in the physics lecture theatre at University College, both memorable occasions in the *Portrait*. Bloom then takes a kettle to the sink and turns the tap to let the water flow:

> Did it flow?
> Yes. From Roundwood reservoir in county Wicklow of a cubic capacity of 2,400 million gallons, percolating through a subterranean aqueduct of filter mains of single and double pipeage constructed at an initial plant cost of £5 per linear yard by way of the Dargle, Rathdown . . .

Not only do we get a bird's-eye view of the workings of the city water supply system, but water itself is surveyed encyclopaedically with full data about its nature, its property, and its uses. Then the heating of the water to boiling point is described in elaborate scientific detail.

The filling out of detail in this way is only one of the devices which give the episode its astonishing flavour of omniscient understanding. The contents of a cupboard, for instance, are catalogued with the same exactitude. Moreover, little incidents are allowed to call back memories of events earlier in the day, and thus to throw fuller light on them. For instance, Bloom sees two torn-up betting-slips on the dresser, angrily torn by Boylan who betted on the favourite (phallic) Sceptre in the Gold Cup race. They bring back a memory of the talk of the race in Barney Kiernan's ('Cyclops' episode) and of the meeting with Bantam Lyons ('The Lestrygonians' episode). Once more the thought impinges that the dark horse, the outsider, the Throwaway, may beat the favourite to the Gold Cup which, by virtue of parallels in the 'Nausicaa' episode, is both chalice and womb.

When Bloom has made cocoa they settle down to drink it, and the relationship between the two of them and previous connections between the two of them are explained in a way that fills out the reader's knowledge satisfyingly, as exact dates and locations are supplied. Bloom is thirty-eight and Stephen is twenty-two. A good deal of quiet humour is involved in comparing the literary ambitions of the two, their respective parentages, their religious initiations, their educational careers and attitudes.

The communion between father and son is at its closest over the cocoa-drinking. There is comparison between the two ancient races, Jewish and Irish, which they respectively represent, both nations that have suffered dispersal and oppression. This theme takes us back to the account of John F. Taylor's celebrated speech quoted in the 'Aeolus' episode. Taylor's speech drew the parallel between the Greeks (resisting the crude Romans) and the Irish (resisting the crude British) as well as between the Jews (resisting the Egyptians) and the Irish. A hint has already been dropped in the 'Circe' episode that the meeting between the philosophically minded Dedalus and the emotional Bloom represents a Hellenic-Hebraic synthesis. In substance and technique this present episode reflects that synthesis; for intellectual clarity and understanding flood everything touched upon by Bloom's thoughts in a new revelatory light. (In this sense, on the Dantean pattern, the episode plays its part in the culminating *Paradiso*.)

Bloom offers Stephen a room for the night, dreaming that he might use Stephen to deflect Molly's attention from Boylan, but Stephen declines. Nevertheless Bloom is anxious to sustain their relationship. He would like Stephen to instruct Molly in Italian while she instructed him in singing. Stephen could come to Eccles Street, and Bloom and he could have intellectual discussions together. But Stephen departs. Bloom leads him to the door, candle in hand, while Stephen raises his ashplant like a cross and sings to himself the 113th psalm of the

Israelites' escape from the house of bondage. Bloom takes him through the back door into the garden. There they stand under the light of the stars and of a lamp from Molly's window upstairs. When Bloom opens the door in the garden wall to let Stephen out, Joyce uses imagery suggesting the drawing of a bow as though the leave-taking somehow represents the beginning of the final acts that restore Ulysses the wanderer to his wife.

Alone, Bloom meditates a while, then returns indoors. He takes off his collar and tie, unbuttons his waistcoat, shirt, and trousers, checks over the day's expenditure and income, then begins to day-dream of his ideal home and its furniture, a suburban villa complete with garden, summerhouse, and tennis court. The day-dream expands, and he sees himself as a squire-like figure in tweeds, with a place in society, and a justice of the peace. Characteristically he figures out the cost of fulfilling this day-dream and the various ways by which he might suddenly be in a position to finance it, for instance by patenting a successful new invention or winning a lottery.

Before going up to bed he unlocks one of his private drawers to put Martha's letter safely away, and ponders the relics of his father kept there, which include his last letter before committing suicide. Other relics, his insurance policy and his bank passbook, set him brooding on the awful possibilities of poverty and how one would escape the disgrace of bankruptcy. He goes upstairs to the bedroom, undresses, then moves a pillow from the head of the bed to the foot and gets in. He is aware that another being has occupied the bed at Molly's side and even begins to list the various 'suitors' who have admired Molly and, however briefly or ineffectively, aspired to occupy the same place. Envy and jealousy are directed at Boylan for his youth and vigour, but he decides against open hostility, accepting the rivalry tolerantly. In a mood of resignation he kisses Molly's bottom, as Odysseus, when he realised that he had landed in Ithaca, passionately kissed the soil of his homeland. Molly and Bloom are side by side but head to toe, in their own way afflicted by the 'foot-and-mouth' disease that is so troubling Ireland. Molly asks him sleepily what he has been doing all day and he mentions especially his encounter with Stephen, 'professor and author'. Both are conscious, as they talk, of the breakdown of their sexual life since little Rudy's birth and death.

Episode 18: Penelope

'Ithaca' leaves us with the impression of husband and wife both conscious of the deficiency in their relationship that has brought a ten-year absence of sexual satisfaction together. Both are consequently toying with other partners. Bloom's repressed condition is evident in his paper-relationship with Martha, in his voyeurism with Gerty

MacDowell, and in his masturbation. But from the beginning of the day to the end Bloom's thoughts have reverted time after time to his wife at home in sexual hunger and in tender memories of their happier days and their former cosy family life together. If he has found a 'son' in Stephen Dedalus, are we to assume that he will be restored after his wandering to a full and happy life with his Penelope? Bloom's real need for this fulfilment has been made plain. It only remains for us to be acquainted with what goes on in Molly's mind.

Joyce's epic therefore ends with an episode in which we are taken into the mind of Molly Bloom. It is night, she is in bed, she has had, one may say, a busy day. So the rambling nature of her musings is to be expected. But she is a woman too, and the book has focused so far on what goes on in the minds of two men, the one of strong material, physical, commercial, and practical interests, the other of sharp intellectual, abstract, and philosophical bent. The down-to-earth pragmatism of Bloom and the uncompromising idealism of Stephen have each their own kind of masculine dryness and incisiveness. When we enter the mind of Molly Bloom we leave this world of masculine aridities and angularities for a world of fluidity. Molly's thought flows, gushes, spurts and tumbles headlong. It is a flood. Joyce gives us fifty pages of unpunctuated prose in which the outpouring of the mind is never impeded by deference to the disciplines of punctuation, syntax, or logic. If there is something sterile about Bloom's sexual life and Stephen's cerebralism, then the antidote to both is here in the outflow of an unstoppable fertility.

Homer's Penelope fobbed off the pressing suitors, who demanded that she should choose between them, by saying that she must first finish making the shroud for Odysseus's father, Laertes. She tricked them by unravelling each night what she had woven during the previous day. In the notion of weaving and unweaving no doubt lay the seed for Joyce's idea of making this great prose tapestry of thought with continuously woven and unwoven themes.

Bloom, it seems, has asked Molly to give him breakfast in bed next morning with a couple of eggs, reminding her of how he used to assert himself grandly in earlier days (and perhaps this is the first sign for the reader that Bloom is once more going to play the man fully in his own home). She thinks he must have 'come' because he is hungry, but it can't be 'love' or he would not be hungry. His story of the day's doings rang hollowly in places. She suspects he may have been with a prostitute. She has seen him furtively writing letters and recalls his flirtation with the servant, Mary Driscoll (a matter made much of during Bloom's hallucinatory 'trial' in the 'Circe' episode). Boylan comes back to mind and also the embarrassments of the confessional. Though Molly asks herself whether she fully satisfied Boylan, she is critical of his patronising familiarity in slapping her behind as he went away. (We recall that what Boylan slapped Bloom kissed.) Reflections on the roughness of his sexual performance and the size of his organ lead to recall of the surprising paucity of his sperm, to a comparison in that respect favourable to Leopold, and to the fleeting thought that it might be nice to have another child. So Bloom and his oddities come to mind again. Molly remembers how knowledgeable he was as a young man and how her engagement to him disappointed her rival, Josie Powell (the Josie Breen Bloom met this morning in 'The Lestrygonians' episode). Josie's bad luck in marriage reminds her that Bloom is at least a respectable husband to have, though she thinks he did pretty well for himself in the marriage market too.

Thinking on the differences between men's behaviour and the ways in which they are attracted by women, Molly recalls her first meeting with Boylan in a café, the approaches made by the tenor Bartell D'Arcy (who sings at the Morkans' party in 'The Dead', *Dubliners*), and Bloom's idiosyncrasies in their courting days, when he begged her to give him a tiny piece cut from her drawers to keep. There are appreciative recalls of Bloom's handsomeness, cleverness, and sensitivity, and of the way Lieutenant Gardner, an early admirer, embraced her, linked up with thoughts of this afternoon's visit by Boylan (who is due again next Monday at 4 o'clock) and the coming trip to Belfast with him. It seems that even the railway journey, if made in a first-class carriage, may provide opportunity for sex. (The trip conveniently coincides with Bloom's anniversary visit to Ennis.) Molly's rapidly shifting thoughts touch so many remembered people and events that only a lengthy account could record and document them. But recurring themes are of course Bloom, Boylan, other earlier admirers, the musical life in which she is involved, and her own past physical experiences and present physical condition.

For instance, thoughts of the coming Belfast engagements lead to reflections on the current musical scene in Dublin dominated by 'little chits of missies they now have singing Kathleen Kearney and her like' which take us back to events in 'A Mother' (*Dubliners*). When Lieutenant Gardner recurs to mind it emerges that he belongs to the Gibraltar days and was killed in the Boer War. And, the military topic having arisen, Molly's thoughts confirm what others have said of Boylan, that his father made money by selling horses to the government (selling them 'twice over', the narrator said in the 'Cyclops' episode). Going thus back to Boylan, she admires the smartness of his clothes and his comparative affluence, out of which she hopes to do well when they go shopping in Belfast, and ponders the appropriate clothes she will take on the trip. She makes clear that Boylan was sexually pretty rough this afternoon and that he lost his temper when he got news of the Ascot Gold Cup result. (Hence the torn tickets Bloom saw.) The desire to make the best of her dress, figure, and complexion provokes comparison with the lot of expensively kept women and reflections on Bloom's failure to get and keep a decent job. There was an occasion when Bloom was sacked for rudeness by Joseph Cuffe, a cattle-dealer, when Molly knew quite well that Cuffe appreciated her bosom so much that she could have got Bloom a managership under him had they played their cards properly.

On the subject of her breasts, Molly recalls how Boylan and Bloom have sucked them and admired them, and concedes that they are indeed more beautiful than the sexual appendages that men carry about in front. Which leads to recalls of various moments in her life at which men have been seen trying to attract women by exhibiting their private parts. She is now feeling restlessly hungry for more sex and is counting the days to next Monday when Boylan is due again. A train whistle sends her thoughts wandering back to Gibraltar days and various acquaintances she made. There were dull days then, and there are dull days now. But at least Boylan has brought some excitement into her life. It would be nice to receive romantic letters from him. She received a letter once in bed in the morning from her first admirer, Lieutenant Mulvey, with whom she spent a romantic last evening on the rocks above the Gibraltar shore the day before he had to sail away. The memories of her affair with Mulvey (though it stopped short of sexual intercourse) are rich with the flavour of her own youthfulness and the colourful Mediterranean background. Molly feels that her female rivals in the Dublin musical world have no such romantic experience behind them. She knew more about men at the age of fifteen than they will know at fifty.

The interweaving of memories grows more complex. Among the numerous threads in the tapestry are concern about what kind of company Bloom is keeping (coming back home at 4 o'clock in the morning and ordering breakfast) and regrets about what a large house it is to be left alone in half the night. It seems that among Bloom's many unrealised ambitions was the notion of making it a musical academy or a small hotel. Milly comes to mind too. Molly thinks that Bloom has sent her off to Mullingar to learn photography because he wanted her out of the way of the liaison with Boylan. There is some rivalry and jealousy in the way Molly reflects on Milly's maturing interests. Milly's dawning adulthood, her relationship with her father, and her readiness to answer back have provoked ill-temper in Molly which she blames on Bloom for not having provided domestic help in the house. The irritations, physical and emotional, now culminate in the beginning of her monthly period. Molly has to get out of bed and sit on the chamber pot, water and blood pouring out of her.

Reflections on her own body bring back again memories of Bloom's devotion to it. But as she gets up, puts on a sanitary towel, and climbs into bed again, she reverts to the frustrating theme of his failure to get or keep a regular job. And why did he come home so late? What has he been doing? Has he been with some woman? She read about the Dignam funeral in the evening paper and she knows that there were men among the mourners whose company Bloom would be better off without. So, in the last pages of the book, Molly's thoughts focus more revealingly on Bloom and on Stephen. She is curious about Stephen as a future author and professor. She recalls how the cards this morning foretold the approach of a young stranger and a rise in society. She can picture herself as appropriate female inspiration for an aspiring poet. Clearly Boylan's crudity and Bloom's restraint have left unsatisfied a craving that the homage of a sensitive young poet might appease. Indeed Boylan's behaviour looks vulgar when measured by this ideal standard. He threw off his shoes and trousers without so much as a by-your-leave. Men are free to choose their women and yet they watch their women possessively. Bloom does not really appreciate her, embracing her only in his sleep and kissing her only on the bottom. His great big carcass of a body snores at her side unconsciously, and she is expected to get his breakfast for him. Men go their ways, quite ignorant of what women go through.

Molly is struck by the irony that parents who have a fine son like Stephen fail to look after him while she and Bloom have lost their son. Thoughts of Stephen thus are intertwined with tender memories of Rudy. Molly is soon dreaming of a domestic threesome in which Stephen has Milly's bedroom and Bloom makes breakfast for two instead of one. Out of this issues perhaps the most significant of all her thoughts in this episode. 'I'll just give him one more chance', she thinks, of Bloom's sexual failure. She will get up early, make Bloom a fine breakfast, sing gaily about the house, put on her most fetching lingerie, give him a real eyeful and then, if he does not respond, give him a full account of her sexual exploits with Boylan. It is all his own fault if she is an adulteress.

This is the nearest thing to a clear indication that Bloom's sexual relationship with Molly will be restored. But Molly has to call a halt to this romantic dream of restoring Penelope to her Odysseus, for she remembers her period. 'Flowers' of course is an old word for menstruation, and Molly now dreams of going out early in the morning to order flowers, then to clean the piano and buy cakes, all in preparation for a possible visit by Stephen. The topic of flowers runs through the rest of her recollections, which turn at last to the day when she and Bloom first made love together on Howth Hill among the rhododendrons and he called her a flower of the mountain. It was by such sensitive touches that he won her. He said what she wanted to hear, and she gave him all he wanted in return.

Finnegans Wake

Degree of experimentation

The vast increase in stylistic experimentation between *Dubliners* and *Ulysses* makes the latter a 'difficult' book by normal standards. But its difficulties are such that interested readers who are prepared to apply themselves to the text with care and thoughtfulness will rapidly find their attentiveness rewarded. They will recognise the devices used by Joyce for enriching the immediate meaning with wider reference as techniques from the metaphorical and allegorical machinery used by poets in many ages. But the increase in stylistic experimentation between *Ulysses* and *Finnegans Wake* is vaster still, so vast that the degree of attention the book demands for even a modest understanding of what it is about is something which only scholars and devout enthusiasts will be prepared to give. Nor is the experimentation merely a matter of style and presentation. Perhaps most taxing of all for the reader is the fact that identities shift and even become interchangeable. Bloom in *Ulysses*, while being representative of the wandering hero, Odysseus, also at various times figured as Moses and Elijah, while Stephen assumed the role of Telemachus, Christ, the first martyr, and the Prodigal Son. In the nightmare hallucination of the 'Circe' episode Bloom became female for a time while Stephen was duplicated in two personae, Philip Drunk and Philip Sober. Such shifts of identity in *Ulysses* remained subordinate to the predominant naturalistic relationship of the thirty-eight-year-old Jewish advertising agent, Leopold Bloom, and the twenty-two-year-old Dublin student, Stephen Dedalus, active in their respective ways in specific parts of Dublin on a specific June day in 1904. In so far as imagery may have transported characters temporarily in imagination or hallucination to, say, an exotic oriental scene, such shifts were essentially decorations of the solid local and temporal placement in twentieth-century Ireland.

In all these respects *Finnegans Wake* pushes experimentation several stages further. Time and place, like individual identity, cannot be pinned down. What is particular is overlaid with such a multiplicity of extensions and variables that universality, instead of enriching particularity, submerges it. The book is about everybody, everywhere, and everything. Nevertheless its base is, of course, Dublin.

Sources of inspiration

Joyce took inspiration from the field of scholarship and from popular Irish balladry. In the world of scholarship he fed on the philosophy of the Italian thinker, Giambattista Vico (1668–1744), who developed a cyclic theory of human history. He saw the historic process represented by three stages of development, the divine age, the heroic age, and the human age, followed by a repetition. For Vico history was an active, creative process made by humanity. His dynamic concept of society and human nature appealed to Joyce. Joyce also drew on the thought of Giordano Bruno (1548–1600), an anti-dogmatic Italian philosopher whose thinking he described as 'a kind of dualism – every power in nature must evolve an opposite in order to realise itself and opposition brings reunion'.

More seminal still, however, was what Joyce took from Irish balladry, the popular verses about Tim Finnegan, a building worker who carries a hod and is too fond of his morning drink. As a result he falls from his ladder one morning and breaks his skull.

> One morning Tim was rather full,
>   His head felt heavy which made him shake,
> He fell from the ladder and broke his skull,
>   So they carried him home his corpse to wake,
> They rolled him up in a nice clean sheet,
>   And laid him out upon the bed,
> With a gallon of whiskey at his feet
>   And a barrel of porter at his head.

Tim's friends gather round the corpse for the wake. Lunch is called for. Tea and cake, then tobacco and punch, are served, but when one of the women threatens to upset the jollity of the occasion by starting to cry over the loss of the deceased, a quarrel breaks out and the party turns into a fight. In the fracas a noggin of whiskey is thrown at Mickey Maloney, misses its target, and in falling washes all over the corpse, who thereupon promptly revives and gets up from the bed. Thus the funeral wake terminates in a 'wakening' and the fun is all the greater.

There is also a popular fragment which children hand on from one generation to another in England, and which must surely have come from Ireland:

> I'll tell you the tale of Michael Finnegan,
> He grew whiskers on his chinnegan,
> The wind came up and blew them in again,

Poor old Michael Finnegan,
Begin again.

'Begin again' of course introduces an endless series of repetitions.

The main characters

The Finnegan of Joyce's book is in the first place Humphrey Chimpden Earwicker (H.C.E.) who keeps a pub in Chapelizod, Dublin. His wife, Anna, has the initials A.L.P. (Anna Livia Plurabelle). They have three children, Shem and Shaun, twins and rivals, opposites and contenders, and a daughter, Isabel. Since Chapelizod is the place from which Tristan fetched Isolde ('Chapel of Isolde'), Isabel's status is that of Isolde. H. C. Earwicker's universal status is made clear by the varied application of his initials, H.C.E., which, for instance, appear as Here Comes Everybody, Haveth Childers Everywhere, and Howth Castle and Environs. In the latter case H.C.E. stands over against A.L.P. as hill and castle over against the ever-flowing, ever-refreshing river Liffey. So time and creativity flow on. In the very first sentence of the book we are reminded of the river's course past the church of Adam and Eve out to sea. In fact the first sentence completes the unfinished sentence with which the book ends, thus indicating the circularity of the historical process with which Vico was concerned. The topographical symbolism also gives the twin sons, Shem and Shaun, balancing opposites and rivals, the status of river banks ('rivae', Latin for 'banks' makes a pun with 'rivals'). The whole landscape of the Dublin area therefore corresponds with Tim Finnegan, or H.C.E. and his family. Finn MacCool, the sleeping giant of Irish legend brings the heroes of the past into the pattern of correspondences. Thus male mountain and giant, along with female river, the flow of life itself, form a natural background to the life of Everyman, his wife and family, which manifests itself in the doings of multiplying parallel personae age after age.

Ulysses is the book of the day. *Finnegans Wake* is the book of the night. The night is the time of dreaming, and in our dreams locales and times shift rapidly and merge incongruously. Similarly individualities are vague, variable, and often even composite. We dream of a person who is at once ourselves and not ourselves, or of a person in whom individualities known to us merge and coalesce. Thus the notion of the dream life comes conveniently to hand to justify the merging of individualities, cutting across all boundaries of place and time, which Joyce required to make his universal history. The substance of that history was to be once more the stuff of Dublin life and above all the stuff of Dublin talk – rich in gossip, anecdote, wit, and inspired inconsequentiality, and laced with history and fable.

Tim Finnegan's story is of fall, death, and resurrection, and as such it contains the seeds of much, in a sense all, of human history. The rivalry of Shem and Shaun is the pattern of all rivalries from that of Cain and Abel to that of James Joyce and Stanislaus, or for that matter the literary 'rivalry' of James Joyce and T. S. Eliot and the musical 'rivalry' of James Joyce and John MacCormack. Certainly Shem the Penman has a great deal of Joyce's own experience focused upon him. Isabel of course is every man's beloved, from Isolde to Jonathan Swift's Stella and Vanessa or the seduced girl of Goldsmith's *Deserted Village*. Naturally Isabel, as the type of the luring beloved, cannot be wholly distinguished from Anna Livia who is the type of all housewives and home-makers, for it is a fact of history that the luring beloved turns into the housewife and home-maker. Thus Joyce's merging of individualities can be justified without having recourse to the defence that the world of *Finnegans Wake* is the world of irrational dreams. The creative feminine principle moves through the historic human body as the Liffey flows between its masculine banks and under the masculine mountain to the sea. All love stories can be comprehended in desire for Isabel as all rivalries can be comprehended in the rivalry between Shem and Shaun.

Central themes

Finnegans Wake is a comprehensive story of fall and resurrection, of love and of rivalry in human history and in literature. But this does not exhaust its basic substance. Another recurring theme is that of assault, especially assault of the young upon the old, the son upon the father, the new upon the established. And a further theme is the exploration of human guilt. Joyce explored human guilt in the 'Circe' episode of *Ulysses* by presenting Bloom under challenge, accusation, and trial. The charges against Bloom are at once so concrete and detailed, so numerous and overwhelming, that ultimately he is bowed down under the burden of mountainous guilt. Yet at the same time he is a man of such simple, harmless, and well-intentioned good-nature that the accusations seem to attribute a degree of guilt grotesquely excessive in his case. In this respect Joyce takes up in *Finnegans Wake* where he left off in *Ulysses*. Early in the book H. C. Earwicker is placed under a questionably founded burden of guilt by gossip which spreads like wildfire. In a key episode Earwicker is walking in Phoenix Park when 'a cad with a pipe' accosts him and asks him the time. Whereupon, quite gratuitously, Earwicker begins to defend himself. Now Phoenix Park had its share of political assassinations, and Earwicker's suspicion when seemingly challenged on what might appear to be a false pretext, need not be regarded as straining credulity. But the book hints at a real misdemeanour committed by Earwicker which seems to involve two girls and three soldiers, though whether it was anything more serious than the fact that Earwicker saw the girls making water is not clear. Be that as it may the 'felix culpa' of Adam ('fortunate sin' in that it led ultimately to Christ's redemption of mankind) becomes the 'phoenix culprit', H.C.E. The cad talks to his wife about Earwicker's seeming guilt, and his wife talks to a priest, and eventually Earwicker's much advertised 'fall' is made the subject of a ballad beginning:

Have you heard of Humpty Dumpty
How he fell with a roll and a rumble
And curled up like Lord Olofa Crumple
By the butt of the Magazine Wall,
(*Chorus*) Of the Magazine Wall,
Hump, helmet, and all?

In so far as there is a naturalistic 'core' to the story, Earwicker's climactic fall occurs in Section xi when his children have gone to bed. The bar is emptied at closing time. Earwicker is left alone and goes round finishing off what is left in all the glasses around him. The mixture does its work and he collapses, dead drunk. It is Adam's fall and Humpty Dumpty's fall, and Everyman's fall. But it is characteristic of Joyce's method that the theme of Father's collapse should be enriched by the memory of a comic story that was one of his father's favourites. The story concerns an Irish soldier, Buckley, who was fighting in the British army in the Crimean War and suddenly found himself ideally placed to shoot a Russian soldier. Buckley raised his rifle and was about to fire when he noticed the Russian's epaulettes. The man was a general. Buckley could not bring himself immediately to shoot such a high-ranking officer and lowered his gun. Then, remembering what his duty was, he raised his rifle again. This time he was delayed by an incident of converse significance. The Russian let down his trousers and began to defecate: Buckley could not shoot a man at such a disadvantage. However, when the general picked up a grassy sod to wipe himself with, Buckley's respect and sympathy alike evaporated and he quickly finished the man off. Richard Ellmann (in *James Joyce*) has given us an interesting sidelight on this story. It appears that Joyce was determined to work it into *Finnegans Wake* for its archetypal quality but did not know how to manage it. However, when telling the story one day to Samuel Beckett, he was interrupted by Beckett at the mention of the grassy sod and the use the general put it to. 'Another insult to Ireland,' Beckett said, and Joyce gave the marksman this clinching motive for firing in *Finnegans Wake*.

Earwicker's tremendous fall reverberates backwards and forwards through the book in successive claps of thunder. On the fateful night, after many intervening interludes, including a long dream-inquest on the fallen father, Kate the servant comes downstairs, finds him, and somehow gets him up to bed. The penultimate section of the book concerns what happens then in the domestic bedroom and elsewhere in the house through the night. It appears that A.L.P. has to get up from her husband's side to attend to a crying child, but, drunk as H.C.E. is, there are attempts at conjugal intercourse in the marital double-bed and prying children share the fun. The last section of the book brings us to the dawning of a new day.

Presentation and style

Finnegans Wake is divided into four numbered parts, seemingly on the pattern of Vico's three ages and the 'ricorso'. The last part is much the shortest. Within these parts the text is sub-divided into seventeen unnumbered sections, eight in Part I, four in Part II, four in Part III, and one in Part IV. Superficially the book as a whole seems to wander shapelessly through a series of ill-defined episodes, but there is no doubt that this superficial inconsequentiality conceals an elaborate design in which subsidiary workings of the Viconian pattern recur within the four main parts.

Succeeding episodes in each section exploit techniques of presentation already used in *Ulysses*. There are a number of mock-lectures, like the learned disquisition of Professor Jones (one of Shaun's personae) on the subject of a letter scratched up by a hen, or Shaun's sermon to the school-girls ('And look before you leak, dears') . There are also pseudo-scholarly commentaries by historians and judges such as the four gospellers, who are compounded into 'Mamalujo' (from Matthew, Mark, Luke, and John) and who also seem to represent the four provinces of Ireland ('Ulcer, Moonster, Leanstare, and Cannought': Ulster, Munster, Leinster and Connaught). There are delightful fables like that of the 'Mookse and the Gripes' and that of the 'Ondt and the Gracehopper', in the latter of which, among particular references, Joyce responds to hostile criticism of his work made by Wyndham Lewis. Perhaps most distinctive of all are the episodes based, in a variety of ways, on the catechetical question-and-answer technique that Joyce used so effectively in the 'Ithaca' episode of *Ulysses*. The questioning takes many forms. Shaun is subjected to prolonged quizzing by Shem in twelve questions in Section vi, Earwicker faces cross-examination in formal trial before judges, counsel, and jurors in Section iv, and Shem himself is tested in a guessing game played with the girls in Section ix. Alongside all the gossiping, lecturing, debating, yarning, and riddling, the stuff of advertisements, newspapers, books, encyclopaedias, and catalogues is parodied, and the listing of comic titles runs sometimes to the irritatingly absurd lengths that one finds in *Ulysses*.

Multiplicity of reference and allusion is central to Joyce's plan and the verbal technique by which he achieved it puts the greatest obstacles before the reader. In this respect the verbal devices of *Ulysses* anticipate the experimentation to only the very slightest degree. In *Ulysses* such compounds as 'pornosophical', 'panthersahib', or 'snaggletusks' speak for themselves. When drunkenness distorts 'temporary insanity' into 'trumpery insanity' the reader readily appreciates the ambiguity. Similarly the invention 'allmoist' is clearly a compound of 'almost' and of 'all moist'. When among the hallucinations of the 'Circe' episode Shakespeare appears to crow like a cock 'Iagogo! How my Oldfellow chokit his Thursdaymomum. Iagogo', it does not tax the reader's ingenuity to recognise the name 'Iago' and to make the connection between 'Othello' and 'Oldfellow' and between 'Desdemona' and 'Thursdaymomum'. But in *Finnegans Wake* these techniques of multiplying significance by fabricated compounds from what Joyce called his 'safety-pun factory' are carried to an extreme where the resources of several languages are drawn upon. While it is not difficult to recognise 'farce of dustiny' as referring to Verdi's *Force of Destiny* or a 'waistend pewty parlour' as a 'west-end beauty parlour', some readers will begin to stumble when faced with 'Askt to whether she minded whither he smuked? Not if he barkst into phlegms'. Provided one recognises the connection between 'smuked' and 'smoked' perhaps the connection between barking into phlegms (which is certainly one possible consequence of smoking) and bursting into flames is readily understandable. But it takes a fairly sophisticated reader to detect that 'Ahdostay, feedailyones' (which, one presumes, calls upon paid daily servants not to leave) mocks 'Adeste, fideles' ('O come all ye faithful') and that 'andrewpaulmurphyc narratives' are anthropomorphic narratives.

There is no doubt that a great deal of fun can be derived from this technique, as Joyce's description of Finnegan's funeral as a 'grand funferall' illustrates. Certainly too a great deal of intellectual satisfaction may be obtained by teasing out that the word 'theuartpeatrick' combines 'therapeutic' with Christ's words 'Thou art Peter', suitably adjusted by reference to Irish Saint Patrick and Irish peat. Indeed the reader appreciative of Joyce's methods in this respect will not be able to open *Finnegans Wake* without coming upon a portmanteau word or pun that gives delight. 'Scheherezade' becomes 'Skertsiraizde', 'Madam Tussaud's' becomes 'Madam Toshowns' and the 'National Gallery' our 'notional gullery'. But it is one thing to pick out such recognisable instances of word-play and another thing to plod word by word, line by line, through pages where recourse to foreign languages helps to impose not only double, but triple and even quadruple meanings on the text. Indeed it can be argued that Joyce never intended the individual reader to grasp what he was saying comprehensively. For not only do his multiple references continually invoke facts of Irish history and Irish topography of which many readers of English literature would be unaware, they also focus on memories of Dublin life and talk from the years of Joyce's adolescence and young manhood which are the stuff of his private life. Similarly, though allusions to Roman Catholic doctrine and practice may be readily understood by readers acquainted with such matters, the more specialised allusions Joyce makes to the particular, and sometimes recondite, theological and philosophical works he himself happened to have read are bound to be inaccessible to most readers. In short Joyce made no clear distinction between experience of what is generally intelligible to all and experience so private as to be generally inaccessible. It was fair enough, no doubt, to poke good-humoured fun at T. S. Eliot by incorporating phrases from his published poems in the tangled text. But to incorporate phrases (as Joyce did) from critical comments made about his own work by Wyndham Lewis was asking too much even of an educated reader.

One effect of the allusiveness is that *Finnegans Wake* (like Eliot's *Four Quartets* and for the same reason) is a richly peopled work. Human presences abound, their names hinted at, and their doings or their sayings grotesquely echoed. Naturally such archetypal figures as Tristan and King Mark, Lancelot and Guinevere put in appearances. Naturally, too, crucially representative figures from Irish history, such as Swift, the Duke of Wellington, Oliver Cromwell, William of Orange, and Parnell, make their presence felt. In addition writers such as Sheridan, Wilde, Byron, Shelley, Carlyle, Newman, Pater, Pope, Gay, Mangan, Sheridan Le Fanu, Ibsen, and Lewis Carroll, not to mention Gilbert and Sullivan and 'Shakessphere', hover at times over the text. And among contemporaries T. S. Eliot, Ezra Pound, Wyndham Lewis, Yeats, and John MacCormack are also in the wings.

The scheme of the book

Anything like an exact summary of the book's substance or narrative is quite out of the question. The reader may however be helped by a rough indication of what is to be found in the succeeding sections. Part I has H.C.E. and his fall as the central pivot of the four sections. Section i is introductory and a good deal of history is thrown into the melting-pot. There is an amusing visit to the Wellington Museum in Phoenix Park. Section ii includes the crucial encounter in the park between H.C.E. and the cad. It concludes with the 'Ballad of Persse O'Reilly' (pun on *perce-oreille*, French for 'earwig' – 'Earwicker') Section iii shows gossip about H.C.E.'s fall spreading around Dublin from mouth to mouth, and also includes a lecture on the subject. Section iv contains the trial of H.C.E. in London.

In Book II the emphasis is shifted from H.C.E. to other members of the family. Section v develops the crucial theme of the 'letter' (representative of literature in general and sometimes of *Finnegans Wake* in particular) dug up in the park from among the litter of history. There is a professorial lecture on it. In Section vi Shaun is quizzed in twelve questions relating to H.C.E., his mother, the pub, the servants, the customers, Isabel and her twenty-eight schoolfellows, and other related (or unrelated) matters. Section vii is devoted to Shem the Penman. Joyce's own dilemma as an exiled writer, misunderstood and persecuted, is projected here with an irony so heavy-handed that one longs for the subtler and more distanced self-portraiture of the *Portrait*. Section viii is A.L.P.'s section and celebrates the feminine flow of life and creativity. Women are washing clothes on the banks of the Liffey and gossiping. Night falls at the end of the section in a lyrical descriptive passage which Joyce read aloud and recorded for posterity.

In Section ix the children, Shem, Shaun, and Isabel and her friends, are playing outside the pub. Shem is put to the test in a guessing game. Eventually H.C.E. calls his family in at bed-time and the friends run off home. The text gets increasingly dense and difficult in Section x which is printed in the form of a learned text equipped with marginal comments along both sides of the page (by Shem and Shaun) and with footnotes underneath (by Isabel). In the basic narrative schema this represents the children's homework, and the studies undertaken are those of the mediaeval trivium and quadrivium (grammar, rhetoric, logic, with arithmetic, geometry, astronomy, and music). Section xi brings us to the climax. Drinkers in the pub gossip, sing, laugh, and yarn until closing time. Then H.C.E., having cleared the bar, finishes off the dregs in all the glasses and falls down drunk. Section xii is a commentary by four annalists, appropriately conducted in an atmosphere of drunken somnolence. It is confused and repetitious, H.C.E. and Shaun seem to stand in relation to Isabel, somewhat incestuously, as King Mark and Tristan in relation to Isolde.

Book III shifts the emphasis to Shaun, H.C.E.'s successor and supplanter. Section xiii opens at midnight. Shaun is Postman as Shem was Penman. He carries the undeliverable letter (work of literature) about Ireland and faces questioning on the subject in a progression which, Joyce claimed, represents Christ's way through the Stations of the Cross. In Section xiv Shaun becomes 'Jaunty-Jaun' and in a sustained 'dream monologue' he preaches a sermon to Isabel and her schoolmates beside the Liffey. The pattern of progress through the fourteen Stations of the Cross is repeated. Section xv is the inquest on H.C.E. In Section xvi H.C.E. is in bed. As so often in the book, it would be impossible to answer here the question 'What is dreamt and what is not dreamt?' as the shifting interludes succeed one another. We do learn, however, that Kate went down and found H.C.E. lying on the floor, and it is clear that H.C.E. and A.L.P. are interrupted at an inconvenient moment by a crying child. A.L.P. goes off to comfort it. When she returns back to bed with H.C.E. there is more love-making, and it is spied on by the twins.

Book IV consists of one section, xvii. It is the beginning of the Viconian replay. H.C.E. wakes up to a new day. A.L.P. calls him down for tea and breakfast. A new letter has arrived.

Whatever may be described as crucial 'events' in the narrative, such as it is, of *Finnegans Wake*, people, gossip, anecdote, history, and sheer foolery cluster around them in such density that they are swamped. To understand Joyce's method in this respect one must recall his deep admiration for the artistry of *The Book of Kells*. This eighth- or ninth-century volume, preserved at Trinity College, Dublin, contains the four gospels with prefaces, summaries, and part of a glossary. The manuscript is decorated with coloured illustrations. There are portraits, representations of scenes from the gospels, and above all pictures of everyday life sprinkled throughout the text. Initial letters are decorated with fanciful designs and pictures extending over the pages. There is a seemingly haphazard elaboration both in the intricate designs and in the lively representation of people and animals, sometimes incongruously comic. Joyce's book, also containing many pronouncements from four 'gospellers', certainly makes its appeal through the seemingly disproportionate (but highly colourful) elaboration of whatever framework there is with the riotously profuse stuff of life sifted through an imagination richer in Irish wit, exuberance, humour, and tantalising obliqueness than perhaps any other in a very rich literature.

Part 3

Studying Joyce

The angle of vision and the narrative voice

Joyce's experiments in style and presentation became increasingly innovative with each successive prose work. Therefore it helps the student if he makes his acquaintance with the works in chronological order. In *Dubliners* we are faced with a text that is straightforward and appears to use a method of presentation that makes no break with established literary convention. The narration of events is clear and unambiguous, the dialogue is directly presented as such and no queries arise over who is speaking at any given point. Nor could there be any doubt about whose thoughts we are following when Joyce takes us into the mind of one of his characters. Yet the surface simplicity seems sometimes too beguilingly obvious, so that, as readers, we stop and ask ourselves 'What exactly is Joyce getting at?' A story in which the outline is clear, and characters have been clearly delineated, may culminate in some event which leaves the reader guessing.

For instance, in 'Eveline' our sympathies are aroused for the girl who struggles to keep the home going after her mother's death, who is brutally treated by her drunken father, and is an overworked victim of exploitation. The chance of escape is offered – but it is presented to the reader wholly through her thoughts. It certainly seems to be a golden opportunity, but we do not, as readers, have a direct introduction to the young man who offers to release her from enslavement, who promises a new life in Buenos Aires, and an end to her miseries. We see him directly only at the end of the story, begging Eveline to follow him. We sense the tragedy of the failure of nerve that holds her back. Then we begin to wonder. Many an oppressed Irish girl might have been offered escape by a seemingly glamorous sailor or other homecomer from abroad, might have accepted, and then found herself left on the streets in Liverpool or London, too ashamed to return home, ruined by a plausible rogue. Does this story then pass judgement on the girl's inability to snatch at escape from Ireland as a prison? Or does it approve the instinctive caution and ingrained moral compunction that prevent a girl from perhaps throwing herself away? And how important in the final inability to leave is the promise Eveline made to her dying mother to keep the home together as long as she could? It would seem likely that Joyce wished to leave precisely these questions afloat in our minds.

The ambiguity derives from the particular angle of vision which Joyce has adopted. We have followed events through Eveline's eyes. Had we been shown them through Frank's eyes, we should have known whether he was a reliable, well-intentioned young fellow who believes that he has found his life's mate or a conscienceless picker-up and dropper of girls who seem to be easy prey. We should know whether his story were true or a tissue of falsehoods. And, if he were not honest and we were taken far enough into his thoughts, we should know whether he were just a rogue deceiving others or a dreamer deceiving himself as well.

Confining the angle of vision in this way is not necessarily a recipe for making a conclusion problematic. It may rather produce irony and pathos. In 'A Painful Case', for instance, we follow Mr Duffy's relationship with Mrs Sinico through his own eyes only. But we can guess a good deal more clearly what Mrs Sinico is thinking than what sailor Frank is thinking. For we see Mr Duffy and Mrs Sinico together in intimate conversation, at first hand, and we are aware that Mrs Sinico's femininity and feeling might soften the shell of a man who has been locked up in arid self-protectiveness. We feel the irony when he talks rather pompously of the 'soul's incurable loneliness' and she impulsively lets herself go so far as to seize his hand passionately and press it to her cheek. The threat of real emotional commitment drives Duffy right back into his shell. We do not need to be told what Mrs Sinico is thinking and feeling, how hungry she is for love. Every word and move in her contact with Mr Duffy has revealed her inmost need to the reader – and sent Duffy scurrying for shelter. The irony is acute.

It adds greatly to the depth of the human study in the *Portrait* that Joyce exploited a peculiar angle of vision with new subtlety. For in the *Portrait* he brings off one of literature's superlative achievements in ironic presentation of his material. He presents experience from Stephen's point of view, letting us into the workings of Stephen's mind, sharing Stephen's reactions with us in the most intimate possible way. We are made to share Stephen's sorrow and anger when he is unjustly treated, to share his delirious excitement when he is stirred by love or by poetry, to agonise with him in his guilt and penitence, and to rejoice with him in his rapturous dreams of artistic achievement. Joyce takes us into Stephen's mental world with great force and thoroughness in this respect. And yet he so manipulates the verbal presentation that we sense the comedy and absurdity of Stephen's attitudes at the very moment when we enter intimately into the earnestness with which he embraces them.

Joyce achieves this effect by withdrawing as author into silence. There is such a thing as an 'authorial tone of voice' which stamps the work of, say, Fielding, Smollett, or George Eliot. Joyce does not have one. The presentational voice heard at any one point in the *Portrait* is that of Stephen Dedalus at a particular stage of development. Thus the idioms of the infant, of the young school-child, of the growing boy making his acquaintance with literature, of the adolescent romanticising his own religious experience and his own artistic aspirations, and of the rebellious student, succeed one another. The young fellow takes himself seriously, very seriously, and through recognising the exaggerations of pose and self-projection that this involves, we form an overall judgement that detaches us from him half in sorrow, half in laughter. Stephen is never so amusing to the reader as when he is in deadly earnest with himself – writing an extravagantly rhetorical poem to Emma Clery and then making sure that she does not see it and that he puts her off when he meets her, or grandiloquently declaiming his artistic faith to unimaginative fellow students like Lynch and Cranly.

In *Ulysses*, similarly, a good deal of what reaches the reader comes through the mind of one of the three main characters, Stephen, Bloom, and Molly, though Molly's thinking is revealed to us only in the very last episode. We have seen how carefully Joyce moulded his representation of the 'stream of consciousness' to fit the thoughts of a bright young intellectual, a sensitive but pedestrian middle-aged advertising agent, and a woman in the emotional vigour of her prime. It is sometimes implied by critics that the most distinctive and characteristic thing Joyce did as a writer was to refine this technique of projecting the inner life on paper. But there are large sections of *Ulysses* where the reader does not find himself or herself carried on the flow of any individual character's thoughts and feelings. Nor is the reader listening to the author's own voice. We cannot list the 'voices' we hear in *Ulysses* as those of the main characters plus that of the author, as we could in the case of many a novelist.

It would be absurd to speak of Joyce's 'narrative voice', as though there were a recognisable one. It is true that there is a narrative voice in the 'Cyclops' episode, but it is so crude and vulgar that no one would mistake it for the author's. It would only be necessary to cite, say, the 'Sirens' episode or the 'Aeolus' episode to establish that there is no Joycean narrative voice. To ask to whose voice we are listening in the 'Sirens' episode would be like asking 'What instrument is that?' when we are listening to a full orchestra. To ask whose voice we hear in the 'Aeolus' episode would be like asking 'Who spoke?' when we are in a busy, packed hall alive with shouting voices. It has been said that Joyce had 'no style', and this is true of *Ulysses*, though it would be equally true to say that Joyce was a 'man of all styles'. What we hear in the 'Sirens' episode is a magnificent literary approximation to music:

what we hear in the 'Aeolus' episode is a magnificent literary approximation to the rush and noise of a newspaper office and the clamant outpourings of the daily press.

Epiphanies

In the short stories of *Dubliners* very often the climax consists in the breaking in of daylight upon a personality in some way shut off from reality, perhaps in the indulgence of his own dreams and aspirations. Joyce had his own word for the brief experience which, whether it is trivial or momentous, impinges on a person with the light of a sudden revelation. He called it an 'epiphany', using the Church's word for the full revelation of Christ's divinity given to the three eastern kings who came to worship him and bring him gifts. A Joycean epiphany is in a small way just such a revelation of a fuller, or stronger, or more joyful reality than has yet been recognised. Stephen Dedalus plans a book of epiphanies in *Stephen Hero*:

> By an epiphany he meant a sudden spiritual manifestation, whether in the vulgarity of speech or of gesture or in a memorable phase of the mind itself.

Thus, at the end of 'A Painful Case', when Mrs Sinico has taken to drink and killed herself and Mr Duffy has reacted initially with predictable distaste, he takes a walk by himself and a new light dawns. 'Why had he withheld life from her?' He is on the crest of Magazine Hill in Phoenix Park and sees lovers lying under the Park wall. 'He gnawed the rectitude of his life; he felt that he had been an outcast from life's feast.' Joyce underlines the irony for those sensitive to his method, for Mr Duffy's home is in Chapelizod, yet its association with the unhesitating romantic love of Tristan and Isolde is something that never enters his mind.

The *Portrait* is peppered with epiphanies which gradually reveal the nature of life to the growing boy and young man. The epiphanies begin in the nursery bedroom when baby Stephen first discovers that the warmth and comfort of wetting the bed is rapidly followed by the let-down of experiencing cold and damp. Thereafter at each crucial stage of development there is a moment of memorable illumination. Some of these moments bring revelations of injustice, bitterness, or squalor, like the brutal bullying of Father Dolan ('Lazy little schemer'), the collapse of the Christmas party in tears and strife, or the reek of horse-urine in the Lotts lane at night. Others are moments in which the potential tenderness, joy, and beauty of life impinge in experiences of release and hope, like the first ease tasted in the arms of the prostitute, or the blissful joy of being absolved from sin, or the inspiration sensed in the glimpse of the wading girl.

Joyce's allusiveness

In order to appreciate Joyce, then, readers must sensitise themselves to Joyce's irony and adjust their minds to a technique of presentation which removes the informative, commentating author from the text, and which hands over thought and utterance, response to the world and to each other, to the beings who inhabit the book's pages. Readers must also be alert to Joyce's practice of locking a vast significance into a sudden experience of sometimes seemingly little moment. Having adjusted themselves to Joyce's narrative method, readers may yet feel overwhelmed by the sheer complexity of substance, in particular the rich allusiveness which becomes so formidable in *Ulysses*.

The allusiveness is often topographical or historical. Joyce knew Dublin inside out. Even so, writing in exile, he pestered people back home by post for factual details in order to ensure that his documentation would be accurate. Could a man drop with safety into the basement yard of 7 Eccles Street by hanging from the railings and letting go? Such enquiries went back from the continent to Aunt Josephine and other correspondents. That particular piece of information was required in connection with the description of Bloom's return home in the 'Ithaca' episode of *Ulysses*. And when Joyce wrote the 'Wandering Rocks' episode, describing the movements of numerous people about Dublin city at mid-day, he worked with a map before him, a ruler, and a stop-watch. Just as he represented the actual topography of Dublin with the strictest accuracy, so too he relied directly on memories of living people for his character studies. In both these respects Joyce's books will prove fascinating for readers keen to explore the character of late nineteenth-century and early twentieth-century Dublin and for readers keen to discover how Joyce portrayed its living personalities in his books.

In this respect the student, in his early days at least, must know where to draw the line between what is essential for a proper understanding of the text, what is helpful and illuminating for a deeper insight into the text, and what is merely interesting for the information one thereby gleans about the connection between Joyce's life and his work. There are three distinct categories of knowledge here, in descending order of importance: what is necessary, what is helpful, and what is purely adventitious. Let us exemplify these three categories in reverse order. The fact that Cranly in the *Portrait* is a portrayal of J. F. Byrne, Joyce's friend at University College, is interesting but sheds no additional light on our understanding of the text. The friendship is full of interest to Joyce's biographer, but the reader of the *Portrait* does not gain any vital new insight from learning that Joyce had a friendship with a man called Byrne on which he modelled the friendship of Stephen Dedalus and Cranly. Such purely adventitious information is neither necessary nor even particularly helpful to the student bent on quick appreciation of the text before him, though of course it is an aid to the reader who wishes to know more of Joyce's life and work as a whole. By contrast it is immediately helpful to the reader following Stephen's experiences and his inner life at Clongowes to know a little of the historical associations of the place. He will enter more fully into Stephen's dreams and fears and excitements if he knows, for instance, that Hamilton Rowan, the eighteenth-century nationalist, was supposed to have escaped pursuit and arrest there. But the third kind of background knowledge, the kind of knowledge which it is absolutely essential to have, is of a much more general kind than knowledge of the special historical associations of Clongowes or of Joyce's personal friendship with J. F. Byrne. It is knowledge of the outlines of Irish history and Anglo-Irish relationships. Plainly no reader can enter feelingly into understanding of the quarrel at the Dedaluses' Christmas party in the *Portrait* unless he or she knows something of what Parnell did and tried to do for Ireland, how he was frustrated, how he fell, and how Irish opinion thereafter divided fiercely for and against him.

Joyce's work is not so formidable in this respect as might seem at first sight. Brief historical sketches like those in the first part of this book are fully adequate to launch a student on the study of Joyce; but of course having general encyclopaedias and reference books to hand will always help to enlarge our understanding. Nevertheless, it is doubtful whether you need to know more of Irish history to appreciate Joyce's work than you need to know of Roman history to appreciate Shakespeare's *Julius Caesar* or of English history to appreciate his *Henry IV*, Parts 1 and 2.

Symbolism

The reason why this is so is that Joyce's imagination, like Shakespeare's, is that of the poet who universalises his material, giving it a significance for all time and all people. We have already remarked how getting to the heart of Dublin was for Joyce a way of getting to the heart of every city, because the particular contains the universal. The universalisation of place parallels the universalisation of character. Joyce called his autobiographical novel *A Portrait of THE Artist*, not *A Portrait of AN Artist*, implying that the struggle against constraints and the aspiration to full self-expression and creativity, experienced by

Stephen Dedalus, has a general validity. In the same way Joyce's identification of his hero Leopold Bloom with the hero of Homer's epic implies that Bloom's struggles and frustrations are essentially those of Everyman, even though they are here seemingly locked into the temporal and local framework of a day in the Irish capital, Dublin, in June 1904.

There is a collection of essays written by Joycean disciples and edited by Samuel Beckett which was published in 1929. It is called *Our Exagmination Round His Factification For Incamination Of Work In Progress* and its purpose is to discuss Joyce's *Finnegans Wake*, then in the process of being written. An interesting point about this collection is that Joyce admitted his direct influence upon the writers of the essays in a letter of 30 July 1929:

> What you say about the Exag is right enough. I did stand behind those twelve Marshals more or less directing what lines of research to follow.

One of the essays, by Thomas McGreevy, called 'The Catholic Element in Work in Progress', has a few paragraphs about *Ulysses* which are crucial to a proper understanding of Joyce's purpose:

> For *Ulysses* is an inferno. As Homer sent his Ulysses wandering through an inferno of Greek mythology and Virgil his Aeneas through one of Roman mythology, so Dante himself voyaged through the inferno of the mediaeval Christian imagination, and so Mr Joyce sent his hero through the inferno of modern subjectivity.

In each case the heroic representative of his age makes his epic pilgrimage.

The literary parallelism is a crucial device for shaping the material and giving it universal status. In *Ulysses* that purpose is also served by an elaborate system of symbols and correspondences which enable the universal to be contained in the particular. Joyce's symbolism is partly traditional and inherited, and partly new in the sense that traditional correspondences are stretched so as to illuminate the detail of contemporary life. In this respect Joyce's experiments began in *Dubliners*. That clay is associated with death in 'Clay' is obvious. Less immediately obvious perhaps is the fact that the snow falling gently over the whole of Ireland in 'The Dead' is associated with the quiet, gentle covering of apathy, respectability, and conformity which has thrown a white wintriness over the spirit of Gabriel Conroy. By contrast the young man out west who died for love of Gretta (and whose very surname was 'Furey') worked in the gasworks, the source of heat and light. He was prepared to stand shivering in the rain to get a glimpse of her, while Gabriel protects himself against nature even to the extent of wearing goloshes. Here, in the references to gasworks and goloshes, we see how Joyce was prepared to extend to the paraphernalia of modern life the range of traditional symbolism inherent in the contrast between natural vitality and power and the protective artifices of civilisation. It is interesting that Mr Browne, who is somewhat out of place at the Morkans' party, being too frank in utterance, too crudely self-assertive, given to bad jokes and rather vulgar in his familiarities, provokes from Aunt Kate the remark 'He has been laid on here like the gas . . . all during Christmas'. When we read 'The Dead' a second and a third time, we notice such overtones. Consider the description of Gabriel as he arrives at the party:

> A light fringe of snow lay like a cape on the shoulders of his overcoat and like toecaps on the toes of his goloshes; and, as the buttons of his overcoat slipped with a squeaking noise through the snow-stiffened frieze, a cold, fragrant air from out-of-doors escaped from crevices and folds.

The cold, fragrant air from out-of-doors that escapes from crevices and folds as Gabriel unwraps himself from the protective covering is a little concrete miniature of the personal psychological experience which the new understanding of Gretta is to bring to him. Thus the detail of weather, snow, clothes, and the like which gives the story its sharp naturalistic force is also alive with additional significances which give a pattern to the material as to a piece of music or a painting. In the *Portrait* recurrent motifs are produced by inherited symbols such as the cow for Ireland, and the green and the red for Ireland and England. Elaborate configurations are involved in references to water, in both its pleasant and unpleasant aspects. The bed-wetting, the fall into the ditch at Clongowes, references to lavatory water and washing in the kitchen, compose a theme whose counter-subject is represented by the sea in which the transfigured girl is seen wading, the sea which must be crossed in escape.

Symbols and correspondences are exploited on an even more complex scale in *Ulysses*, and their effect is to pull into shape what otherwise might have seemed a very sprawling text. In the essay already quoted from the *Exagmination* Thomas McGreevy has this to say of Joyce's work:

> The author of *Ulysses* [is] . . . a prose writer who combines a wellnigh flawless sense of the significance of words with a power to construct on a scale scarcely equalled in English literature since the

> Renaissance, not even by the author of *Paradise Lost*. The splendour of order, to use St Thomas's phrase, has not been the dominating characteristic of modern English prose and it is partly because the quality was demonstrated on a vast scale in *Ulysses* that that book marked a literary revolution.

It is indeed one of the great Joycean ironies that modernism's seemingly most extreme literary experiment in faithfully reproducing the flux of discrete thoughts and feelings, of evanescent moods and impulses, which make up our inner life, is in fact at the same time a highly patterned and unified network of metaphor and symbol.

The method of this patterning may be seen in the way Joyce detaches himself in *Ulysses* from current political issues. He can align himself neither with Irish nationalism nor the British establishment. The Cyclopean nationalist in his cavelike pub is as one-eyed as is Nelson, the representative of the British empire on his column in O'Connell Street. In Minos Daedalus had made the shell of a cow in gold so that Pasiphae might squat in it and indulge her perverted passion for the bull, and the cow is the symbol of Ireland as John Bull is of England. Joyce would emulate Daedalus as a labyrinth-maker, but refused to follow him in creating a glittering artificial cow for John Bull to take his pleasure in. *Ulysses* shows Ireland betrayed from without and from within. She is betrayed by those who sell her horses to the enemy (like Boylan's family), by those who sell her artistic soul (as Stephen is tempted to do and as Gabriel Conroy does), and by those who sell her young womanhood in the Dublin brothels. Ireland is also betrayed by her supposed patriots, the fanatical revolutionaries like the Citizen with his foaming, irrational hatred of the British, and the sentimental idealisers of Ireland in the newspaper office who are so obsessed with the past glories of Irish culture that they ignore the human claims of the living present.

If Ireland suffers a double betrayal, from without and from within, so too does Bloom's home. For the hero's household reflects microcosmically the wider situation in the country as surely as it does in *King Lear*. Bloom's home is betrayed by the usurping adulterer, Boylan, as Ireland is betrayed by the British – and as Eve was betrayed by the serpent, for the shock of red hair sprouting out of Boylan's anus is indubitably a diabolical tail. But the betrayal is abetted from within by Leopold Bloom's sterile idealism – the fastidiousness of his recoil from the demands of fertility. He is tired of the discomforts and messiness of labour and babies. Moreover, ever since the traumatic loss of baby Rudy he has misread his wife's uneasy, superficial feminine 'No' to sex.

The 'No' has really been a 'Yes/No' as we know from Molly's own thoughts at the end of the epic, and indeed as is indicated in Molly's first utterance in the book: 'You don't want anything for breakfast? A sleepy soft grunt answered – Mn.'

Mn. That is Molly's first word as 'Yes' is her last. A lot happens in between. Bloom reads 'Mn' as 'No'. Molly does not want any meat, and meat is a thematic thread in the symbolic web. We know by the end of the book that Molly *does* want meat, sexually at least, and that Boylan's potted meat by no means answers the need. She would be better fed, like Mina Purefoy, the symbol of Ireland's poverty-stricken fertility, on beefsteaks raw and bleeding. But the rampant animality has been knocked out of Leopold Bloom. Molly calls him 'Poldy', knocking the *Leo*, the lion out of him. (She is keen on fictional lion-tamers too and the lush novels of Paul de Kock . . . 'Poldy Cock'.) Not until we get LEO sorted out and put back inside Molly's MN do we catch sight of the real substantial MELON, the longed-for fruit of the Promised Land so often conjured up in Bloom's day-dreams: 'He kissed the plump mellow yellow smellow melons of her rump, on each plump melonous hemisphere.'

What makes *Ulysses* so fascinating is that it is a life-long delight to explore. There is always something new to discover in it. It will justify any number of re-readings. T. S. Eliot, who usually chose his words with precision, called it 'the most considerable work of imagination in English in our time'. It is notable that he avoided use of the word 'novel'. Why he did so may be guessed from his complaint in 1937 (in his Introduction to Djuna Barnes's *Nightwood*):

> Most contemporary novels are not really 'written'. They obtain what reality they have from an accurate rendering of the noises that human beings currently make in their daily simple needs of communication; and what part of a novel is not composed of these noises consists of a prose which is no more alive that that of a competent newspaper writer or government official. A prose that is altogether alive demands something of the reader that the ordinary novel-reader is not prepared to give.

Perhaps *Ulysses* ought not to be called a 'novel'. W. H. Auden made the point that Joyce should be judged as a poet. Already we have seen that one cannot discuss his predecessors except by reference to Homer, Virgil, Dante, Milton, and Shakespeare; and these are not novelists.

Certainly Joyce's prose is always altogether alive. From the start, in *Dubliners*, his fascination with the symbolic potential of words enriches texts which on the surface are beguilingly bare. His verbal sensitivity is unfailingly acute. Frank O'Connor tells how, visiting Joyce one day, he pointed to a framed picture on the wall. 'What's that?' he asked. 'Cork', Joyce replied. 'Yes, I know', O'Connor said, for it was his native city. 'But what's that?' tapping the frame. 'Cork', Joyce repeated. If *Finnegans Wake* was to carry this obsessive delight in word-play out of reach of any but the passionate devotees, the same could not be said of *Ulysses*.

Structure

When Thomas McGreevy spoke of the 'splendour of order' in Joyce's work and compared *Ulysses* in this respect with *Paradise Lost*, he drew attention to qualities in Joyce which have been all too often overlooked by critics obsessed with Joyce's innovations in managing the 'stream-of-consciousness' paragraph by paragraph. Even in the short stories of *Dubliners* the design is planned with great care so as to give the maximum impact to lesser epiphanies and to the final climax. Joyce's full effect upon the reader depends on that reader's sensitivity to structure. 'Counterparts', for instance, is shaped like a sandwich in what the musicians would call 'ternary' form. There are three sections, the first and the third having a relationship of similarity, and the two of them standing in joint contrast to the middle one. The first part presents Farrington being resentfully and, as he thinks, unjustly bullied in his office, and the third part presents Farrington resentfully and unjustly bullying his little boy at home. Sandwiched between these presentations the second part shows Farrington boosting himself vainly to fellow-drinkers in the bars. The Farrington ego is ruthlessly analysed in a sequence which depends for impact upon the reader's responsiveness in relating part to part.

In the later works Joyce's method continues to require the reader to detect recurring motifs that contribute to the overall design. In the *Portrait* the demand for an apology from the infant in the opening episode has to be related to the terrifying exhortation to repentance preached to the adolescent in the retreat. Similarly the jotted notes of the final episode in the book in which the young artist prepares to set out on life's adult pilgrimage have to be mentally connected by the reader with the inarticulate jottings of the book's opening episode which represent the infant's first setting out on life's journey. Because Joyce thus requires the reader to connect section with section, theme with theme, symbol with symbol, over a work as a whole, students will find it helpful to make their own summary-scheme of a work to impress its overall pattern on their mind. Though this grasp is not something which can be attempted for *Finnegans Wake* except by the advanced specialist, it is not difficult to sketch out the pattern of the *Portrait* and the pattern of *Ulysses* in such a way that when reading any given section, one can readily sense its place in the whole design.

Structure of *A Portrait of the Artist as a Young Man*	
Chapter 1:	**Infancy and Childhood**
Section i	Jumbled memories of Stephen's infancy at home, culminating in the demand for an apology.
Section ii	Unhappy memories of games, lessons, and bullying at Clongowes, culminating in sickness and delirium.
Section iii	Christmas party at home, starting in jollity and friendliness, soured by quarrel over Parnell, and culminating in uproar.
Section iv	Back at Clongowes Stephen's broken glasses prevent him from working and he is unjustly caned. His protest to the rector brings a personal triumph.
Chapter 2:	**Adolescence**
Section i	Summer at home at Blackrock. Stephen walks with Uncle Charles, plays in a gang, goes on rounds with the milkman. The family situation deteriorates. Stephen romanticises his role after reading *The Count of Monte Cristo*.
Section ii	The Dedaluses move to Dublin into a meaner house. Stephen is stirred by Emma at a party, fails to respond to her afterwards, but writes a poem to her. Father Conmee offers him a place at Belvedere. He learns that his protest at Clongowes was a great joke to the masters.
Section iii	At Belvedere Stephen has brushes with authority and with other boys. He performs on stage with great éclat, then finds that Emma was not there to see him. He rushes off into the city in despair.
Section iv	Mr Dedalus takes Stephen to Cork by night train, and next day they visit his old haunts at Queen's College. On the college visit and on the subsequent round of pubs Mr Dedalus's vanity and shallowness disgust Stephen. He feels isolated and old beyond his years.
Section v	Stephen wins prize money, treats the family and tries vainly to ameliorate the squalor at home. Restless and dissatisfied, he meets a prostitute and finds relief.
Chapter 3:	**Repentance**
Section i	At school Stephen is uneasily conscious of his double life. The rector announces a retreat. Stephen wilts.
Section ii	Father Arnall's introductory sermon stirs self-disgust in Stephen. Second day sermons on death and

	judgement induce an agony of shame. Third day sermons on hell totally overwhelm him.
Section iii	At home Stephen is overcome with horror and terror at his sinfulness. He goes out to confess. Absolved, he finds relief and peace.
Chapter 4:	**Reformation and a new 'Conversion'**
Section i	Stephen amends his life with rigorous discipline of devotions and self-mortification.
Section ii	The director interviews Stephen and suggests vocation for the priesthood. Stephen has felt the attractions of the priestly role, but on leaving the director he realises that he belongs with the life of the world outside.
Section iii	Mr Dedalus enquires about a place for Stephen at the University. Stephen takes a walk out towards the sea. He senses his vocation to be an artist with words. A girl he sees wading becomes a symbol of beauty reinforcing his dedication to life and creativity.
Chapter 5:	**Student Days**
Section i	Stephen leaves his squalid home for college, where he attends a lecture and is involved in discussion with other students. On a walk with Lynch he propounds his aesthetic theory. The sight of Emma stirs him.
Section ii	The effect of brooding romantically on Emma is a burst of rapturous creativity. Stephen writes a villanelle to her, but does not send it to her.
Section iii	Stephen drags Cranly away from gossiping students and on a long walk explains his rebelliousness and his personal credo.
Section iv	Final diary jottings on various friends and on Emma end in an account of preparations to leave.

Structure of *Ulysses*

Book I:	**The Search**
Episode 1	Telemachus (Odysseus's son). 8 a.m. The Martello Tower, Sandycove. Stephen Dedalus, Buck Mulligan, and Haines have breakfast, then go to the beach. Mulligan bathes. Stephen leaves the tower key and goes off to school.
Episode 2	Nestor (the old warrior from whom Telemachus sought news). 10 a.m. The school at Dalkey.

	Stephen gives history and poetry lessons, then goes to the headmaster's room where Mr Deasy pays him, gives him good advice and a letter for publication in the press.
Episode 3	Proteus (the chameleonlike god of the sea). 11 a.m. Sandymount strand. Stephen walks on the shore brooding on the nature of being. Eventually the creative urge seizes him and he writes some verse.
Book II:	**The Wanderings**
Episode 4	Calypso (the nymph who held Odysseus captive). 8 a.m. 7 Eccles Street. Leopold Bloom leaves home to buy meat for breakfast; returns, takes breakfast up to his wife in bed and also a letter from Boylan. After his own breakfast he goes to the outside privy.
Episode 5	The Lotus-Eaters (who were drugged to forgetfulness of home). 10 a.m. The streets. Bloom collects a letter from Martha from the post office, drops into All Hallows' church, calls at the chemist's, and goes to the bath.
Episode 6	Hades (the Underworld). 11 a.m. Journey across Dublin to Glasnevin cemetery. Bloom, Cunningham, Power, and Mr Dedalus share a carriage in the funeral procession. At the cemetery they follow Paddy Dignam's coffin to the chapel and to the grave.
Episode 7	Aeolus (the god of the winds). 12 noon. The newspaper office. Bloom comes to negotiate the renewal of the Keyes tea advertisement. Dubliners, gassing in the office, sentimentalise Irish history. Stephen brings Deasy's letter. Bloom is rebuffed by the *Evening Telegraph* editor.
Episode 8	The Lestrygonians (cannibals). 1 p.m. The streets, the Burton Restaurant, Davy Byrne's. Bloom walks brooding, meets Josie Breen, hears about Mina Purefoy in labour. Repelled by the guzzling in the Burton, he goes for a sandwich and a glass of wine at Davy Byrne's. Afterwards he catches sight of Boylan in the street and slips into the museum.

Episode 9	Scylla and Charybdis (the monster and the whirlpool). 2 p.m. The library. Stephen converses with AE and the librarians. He begins to expound his theory of *Hamlet*. Mulligan arrives. Bloom comes, seeking to consult the files of the *Kilkenny People*. Stephen completes his account of *Hamlet*. Bloom passes between Stephen and Mulligan as he leaves.
Episode 10	The Wandering Rocks. 3 p.m. The streets. Episode opens with Father Conmee's journey across Dublin and closes with the Viceroy's journey across Dublin. Between them there is a cross-section of Dubliners' movements at that time in the city.
Episode 11	The Sirens (the irresistible singers). 4 p.m. The Ormond Hotel. Two barmaids watch the vice-regal procession. Simon Dedalus comes in, then Lenehan, then Ben Dollard and Father Cowley, and then Boylan. Bloom meets Richie Goulding at the door and they enter together for a meal. Bloom sees Boylan leave. Simon Dedalus sings 'M'appari'. Bloom secretively writes a reply to Martha. Dollard sings 'The Croppy Boy'. Meanwhile Boylan is riding across the city to Molly's.
Episode 12	The Cyclops (the one-eyed giant). 5 p.m. Barney Kiernan's bar. Bloom goes to the bar looking for Martin Cunningham and runs into the coarse gossip of the drinkers and the violent nationalistic tirades of the Citizen. There is mockery of Bloom's moderation and his Jewishness. When Bloom finally leaves with Cunningham and Power, he defends himself against the Citizen's abuse and the Citizen throws a biscuit tin at him.
Episode 13	Nausicaa (the princess who rescued Odysseus on the shore). 8 p.m. Sandymount strand. Gerty MacDowell sits on the rocks while her girl friends look after their infant charges. Bloom, at a distance, stares at her. Conscious of his gaze, she leans backwards, revealing her thighs and knickers, so that Bloom has a voyeuristic emission.
Episode 14	The Oxen of the Sun (sacrilegiously killed by Odysseus's men).

10 p.m. The Holles Street Maternity Hospital.
Bloom comes to enquire after Mina Purefoy. He is invited to join a group of roistering students and their friends. The baby is born. The young men go off to Burke's pub. Bloom follows.

Episode 15 Circe (the enchantress who turned men into swine).
12 midnight. Nighttown and Bella Cohen's brothel.
Bloom follows Stephen and Lynch to Monto. Zoe Higgins accosts him and they go to Bella Cohen's where Stephen and Lynch are with Florry Talbot and Kitty Ricketts. Stephen is drunk. After a wild dance he breaks a chandelier and dashes out into the street. Bloom follows him again and finds him in a row with two British soldiers, one of whom knocks him down. Bloom watches over him.

Book III: **The Return**

Episode 16 Eumaeus (Odysseus's swineherd).
After midnight. The street and the cabmen's shelter.
Bloom helps Stephen to his feet and guides him to the cabmen's shelter where they can get coffee in the early hours. Bloom finds himself relishing Stephen's company and takes him along to his home.

Episode 17 Ithaca (Odysseus's homeland).
The early hours. 7 Eccles Street.
Bloom takes Stephen to his kitchen and makes cocoa. There is some sympathy between the two of them – but not as much as Bloom thinks. He offers Stephen a room for the night, but Stephen declines and Bloom sees him out by the back gate. Bloom day-dreams a while, then goes up to bed, getting in beside Molly. She questions him sleepily about his day's doings.

Episode 18 Penelope (Odysseus's wife).
The early hours. The Blooms' bed.
Molly broods about her husband, Boylan, and other admirers. She looks forward to her visit to Belfast and back to her Gibraltar days. She plans to give Bloom 'one more chance' to re-establish their relationship.

Chronology

Date	Joyce's life	Historical events
1882	Joyce born in Dublin, 2 February	Phoenix Park murders
1884	Joyce's brother Stanislaus born	
1886		First Home Rule Bill defeated
1887	Joyce family moved to Bray	
1888	Joyce admitted to Clongowes Wood College	
1890		O'Shea divorce; fall of Parnell
1891	Joyce withdrawn from Clongowes	Death of Parnell
1892	Joyce family moved to Blackrock	
1893	Joyce family moved to Dublin: Joyce admitted to Belvedere College	Second Home Rule Bill rejected by the House of Lords. Gaelic League founded
1896	Joyce's first encounter with a prostitute	
1898	Joyce left Belvedere; was admitted to University College	Yeats founded the Irish Literary Theatre Society
1899		Yeats's *The Countess Cathleen* produced
1900	*Fortnightly Review* published Joyce's 'Ibsen's New Drama'	Oscar Wilde died
1901	Joyce's pamphlet 'The Day of the Rabblement' published	Queen Victoria died; Edward VII succeeded
1902	Joyce took his BA degree; made himself known to AE (George Russell), Yeats, and Lady Gregory; in December left for Paris (returning home briefly at Christmas)	The Irish Literary Theatre became the Irish National Theatre; Yeats's *Cathleen ni Houlihan* produced. Electric trams replaced Dublin horse trams
1903	Joyce returned to Dublin in April; his mother dying	

Date	*Joyce's life*	*Historical events*
1904	Joyce started *Stephen Hero*; published two short stories in *The Irish Homestead*; in June met Nora Barnacle; left with her for Pola in October	The Abbey Theatre founded
1905	Joyce and Nora moved to Trieste; Giorgio was born; *Dubliners* offered to publishers	
1906	Temporary attempt to settle in Rome	
1907	Joyces returned to Trieste; *Chamber Music* (poems) published; Lucia was born	Synge's *The Playboy of the Western World* produced at the Abbey Theatre
1909	Joyce paid a visit to Dublin and Galway	
1910		Edward VII died; George V succeeded
1912	Joyce visited Dublin and Galway again; this time with his family	Third Home Rule Bill introduced
1914	*A Portrait of the Artist as a Young Man* serialised (*Egoist*); *Dubliners* published; Joyce started *Ulysses*	First World War began, 4 August; Home Rule Bill became law, but implementation suspended for the duration of the war
1915	Joyces moved to Zürich	
1916	The *Portrait* published in New York	Easter Rising in Dublin; Irish Republic proclaimed; leaders executed
1917	Harriet Shaw Weaver made her first gift to Joyce	
1918	*Exiles* published; sections of *Ulysses* began to appear (*Little Review*, New York)	Armistice in European war; Anglo-Irish war began
1920	Joyces moved to Paris	
1921		Anglo-Irish Treaty, establishing the Irish Free State, signed in London
1922	*Ulysses* published in Paris; Nora took the children to visit Galway	Treaty ratified in Dublin; Civil War followed between Free-Staters and anti-Treaty republicans

Date	*Joyce's life*	*Historical events*
1923	Joyce began work on *Finnegans Wake*	Anti-Treaty forces conceded defeat
1924	First fragment of 'Work in Progress' (*Finnegans Wake*) appeared (*Transatlantic Review*, Paris)	Sean O'Casey's *Juno and the Paycock* produced at the Abbey Theatre
1926	*Exiles* produced in London	
1929	*Our Exagmination*, edited by Samuel Beckett, published	
1931	Joyce and Nora visited London and were married there	
1932	Lucia's first breakdown from schizophrenia	Lady Gregory died. Fianna Fail party came to power
1933		George Moore died
1939	*Finnegans Wake* published in London	Second World War began. Yeats died
1940	Joyces left Paris for Zürich	Fall of France
1941	Joyce died, 13 January	

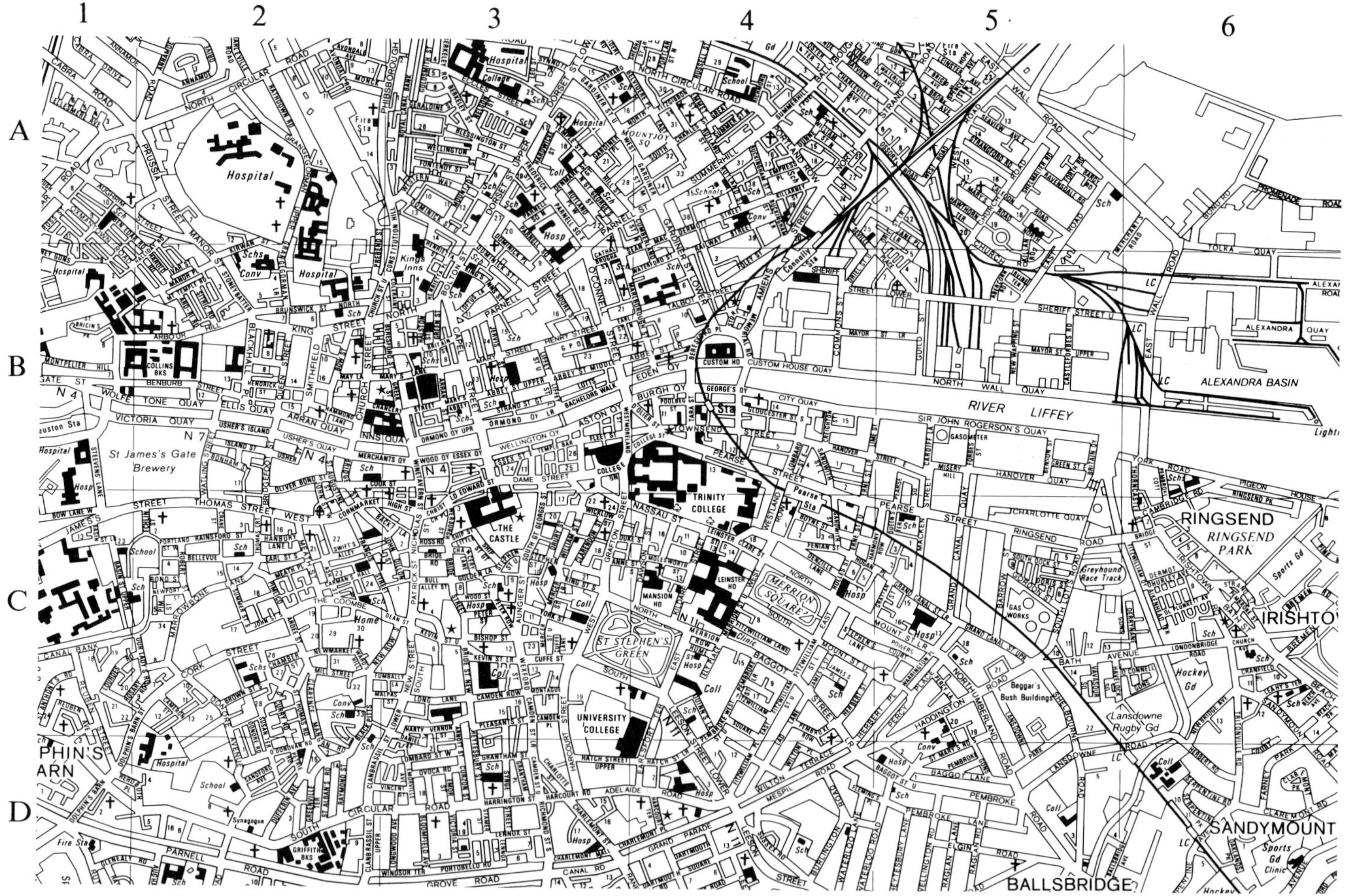

1
2
3
4
5
6
A
B
C
D
RIVER LIFFEY
ALEXANDRA BASIN
TRINITY COLLEGE
THE CASTLE
ST STEPHEN'S GREEN
MERRION SQUARE
UNIVERSITY COLLEGE
MOUNTJOY SQ
CUSTOM HO
St James's Gate Brewery
RINGSEND
RINGSEND PARK
IRISHTOWN
SANDYMOUNT
BALLSBRIDGE
Lansdowne Rugby Gd
Beggar's Bush Buildings
Greyhound Race Track
GAS WORKS
COLLINS BKS
GRIFFITH BKS
Kings Inns
MANSION HO
LEINSTER HO
NORTH CIRCULAR ROAD
SOUTH CIRCULAR ROAD
O'CONNELL STREET
NASSAU ST
DAME STREET
THOMAS STREET WEST
NORTH WALL QUAY
SIR JOHN ROGERSON'S QUAY
CUSTOM HOUSE QUAY
CITY QUAY
ARRAN QUAY
INNS QUAY
USHER'S QUAY
VICTORIA QUAY
WOLFE TONE QUAY
ELLIS QUAY
PEARSE STREET
GRAND CANAL
ROYAL CANAL BANK
PHIBSBOROUGH

Map of Joyce's Dublin

The map opposite is a section of a modern Ordnance Survey of Ireland plan of Dublin. Many of the names of streets and places would have been known to Joyce, but Dublin has also changed considerably since his day. In the key below, the modern names are indicated in brackets where former names have been replaced.

All Hallow's Church, Westland Row	4C
Amiens Street Station (now Connolly Station)	4B
Bachelor's Walk	3B
Bank of Ireland, College Green	3B
Barney Kiernan's Pub, Little Britain Street	3B
Belvedere College, Denmark Street	3A
Butt Bridge, over the Liffey, Beresford Place	4B
City Hall, Dame Street	3B
Custom House	4B
Davy Byrne's, Duke Street	3C
Dodder, river, from south (5D, 6D, 6C) under Ringsend Road (5C) into the Liffey by Britain Quay	5B
Dolphin's Barn	1D
Dorset Street	3A
Dublin Castle	3C
Eccles Street	3A
Essex Bridge/Grattan Bridge, Capel Street	3B
Four Courts, Inns Quay	2/3B
Gardiner Street	4A/B
Glasnevin Cemetery, *off map to the north*	2A
Grafton Street	3C
Grand Canal, by Parnell Road (1/2D), Grove Road (3D), Grand Parade (4D), to Grand Canal Quay	5C/B
Great Britain Street (now Parnell Street)	3B/A
Great Brunswick Street (now Pearse Street)	4B
Holles Street Maternity Hospital	4C
Little Britain Street	3B
Mecklenburg Street (now Waterford Street and Railway Street)	4B/A
Merchants Quay	2/3B
Montgomery Street (now Foley Street)	4B
National Library, Kildare Street	4C
Nelson's Pillar, O'Connell Street, end of Henry Street	3B
Newbridge Avenue (the Dignams'), Sandymount	6C
Newcomen Bridge, North Strand Road over Royal Canal	4A
O'Connell Bridge, O'Connell Street	3B
Ormond Hotel, Ormond Quay	3B
Pigeon House Road	6B
Rotunda, Rutland Square (now Parnell Square)	3A
Royal Canal swings north-west from beside North Wall Station	5B
St Mary's Abbey	3B
St Stephen's Green	3/4C
St Werburgh's Church, Werburgh Street	3C
Sir John Rogerson's Quay	5B
Talbot Street	4B
Trinity College	4B/C
University College, in Joyce's time, south side of St Stephen's Green	4C
Westland Row Station (now Pearse Station	4B/C
Westmoreland Street	3B

Bibliography

Works by James Joyce

Dubliners, Panther, Granada, London, 1977.

A Portrait of the Artist as a Young Man, Panther, Granada, London, 1977.

Stephen Hero, Panther, Granada, London, 1977.

Exiles, Penguin Books, Harmondsworth, 1973.

Ulysses, Bodley Head, London, 1960; paperback, Penguin Books, Harmondsworth, 1969.

Finnegans Wake, Faber, London, 1969; paperback, 1975.

A Shorter Finnegans Wake, (ed. A. Burgess), Faber, London, 1966.

Chamber Music, Jonathan Cape, London, 1980.

Pomes Penyeach and other verses, Faber, London, 1966.

Critical Writings (ed. E. Mason and R. Ellmann), Faber, London, 1959.

Letters, biography, and memoirs

BRADLEY, BRUCE: *James Joyce's Schooldays*, Gill and Macmillan, Dublin, 1982.

COLUM, PADRAIC and COLUM, MARY: *Our Friend James Joyce*, Doubleday, New York, 1958.

COSTELLOE, PETER: *James Joyce* (Irish Lives), Gill and Macmillan, Dublin, 1980.

CURRAN, C. P.: *James Joyce Remembered*, OUP, London, 1968.

DAVIES, STAN GELBER: *James Joyce: A Portrait of the Artist*, Davis-Poynter, London, 1975; paperback, Panther, Granada, London, 1982. A shorter study.

ELLMANN, RICHARD: *James Joyce*, OUP, London, 1966, revised 1982. The standard full-scale biography.

ELLMANN, RICHARD (ED.): *Selected Letters of James Joyce*, Faber, London, 1976.

HEALEY, GEORGE H. (ED.): *The Complete Dublin Diary of Stanislaus Joyce*, Cornell University Press, Ithaca & London, 1970.

JOYCE, STANISLAUS: *My Brother's Keeper: James Joyce's Early Years*, (ed. R. Ellmann), Faber, London, 1982.

POTTS, WILLIAM (ED.): *Portrait of the Artist in Exile: Recollections of James Joyce by Europeans*, Wolfhound Press, Dublin, 1979.

Guides to the works

BENSTOCK, SHARI and BENSTOCK, BERNARD: *Who's He When He's At Home: A James Joyce Directory*, University of Illinois Press, Urbana, 1980. List of characters in Joyce's works.

BIDWELL, BRUCE and HEFFER, LINDA: *The Joycean Way: A Topographical Guide to 'Dubliners' and 'A Portrait of the Artist'*, Wolfhound Press, Dublin, 1981.

BLAMIRES, HARRY: *The Bloomsday Book: A Guide through Joyce's Ulysses*, Methuen, London, 1966. A page-by-page guide.

BLAMIRES, HARRY: *James Joyce, A Portrait of the Artist as a Young Man*, York Notes, Longman, Harlow, 1984.

GIFFORD, DON: *Joyce Annotated: Notes for Dubliners and A Portrait of the Artist as a Young Man*, University of California Press, Berkeley, Los Angeles, 1982.

GLASHEEN, ADALINE: *A Third Census of Finnegans Wake: An Index of Characters and their Roles*, University of California Press, Berkeley, Los Angeles, 1977.

HODGART, MATTHEW: *James Joyce: A Student's Guide*, Routledge and Kegan Paul, London, 1978.

McHUGH, ROLAND: *Annotations to Finnegans Wake*, Routledge & Kegan Paul, London, 1980.

THORNTON, WELDON: *Allusions in Ulysses: An Annotated List*, University of North Carolina Press, Chapel Hill, 1968.

TINDALL, WILLIAM YORK: *A Reader's Guide to James Joyce*, Thames & Hudson, London, 1960.

TINDALL, WILLIAM YORK: *A Reader's Guide to Finnegans Wake*, Thames & Hudson, London, 1969.

Critical studies

ADAMS, ROBERT MARTIN: *Surface and Symbol: The Consistency of James Joyce's Ulysses*, OUP, New York, 1962.

ANDERSON, CHESTER: *James Joyce and His World*, Thames & Hudson, London, 1967. An illustrated book.

BECKETT, SAMUEL (ED.): *Our Exagmination Round His Factification For Incamination Of Work In Progress*, Faber & Faber, London, 1929.

BEJA, MORRIS (ED.): *James Joyce: Dubliners and A Portrait of the Artist as a Young Man: A Casebook*, Macmillan, London, 1973. A selection of critical essays.

BOLT, SYDNEY: *A Preface to James Joyce*, Longman, London, 1981.

BUDGEN, FRANK: *James Joyce and the Making of Ulysses*, introduced by Clive Hart, OUP, London, 1972.

DEMING, ROBERT W. (ED.): *James Joyce 1907–1942: The Critical Heritage*, 2 vols, Routledge & Kegan Paul, London, 1970.

ELLMANN, RICHARD: *Ulysses on the Liffey*, OUP, New York, 1972.

ELLMANN, RICHARD: *The Consciousness of Joyce*, Faber, London, 1977.

GILBERT, STUART: *James Joyce's Ulysses: A Study*, Faber & Faber, London, 1930.

GOLDMAN, ARNOLD: *James Joyce, Profiles in Literature*, Routledge & Kegan Paul, London, 1968.

KAIN, RICHARD: *Fabulous Voyager: James Joyce's Ulysses*, University of Chicago Press, Chicago, 1947.

KENNER, HUGH: *Joyce's Voices*, Faber, London, 1978.

Background and reference

BECKETT, J. G.: *The Making of Modern Ireland 1603–1923*, Faber, London, 1966.

BLAMIRES, HARRY (ED.): *A Guide to Twentieth-Century Literature in English*, Methuen, 1983. Contains encyclopaedic articles on writers of the century.

BLAMIRES, HARRY: *Twentieth-Century English Literature*, The Macmillan History of Literature, Macmillan, London, 1982. A chronological survey of the century's literature.

BOYLAN, HENRY: *A Dictionary of Irish Biography*, Gill & Macmillan, Dublin, 1978.

CURTIS, EDMUND: *A History of Ireland*, Methuen, London, 1936, paperback, 1961.

DELANEY, FRANK: *James Joyce's Odyssey: A Guide to the Dublin of Ulysses*, Hodder & Stoughton, London, 1981. Fully illustrated.

HICKEY, D. J. and DOHERTY, J. E.: *A Dictionary of Irish History since 1800*, Gill & Macmillan, Dublin, 1980.

JEFFARES, A. N.: *Anglo-Irish Literature*, The Macmillan History of Literature, Macmillan, London, 1982. A chronological survey.

LIDDERDALE, JANE and NICHOLSON, MARY: *Dear Miss Weaver: Harriet Shaw Weaver 1876–1961*, The Viking Press, New York, 1970. A biography of Joyce's patroness.

LYONS, F. S. L.: *Ireland Since the Famine*, Collins, London, 1973.

NORRIS, DAVID: *James Joyce's Dublin*, Eason & Son, Dublin, 1982.

O'CONNOR, FRANK (ED.): *A Book of Ireland*, Collins, London and Glasgow, 1959

O'CONNOR, ULICK: *Oliver St John Gogarty: A Poet in His Time*, Cape, London, 1964.

PEARL, CYRIL: *Dublin in Bloomtime: The City Joyce Knew*, Angus & Robertson, London, 1969. Fully illustrated, contains some fine photographs.

Index

YORK HANDBOOKS

Further titles

THE ENGLISH NOVEL
IAN MILLIGAN

This Handbook deals with the English novel from the historical, thematic and technical points of view, and discusses the various purposes of authors and the manner in which they achieve their effects, as well as the role of the reader. The aim is to bring to light the variety of options at the novelist's disposal and to enhance the reader's critical and interpretive skills – and pleasure.

Ian Milligan is Lecturer in English at the University of Stirling.

A DICTIONARY OF LITERARY TERMS
MARTIN GRAY

Over one thousand literary terms are dealt with in this Handbook, with definitions, explanations and examples. Entries range from general topics (comedy, epic, metre, romanticism) to more specific terms (acrostic, enjambment, malapropism, onomatopoeia) and specialist technical language (catalexis, deconstruction, *haiku*, paeon). In other words, this single, concise volume should meet the needs of anyone searching for clarification of terms found in the study of literature.

Martin Gray is Lecturer in English at the University of Stirling.

AN INTRODUCTION TO LITERARY CRITICISM
RICHARD DUTTON

This is an introduction to a subject that has received increasing emphasis in the study of literature in recent years. As a means of identifying the underlying principles of the subject, the author examines the way in which successive eras and individual critics have applied different yardsticks by which to judge literary output. In this way the complexities of modern criticism are set in the perspective of its antecedents, and seen as only the most recent links in a chain of changing outlooks and methods of approach. The threads of this analysis are drawn together in the concluding chapter, which offers a blueprint for the practice of criticism.

Richard Dutton is Lecturer in English Literature at the University of Lancaster.

STUDYING CHAUCER
ELISABETH BREWER

STUDYING SHAKESPEARE
MARTIN STEPHEN AND PHILIP FRANKS

STUDYING MILTON
GEOFFREY M. RIDDEN

STUDYING THE BRONTËS
SHEILA SULLIVAN

STUDYING CHARLES DICKENS
K. J. FIELDING

STUDYING THOMAS HARDY
LANCE ST JOHN BUTLER

AN A·B·C OF SHAKESPEARE
His Plays, Theatre, Life and Times
P.C. BAYLEY

ENGLISH LITERATURE FROM THE THIRD WORLD
TREVOR JAMES

EFFECTIVE STUDYING
STEVE ROBERTSON and DAVID SMITH

AN INTRODUCTORY GUIDE TO ENGLISH LITERATURE
MARTIN STEPHEN

PREPARING FOR EXAMINATIONS IN ENGLISH LITERATURE
NEIL McEWAN

ENGLISH POETRY
CLIVE T. PROBYN

DRAMA
MARGERY MORGAN

ENGLISH USAGE
COLIN G. HEY

ENGLISH GRAMMAR
LORETO TODD

STYLE IN ENGLISH PROSE
NEIL McEWAN

AN INTRODUCTION TO LINGUISTICS
LORETO TODD

READING THE SCREEN
An Introduction to Film Studies
JOHN IZOD

The author of this Handbook

HARRY BLAMIRES is a graduate of University College, Oxford. He spent a large part of his teaching life as Head of the English Department at King Alfred's College, Winchester. He has been writing steadily since 1950 and has now published over twenty books in the fields of literature, fiction, and theology. Over half of them are currently in print in the United Kingdom or in the United States, where he has been a frequent visiting lecturer since he gave up teaching in 1976. His first book on Joyce, *The Bloomsday Book*, *A Guide through Joyce's Ulysses*, has been in continuous demand by students since its publication in 1966. He is also the author of the York Notes on Joyce's *Portrait of the Artist as a Young Man* (1984). He has presented twentieth-century writers in *Twentieth-Century English Literature* (1982), a volume in the Macmillan History of Literature, and also in *A Guide to Twentieth-Century Literature in English* (1983), which he edited and to which he contributed the articles on United Kingdom and Irish writers. His popular survey, *A Short History of English Literature* (1974), was published in an expanded version in 1984.